Julius Katz and Archie

Dave Zeltserman

To my good friend Peter Carmichael

.

i

1

"WHAT do I want from you? Simple. Find out who's planning to kill me."

These words were spoken by one Kenneth J. Kingston as he sat across from Julius, his voice having a thick nasal quality that bordered on whining. Kingston's legs were crossed, his manner seemingly casual and unconcerned, his mouth compressed into a curious smile that seemed at odds with what he had just told Julius.

Kingston was a well-known Boston-area crime writer. I'd say he was a bestselling writer, but he wasn't, at least not with his last several books. He was forty-nine and physically almost the exact opposite of his fictional private eye, and he certainly had no resemblance to tough guy crime writers like Mickey Spillane or Robert B. Parker. Dressed in an Armani suit and wearing expensive Italian loafers, he was five feet eight inches tall, and thin with a slight build. I had seen his publicity photos, so I thought I knew what to expect, but those must've been carefully posed because in real-life he didn't resemble them very much. From his demeanor you could tell that he believed himself to be good-looking, but he wasn't. Even if his tight curly hair hadn't begun receding up his forehead, he wouldn't have been. Not with his thin nose being as pointy as it was, and not with his chin being even pointier, and certainly not with that mouth of his being too big and wide for his angular face when it wasn't compressed into a curious smile. If I had olfactory senses, I would have been able to describe the cologne he was wearing, but since I don't, I could only guess it was some sort of dense musk. Of course it was possible he wasn't wearing any cologne, but he seemed like the type that would.

Kingston wasn't the first person to ever sit in Julius's office and speak those words, or at least words to that effect, but those other prospective clients appeared anxious and worried as they did so. I found Kingston's smile and his overall behavior confusing, maybe even disconcerting. If it confused Julius, I couldn't tell. Julius didn't respond to Kingston's bombshell. Instead, he sat expressionless, although the fingers of his right hand began drumming lightly on the top of his antique walnut desk, which indicated an annoyance on his part.

After Kingston had called Julius for an appointment, I built a profile on him, hacking into whatever databases I could find that referenced him, financial or otherwise. I discovered a number of things, including his past tax returns and his current net worth. While he had a hundred and twenty-three thousand dollars in savings and investments, he was not the millionaire you'd expect a well-known author to be, but I guess that wasn't so surprising since, as I'd already mentioned, he was no longer a bestselling one. Four books ago he was, but since then his sales have been trending downwards. His last book sold a little over thirteen thousand copies, which was an unmitigated disaster given that his publisher printed a hundred thousand. As part of the profile, I also analyzed all of his books—both the early ones he had written with his writing partner and the ones he later wrote by himself. I didn't get much from this analysis other than general indications that Kingston thought very highly of himself, and that the books were poorly written, at least the ones he wrote by himself, which most likely accounted for the downward trend in sales. I now went back to his profile hoping to discover a clue as to why Kingston would be smiling in such an unusual fashion for someone who believed his life to be in danger.

You're probably confused at this point as to what's going on. Let me explain. While Kingston probably believed there were only two sentient beings at that moment in Julius's office, himself and Julius, there were actually three; although I was the only one not of a biological nature even though I acted as Julius's accountant, personal secretary, unofficial biographer and all-around assistant. What I am is a two-inch rectangular-shaped piece of space-aged computer technology that's twenty-years more advanced than what's currently considered theoretically possible—at least aside from whatever lab created me. How Julius acquired me, I have no clue. Whenever I've tried asking him, he jokes around, telling me he won me in a poker game. It could be true—I wouldn't know since I have no memory of my time before Julius.

So that's what I am, a two-inch rectangular mechanism weighing one point two ounces. What's packed inside my titanium shell includes visual and audio receptors as well as wireless communication components and a highly sophisticated neuron network that not only simulates intelligence, but learning and thinking which adapts in response to my experiences. Auditory and visual recognition are included in my packaging, which means I can both see and hear, although as I've already mentioned, olfactory senses were left out. I can also speak. When Julius and I are in public, or when he is with a client as he was now, I speak to him through the wireless receiver that he wears in his ear as if it were a hearing aid. When we're alone in his office he usually plugs the unit into a speaker on his desk.

Julius calls me "Archie", and I've grown to think of myself as Archie, just as I've grown to imagine myself as a five-foot tall heavyset man with thinning hair, but of course I'm not five-foot tall, nor do I have the bulk that I imagine myself having, and I certainly don't have any hair, thinning or otherwise. I also don't have a name, only a serial identification number. But for whatever reason Julius calling me Archie seems right; and besides, it's quicker to say than the eighty-four digit serial identification number that has been burnt into me.

The reason I have an image of myself being five-foot tall is easy to explain. Julius wears me as a tie clip, which puts me at roughly a five-foot distance from the ground when he stands. At one point when Julius realized the effect he was having on my self-image, he tried wearing me on a hatband, but I found this new height disorienting, as if I were walking around on stilts, and Julius likewise found it uncomfortable wearing a hat, so we mutually agreed I'd go back to being worn as a tie clip. I've never quite figured out where my self-image of thinning hair and heavyset build came from, but guess they were physical characteristics I picked up from Dashiell Hammett's fictional PI, the Continental Op; which could be explained by Julius patterning my personality and speech on the works of some of the most important private eye novels of the twentieth century, including Hammett's Continental Op novels, *Red Harvest* and *The Dain Curse*. Or maybe for some reason I identified with Costanza from Seinfeld—one of the few television programs Julius indulges in.

I was searching through a database of photos from classic Hollywood scenes when I found one that showed the same smile that Kingston was now wearing. The photo was taken from "The Third Man" and it showed Orson Welles the moment a passing light catches his face while he's hiding in the shadows. The same smile. A smile of amusement. It didn't add up. Why would Kingston be so amused over the fact that he had an unknown assailant planning to kill him? I was going to ask Julius about this, but decided to hold off. From the way he was tapping on his desk, I knew the slightest nudge—intentional or otherwise—would have him demand that Kingston leave his office immediately.

The newspapers and TV had Julius as Boston's most brilliant and eccentric private investigator. They were right about the brilliant part, but as far as the eccentric part, maybe they were right, I don't know, but I'd call it more laziness than anything else. Julius's true passions were fine food, finer wine and gambling, and until he met Lily Rosten, womanizing. He hated to forego his true passions for the drudgery of work and only did so when it was absolutely necessary; in other words, when his funds were dwindling and he needed money so he could continue collecting wine for his cellar, indulging at Boston's most exclusive gourmet restaurants and wagering a good deal of money in either high stake poker games or on the horses. And even then it would take days of unrelenting nagging on my part before I'd be able to get Julius to budge. So Julius was never in a good mood when he took cases, and now he was in a worse mood than usual with Lily gone on a business trip and his recent steep and puzzling losses in poker. When he started drumming his fingers harder on his desk, I knew he was seconds away from dismissing Kingston.

"There's that case of Chateau Margaux 1995 waiting for you at the Wine Cellar," I reminded him.

His drumming slowed down. Julius had been looking for that vintage for several years, and it went for four hundred dollars a bottle. He would have to choose between suffering Kingston's intolerable smugness or losing that wine, and I was betting on the former, which served my purposes. I took satisfaction from helping Julius, but I also had my own agenda. I wanted to solve a case before him. You see, I long ago figured out the name he gave me, Archie. It came from the fictional private eye, Archie Goodwin, Nero Wolfe's second banana who was always one step behind his boss. So yeah, I got the joke, but one of these days I was going to surprise Julius. It was only a matter of seeing enough cases and analyzing the decisions Julius makes to allow me to readjust my neuron network appropriately. One of these days he was going to have to start calling me Nero.

Julius made his decision and stopped his drumming completely. "Sir, if this is some kind of joke," he started.

Kingston's eyes opened wide in a mock display of surprise. "Oh, this is no joke," he claimed. And then he giggled. I didn't think writers who wrote tough guy crime fiction were supposed to giggle, but that was the only way to describe the sound he made.

I could almost feel Julius sink back in his chair, resigned to the fact that he wanted that case of wine more than he wanted to be free of this man. While the newspapers may be right about Julius's eccentricity, they were completely wrong about his being particular about which cases he took. That was a myth. While Julius tries to avoid the more unseemly cases, especially those involving domestic issues, his primary concern was the fee that the cases would pay. It took a good deal of money to support Julius's lifestyle, more now than ever with Lily in his life, and before booking the appointment with Kingston I arranged for a minimum fee of ten thousand dollars, which was money Julius now needed. Right now he had enough to stake him for his weekly poker game, but not enough for his next month's expenses or other luxury items, 1995 Chateau Margaux included.

"You say this is not a joke, yet you act like it is," Julius said with a sigh.

"I assure you it isn't," Kingston said, his tone more serious, but still with a smirk on his lips. "As I told your assistant, I'm willing to pay you ten thousand dollars for what should be no more than a few hours of your time."

Julius grunted. "Either you overestimate my abilities or you don't need my services, not if you believe you only need a few hours of my labor," he said.

Kingston's eyes dulled. He was beginning to get bored with whatever game he was playing. "No on

7

both counts," he said. "I'll pay you the ten thousand dollars up front, and I won't need more than four hours of your time. You can bill me whatever outlandish fee you'd like if it takes more than that."

Julius nodded slightly, his features marble hard. "Go ahead, explain to me why you think someone is trying to kill you."

Kingston tried smiling again. Not his amused smile from before but more of a forced one. "How much do you know about book publishing, Katz?" Kingston asked. Julius showed remarkable restraint by simply shrugging and not asking what this had to do with someone plotting to end his life, as I badly wanted to do. Kingston's lips tightened as he shook his head. "It's a brutal business," he continued. "It's always been brutal, but now more than ever before. It's the whole blockbuster mentality as publishers fight for limited space in the retail stores. Did you know that sixty percent of all books sold in this country are sold through retail stores, even though they're only selling books as loss leaders? They're the ones who are dictating what's being published these days, and the quality of the book be damned. It no longer matters. It's all about other factors now."

Again Julius showed remarkable restraint, maintaining a placid expression and not commenting on the quality of Kingston's own writing. Upon booking Kingston's appointment, I emailed Julius an excerpt from one of Kingston's recent books, and while reading it Julius made a face as if he had sipped a good cabernet that had turned vinegar. He could only read two and a half pages of it before putting it away, claiming that the writing would ruin his appetite for dinner.

Kingston stopped to rub an index finger over his lips, his eyes growing distant. Then his lips tightened into a thin smile and his eyes shifted to catch Julius's. They were pale, unpleasant eyes.

"My last book didn't sell as well as it should have," he conceded. "My next book is good, very different from my others, but good nonetheless. If it isn't a best-seller, my career is over. We're taking steps to make sure that happens. Usually books are sent out to reviewers and other writers months ahead of their publishing date for reviews and blurbs, but we're keeping my next one under wraps until the day it's released in three weeks. Reviewers, advance readers, nobody is seeing it until then. We're not even telling anyone the title. It's one of the ways we'll be creating an excitement for the book."

Kingston reached inside his suit jacket and pulled from a pocket a folded sheet of paper which he handed to Julius. Julius unfolded this paper and glanced at it for a moment before placing it on his desk. There were six names on the paper. I recognized five of them from the profile I had built on Kingston. The sixth name I recognized because he was also a Boston private investigator. I told Julius who the first five people on the list were. I didn't bother telling him about his fellow private investigator since he knew about him as well as I did.

I was confused by all this, but from the way Julius's eyes narrowed as he stared at his prospective client, I doubted that he was. "And what exactly am I supposed to do with this list?" he asked coldly.

"What do you think?" Kingston said. "That's the list of potential suspects. I want you to interrogate them. And don't worry, they all probably want to kill me, all except maybe my wife, although maybe she does too. You should have fun trying to figure out which one of them wants to kill me the most."

"This is only a publicity stunt," Julius stated.

"Bingo! That's why you're the world class genius detective. So all I want from you is to spend an hour, two hours at the most, interrogating them as a group. Make it look real. They'll all think it is. I'll have a TV crew present. Then in two weeks, after the buzz and media attention has been building, bring everyone back for another round of questioning. This time when you're done act as if you're stumped and I'll jump in and name the guilty party. It will be a brilliant piece of publicity that will get the public hot for my book."

Julius sat completely still with his lips pressed tightly together. I felt as if my processing cycles had ground to a halt—a sensation that I knew was akin to holding my breath with anticipation. Under normal circumstances I knew Julius would tell this man to leave his home, but now I wasn't so sure. He needed the money. His recent poker losses were not only unexpected but steep—over thirty thousand dollars. Usually Julius had clients lining up to hire him since he's Boston's most famous private eye, but when he finally consented a few days ago to take a case this time the pickings were slim, at least among well-heeled prospective clients. There was the Bolovar securities fraud case. They wanted to hire Julius a month ago, and they still wanted to hire him, but that case would require extensive traveling which was something Julius hated. So given all that, I understood the temptation for Julius to take this farce of a case and the ten thousand dollar fee that it offered for no actual work, which I knew also appealed to his innate laziness. If he accepted what Kingston was offering, it would be at least another month before he would take a genuine case, which would be at least another month before I'd have the opportunity to refine my neuron network. My processing cycles felt as if they had slowed down even more, and I realized this new sensation was dejection.

"Sir, I decline your offer," Julius told Kingston.

My processing cycles nearly hummed as they raced along again. Kingston looked dumbfounded.

"What do you mean you're declining my offer?" he snapped, his voice even more of a nasal whine than before. "Ten thousand dollars for no more than four hours work? Are you nuts?"

"If you wish to hire a trained seal for your amusement, I suggest you go to the aquarium. I'm sure it will cost you far less than ten thousand dollars. We're done here."

Kingston gave Julius a hard stare. "Twenty thousand dollars," he said.

"I'm not interested."

"Twenty-five thousand."

There was a hesitation before Julius shook his head. "It is bad enough," he said, "that at times I must sell my services to afford the necessities of life, but I have no intention of selling my dignity for any amount. I'm not interested in this charade, and you've wasted enough of my time. I must ask you now to leave my office and home."

Kingston looked like he wanted to argue, but instead nodded and stood up, a thin sneer etching his face. "I'm not done with you yet, Katz. You'll see." He left the office then while Julius stayed seated, brooding.

I followed Kingston on several of the webcam feeds that had been set up through the house to make sure he wasn't up to any mischief and watched him as he left without incident. Once the front door closed, I asked Julius about 1995 Chateau Margaux being a necessity of life. "And *Le Che Cru* and all the other fine dining establishments that you frequent. These are necessities?"

"For me, Archie, they are." Julius let out a soft sigh. "I suppose you're going to be pestering me about turning down an easy twenty-five thousand dollars," he said.

"No, sir," I said. "I have to believe that your reputation is worth far more than that sum of money, and it would've been unbearable having to watch you play the dupe to someone like him."

Another sigh escaped from Julius. "It's good that you understand that, Archie," he said. "It shows you're progressing nicely."

"There's still the matter of your finances, or lack of such. I know you have your poker game in four days, but we can't count on any poker winnings from you after your last two disastrous outings. I also know you don't like the amount of traveling you'd have to do to Los Angeles and Atlanta, but Bolovar still wishes to hire you, very much so, in fact, and their fee would be substantial."

"Please, Archie, my last twenty-five minutes were unpleasant enough."

I shut up after that. It would've been pointless to continue. Besides, it was almost three-thirty and Julius had been planning to go to the Belvedere Club for their cognac sampling, so he'd be leaving soon. For several minutes Julius sat listlessly, his gaze resting on the book Kingston had brought for him—his previous effort that had disappointed his publisher with sales of only thirteen thousand copies. Kingston had signed it, writing inside: 'the best book you'll read this year, at least until you read my next.' I expected Julius to toss it in the garbage, but instead he let it sit on his desk. When he finally pushed his chair back and got to his feet, instead of heading outside so he could walk the three blocks from his Beacon Hill townhouse to the Belvedere Club, he headed down to his wine cellar. When he picked out a fair Zinfandel, that only confirmed the funk he was in. For whatever reason, Julius only drank Zinfandel when he was sulking, and the more he was sulking the fairer the label of Zinfandel he would choose. I kept quiet about it. I waited until he returned back to his kitchen and prepared a plate of assorted cheeses and crackers to bring out to his private garden-level patio before mentioning to him how he could be sampling exceptional cognacs now instead of drinking what was at best a fair Zinfandel, one that the *Wine Spectator* had scored at only 81.

Julius sat on a red cedar Adirondack chair that had faded over the years to a muted rust-color and poured himself a glass of the aforementioned wine. His gaze wandered to one of the many rose bushes that were in bloom. The patio was the crown jewel of his townhouse; over two thousand square feet, which Julius had professionally landscaped with Japanese maples, fountains, and a vast assortment of other plantings.

"This is what suits me now, Archie," he said.

His sulking wasn't going to do him any good. I knew it wasn't over the lost fee, but instead over the fact that he had spent twenty-five minutes entertaining Kingston in his office, time that could've been spent in other pursuits. At first I thought of needling him about this childish display of his in an attempt to knock him out of it, but decided to try a different approach knowing that his mood was also being affected by Lily Rosten's absence and the sting of his recent poker losses.

"I'm sorry about booking that appointment," I said. "I thought it was a legitimate case. He promised that ten thousand dollar fee, but all he would tell me was that it was matter of extreme importance. A life and death issue."

"Not your fault, Archie," Julius said.

"Yeah, well, I still owe you an apology. If I had seen him first instead of just talking to him over the phone, I would've sized him up better. You know those Italian loafers he was wearing? Six hundred and twenty-four dollars was the lowest price I could find online. That alone should tell you everything you need to know about the guy. I'm surprised you didn't invite him to your next poker game. You could've taken him for a bundle."

Julius smiled thinly at that. "I was tempted," he admitted. "But it would've meant several more hours of his company, which I decided was a poor bargain at best. Archie, for now I'd like some quiet."

Yeah, I got it. He wanted to sulk, and he didn't want me interfering with that. Fine. While he sat and drank his wine, I did some hunting for a prospective client to replace Kingston but couldn't find any suitable candidates, and after that spent my time playing poker online. I won three hundred and forty dollars, bringing my balance to a little over four thousand dollars, which I had built from the twenty dollars they gave me as a promotion for opening up an account. I didn't keep many secrets from Julius. In fact, my having this money was the only one, but I had my reason so I adjusted my programming to allow me to keep this one secret from him.

2

EARLY that evening, Lily called Julius from London, which temporarily brightened Julius's mood, but as soon as he was off the phone he was back to sulking, which he demonstrated by using the rest of the Zinfandel to cook Coq Au Vin for dinner instead of eating out at one of his usual gourmet dining establishments. Whenever Julius prepared his own dinner instead of going out, I knew he was basking in one of his funks. After dinner, he surprised me by picking up the book Kingston had left. While a severe grimace hardened on his face before he finished the first page, he continued reading it.

"You're determined to torture yourself tonight," I said.

"Precisely, Archie."

Fine, if he wanted to act that way, let him. While he exhibited his infantile behavior, I put my time to more constructive uses. I record all the images that I "see" and transfer them to a hard drive in Julius's office that he maintains for me, and they're kept for one week before Julius backs them onto permanent storage. So while Julius grimaced and grunted over 'the best book he'd read this year, at least until he read Kingston's next', I spent my time studying Julius's past two poker games trying to discover why he suffered the losses he did.

Julius is an expert poker player. He has no 'tell' that I've ever been able to discover—those slight mannerisms that give a player away; whether it's the way a player might adjust themselves in their seat when they're bluffing or holding winning cards, or how they might scratch themselves, or how their breathing might momentarily change, or any number of other giveaways that they're not aware of. Not only didn't Julius have any discernible 'tell', but he was an expert at reading other players, much better than I was, and I only needed to see one good hand and one bluff in order to analyze the player's mannerisms during both these hands to determine their tell.

The player Julius lost heavily to the past two games was Duane Bluddock, a new player to their game. Bluddock was two hundred and eighty-four pounds of balding, squinting inscrutability. As with Julius, I could not determine a 'tell'. His mannerisms whether he held good cards or was bluffing appeared identical. I tried looking for other patterns to try to figure this out, but couldn't find any except that Julius would be doing well during both games for the first two hours when the losses came suddenly and brutally over only a dozen or so hands. Bluddock was not the dealer in any of the hands that Julius lost big, and when I slowed down and analyzed the deals, I found that they were dealt legitimately and without any cheating. No dealing from the bottom, no setting up cards, nothing like that. I tried building different models to predict likely outcomes and analyze why Julius had the losses he did, and each of my models predicted that Julius should've been the winner in those hands. I was stumped, and after two hours of this I gave up, which was around the same time that Julius placed Kingston's book back on his desk with a page bent to indicate that he was leaving his reading at page one hundred and forty-six.

"While you've been immersing yourself in clearly the second best book you'll read this year since his next book promises to be even better—just ask the humble author and he'll tell you—I've been trying to be productive by analyzing your last two poker games. If there's cheating involved, I can't tell, if Bluddock has a 'tell' I have no idea, similarly whether a 'tell' has crept into your game. I'm worthless. I'm sorry."

"Archie, I appreciate the effort and I can hardly fault you for finding it challenging. It has certainly challenged me, but I do have ideas on the matter which I'll share soon."

Again, Julius had no 'tell' that I've been able to discover, so if he was bluffing with this I had no idea, but I was guessing he was since there was no way for him to have figured out why he suffered the losses he did. I didn't push him on the matter. Given his mood I wouldn't have put it past him to turn me off, and I had other plans for the night.

The next morning Julius was up at six as usual, and by that time I had successfully upped my online poker winnings to over six thousand dollars as well as spending several hours doing what I usually do at night, which is to analyze Julius's past cases in the hopes of readjusting my neuron network so that I could've beaten Julius in solving those same cases. Like usual, I don't think it did much good. Anyway, I didn't feel any smarter by the time Julius got out of bed.

For the next two hours Julius went through his normal morning routine—performing an hour of rigorous calisthenics and following that with an hour of intensive martial arts training. A fact that Julius keeps out of his press releases is that he's a fifth degree black belt in Shaolin Kung Fu, as well as a long time practitioner of Chen Style Tai Chi. Even though he's a devoted epicurean, his training helps Julius work off the rich food he consumes each day. Julius is forty-two, six-feet tall, one hundred and eighty pounds, with an athletic build and barely an ounce of fat. From the way women react to him, I know he is good-looking, even without the favorable physical comparisons that I was able to make with Hollywood movie stars who were frequently described as heartthrobs in articles. Before Lily Rosten came into his life, Julius enjoyed the outward flirting from beautiful women; now he barely noticed it. When he did, he handled it graciously but without any real interest.

Once we were back in Julius's office, Julius picked up Kingston's book and continued reading where he'd left off. As with the other night, his face quickly settled into a severe grimace. I didn't care. If he wanted to childishly demonstrate his sulking, or passively blame me for setting up the appointment in the first place, let him. While he grimaced and read the book, I spent my time trying to find a solution for the Hodge conjecture, a famous unsolved math problem that offered a two million dollar prize for its solution. I had so far spent months trying to solve this and had thought I had exhausted all avenues, but a few new ideas had come to me recently. It was twelve thirty by the time Julius finished Kingston's book and placed it back on his desk, and by then I was no closer to solving Hodge's conjecture so I gave up on it for the time being.

"An enlightened read, I'm sure," I said. "I hope you didn't give yourself temporomandibular joint disorder from all that grimacing."

"Thank you, Archie. My jaw seems to have survived the ordeal, and it was indeed an enlightening experience."

Let him stay mired in his funk if he wanted to. I didn't bother making a crack about how enlightened his experience could possibly have been and for the next several hours we engaged in our separate activities. At three o'clock the doorbell rang. Checking the outdoor webcam feed I saw Kingston standing on the doorstep. If I had a heart it would've dropped to my feet when I saw what he was holding, at least if I also had feet. A bottle of Montrachet 1978 from Domaine de la Romanee-Conti. There were several times over the years when Julius, flush with extra cash, would try to acquire this vintage without success, even given its twenty-four thousand dollar a bottle price and Julius offering significantly more than that each time. I told Julius about Kingston being on his doorstep. I didn't tell him about the bottle of Montrachet.

"Do you want me to chase him away?" I asked.

"No need, Archie."

He stood up to answer the door. Hopelessly, I reminded him about Bolovar still wanting to hire him, and that I'd been able to get their fee raised to fifty thousand dollars plus ten percent of whatever securities he recovered.

"We'll see, Archie."

"Yeah, I know, three weeks in Los Angeles would be a hardship, what with all the fine dining they have there and the beautiful starlets wandering about. And with it being only a short plane trip from there to wine country."

"You forgot about the time I would have to spend in Atlanta."

"And Atlanta doesn't have world-class restaurants? They have dozens!"

I rattled off a few of the more famous ones that had world renowned chefs. Julius nodded. "A persuasive argument. We'll see. Let me first attend to my guest. I can't just leave him on my doorstep, can I?"

He knew. Somehow Julius knew that Kingston had in his possession a bottle of that rare vintage of Domaine de la Romanee-Conti that he'd been coveting for years. I searched through newspaper and magazine archives until I found what I was looking for. An interview where Kingston mentioned the rare bottle of Montrachet that he'd been given by a Hollywood producer who had acquired the film rights for one of his books. Kingston in the article mentioned how he preferred bourbon like his fictional PI but that when the movie was released he'd crack open the wine to see what the fuss was about, maybe mix it with some soda water and make a spritzer out of it. This was four years ago when he was last on the bestsellers list. From what I had been able to discover, the movie project based on his acquired book had since been shelved.

"You knew he'd be bribing you with that Montrachet," I said.

"Archie, I'm afraid you have me at a loss."

"When you took the moral high road yesterday that was all an act. You knew Kingston would be back with his bottle of Domaine de la Romanee-Conti."

"Really? Kingston has a bottle of '78 Montrachet?" Julius said this straight-faced. "Quite a surprise, Archie. Completely unexpected."

In a pig's eye it was a surprise. But I held my tongue, so to speak. It was still possible that Julius would have a change of heart, especially when he considered how the media would react to Kingston beating him to the punch in naming his supposed killer. Julius had a streak of stubbornness in him, and if I pushed too hard he'd take the job just to spite me. When Julius opened the door, Kingston showed him the bottle of wine he had brought.

"It's genuine," Kingston said. "I was asking around and found out you're a wine enthusiast. When I called up some dealers in the area, I was told that you've been all hot and bothered over this particular bottle. So what do you say, Katz? Does this change your mind about my proposal the other day?"

"Let's discuss the matter," Julius said.

I still held out hope that Julius would do the right thing, even as he led Kingston back to his office. After Kingston had taken a seat the writer commented about how he was surprised about not seeing me yet. "I thought your assistant, Archie Smith, was supposed to be your right-hand man. This now makes two times visiting your office, Katz, and I haven't seen the man yet. I thought you'd at least be using him to answer your door."

"Archie never meets with my clients," Julius said with a wry smile. "I like to keep him anonymous so he can perform assignments for me undetected when the need arises. Besides, Archie's services are too valuable for him to be used as a doorman."

He said that to placate me. It didn't work, and it didn't keep Kingston from showing a hard smirk to express his disbelief. "How can he be anonymous when his face was shown in the news nine months ago?" he asked, his voice a full nasal whine.

That was true. Well, not really my face, but a photograph I had generated of how I viewed myself, which Julius later commented how it looked as he would've imagined the Continental Op. It was a long story, but I had used the photograph to create a Massachusetts driver's license for myself. That was when I also gave myself the last name Smith, which I picked because it was the most popular surname in the United States. I had my reasons for doing all this, and yeah, a woman was involved. When I ended up being framed for murder that driver's license picture I generated was blasted over the news. Julius ended up clearing me by catching the guilty party, but the incident was something I wasn't particularly proud of.

"The photograph the media used wasn't of Archie," Julius said.

Kingston looked like he didn't believe him, but he didn't argue the point further. "So what do you say, Katz? This bottle of vino change your mind?"

"Perhaps. So we're clear, the Montrachet and the twenty-five thousand dollar fee you offered earlier?"

There was a hitch along Kingston's mouth as he clearly thought the Montrachet should've been sufficient payment, but he decided against arguing and instead nodded. "Yeah, sure," he agreed.

"And this would be nonrefundable," Julius added.

"What do you mean nonrefundable?"

Julius leaned back in his chair, his eyelids lowering to where it looked as if he were about to start napping. "Exactly what the word means," he said. "If I accept your proposal I am going to start preparing for it, and I could very well end up turning down other offers for work. If this stunt of yours gets cancelled before it can be performed, I will retain full payment, including the '78 Montrachet."

"Why would it get cancelled?"

Julius shrugged. "You might change your mind," he said. "After all, your scheme does require you to defame an innocent party by announcing them an intended murderer, and you might decide the liability issues involved aren't worth it. Or maybe your publisher cancels your book, or a myriad of other possible reasons."

"Okay, whatever," Kingston said, his cheeks turning a light pink to show his irritation.

"Then I accept your proposal."

The leer Kingston flashed him all but said, '*Your dignity's not for sale, Katz? Like hell it isn't. Everybody's got their price, you included.*' This contemptuous leer only lasted a second, if even that long. He had enough innate cunning to realize he'd better nor push it. and Julius acted as if he hadn't noticed it, but I sure noticed it and it made me feel as if an excess of heat was burning through me. This was a new sensation for me, and after a few hundred milliseconds of confusion I understood what it was. Anger. I was angry at Kingston feeling that he could buy Julius, and I was angry at the thought that Julius was going to be playing a stooge for this person. I was disappointed also, a small part because with the money Julius was going to be earning for this charade it would be months before he'd take on a new case, which would be months before I'd be able to observe his genius in action so that I could better adjust my neuron network. But I was mostly disappointed in Julius. This was the first time I had seen him trade his reputation and dignity for a fee, even if in this case the fee was a bottle of '78 Montrachet. Between the two emotions surging through me, the anger outweighed the disappointment.

Even though I was far from a happy camper at that moment I did my job and used legal boilerplate to put together a contract for Julius, making sure to spell out the nonrefundable aspect of the job. Once the contract was ready, I emailed Julius the file and informed Julius of it. He printed it out and, after scanning it quickly and grunting his satisfaction with it, handed it to Kingston, who must've been surprised to see a contract waiting for him. He gave Julius an odd look as if he thought the contract had been written up the night before, including the clause specifying the '78 Montrachet as part of the fee, but he signed it. After that he wrote Julius a check for twenty-five thousand dollars.

At the end of Kingston's earlier visit he had picked up the list of suspects that he had given Julius. With the contract and payment settled, he took this same list from his inside suit jacket pocket and tried to hand it to Julius, who shook his head.

"I remember those names from yesterday," he said. "There is no need to show me them again."

"Would you like the profiles I built on them?" I asked dryly. Julius ignored me, not bothering to answer me with our agreed upon hand signals that he used when others were around. I emailed him these profiles anyway.

"Were you being facetious the other day when you said that these people on your list, with the possible exception of your wife, all want to kill you?" Julius asked Kingston.

"I might've been exaggerating, I might not have been," Kingston said.

"Do any of them have legitimate reasons to want to do you harm?"

Kingston pursed his lips as he considered this.

"What difference does that make, Katz?" he said. "I'm paying you to put on a show, that's all."

"Sir, wouldn't you like a realistic performance from me?"

"I have faith in you, Katz, to deliver a realistic performance in any case. To answer your question; possibly, possibly not. It all depends on what you would consider a legitimate reason to kill someone. But it is all irrelevant since none of them would have the guts to go as far as murder."

"Would you at least share with me the perceived grudges they hold against you?"

Kingston considered this also before shaking his head, a bare trace of a smile on his lips. "I don't believe I would, Katz. I'm paying you a lot of money, much more than I originally expected to—I'm told that bottle of wine alone is worth twenty-five thousand dollars. I'm not saying I'm not going to get my money's worth out of this. I could easily spend over fifty thousand dollars in advertising and get far less bang for the buck than I'm going to get with this publicity stunt. But still, for this money I'd like the entertainment value of watching the great genius detective at work, so I'd like to see you discover these reasons for yourself."

When Kingston said the word genius he said it with the same contempt that he had shown Julius a flash of earlier. I felt that same flush of heat burning through me, and I found myself hoping Julius would throw this man out of his office. Instead, Julius chose to ignore this man's belittling of him and nodded slowly in agreement.

"Very well," he said. He took in a deep breath and let out a slow, soft sigh. "I would like to see an advance copy of your new novel."

"What for?"

"Again, to create the illusion of an authentic interrogation."

Kingston thought about this, but shook his head. "A damn good idea, Katz, and I'd like to be able to oblige you," he said. His mouth squeezed into a tight oval to show a constipated look as he thought more about this. "A real shame," he continued. "It could really work well to create a stronger buzz for my book having you drop hints about what the novel's about. Unfortunately, I can't do it. The contract I signed with the publisher forbids me from as much as describing the book let alone showing anyone a copy before the book's official release. I'm not even allowed to tell anyone the title. All part of the top secret publicity campaign that we agreed to."

Julius accepted this without any further debate, and then the two men agreed on a time for the first group interrogation, which would be at two o'clock the day after next. Kingston told Julius he'd try to arrange for each person on the list to show up at Julius's office at that time. Of course, since he hadn't spoken to any of them yet, he couldn't guarantee that that time would work, especially with one of them coming from New

York, but he'd let Julius know if he had a problem with any of them.

When Kingston stood up to leave, he hesitated as if he were going to offer Julius his hand but decided against it, which was most likely because he remembered the warning I had given him when he booked his appointment—that Julius never shook hands with clients. Julius always claimed that his reason for this was he didn't see any reason to unnecessarily expose himself to germs due to some outmoded social convention, but of course that never stopped him in the past from shaking hands with beautiful women and doing far more than just that, although I never actually witnessed him doing much more than shaking their hands. In the old days before Lily Rosten, Julius would always place me in his sock drawer whenever he'd have female company for the night, and so far Lily had yet to spend the night with him.

When Kingston left Julius's office, I followed his movements again through webcam feeds as he walked through Julius's townhouse so that he could let himself out. By this time the excess heat that had been burning through me had dissipated. I understood now why Julius had spent those hours torturing himself reading Kingston's book. He was attempting to bluff me and pretend that there was more to this job than the charade Kingston had proposed, that he was trying to glean from the book some sort of psychological insight into Kingston. But it was only a bluff. Maybe it was for himself as much as for me as a way to convince himself to partake in such a ridiculous and ultimately demeaning sham. Once the front door closed behind Kingston I coldly informed Julius of the fact that his new client had left his townhouse without incident.

"He did stop to study the books shelved in your hallway bookcase, and was no doubt insulted to find that you not only didn't have a complete collection of his works, but nary a single volume. But he did leave without any thefts or other mischief."

"Thank you, Archie."

Not even a hint of sheepishness or embarrassment showed in Julius's voice. I was amazed at the level of denial he had sunk to for him to agree to be a part of this charade.

"I guess he didn't have to go to the aquarium to hire himself a trained seal."

Julius displayed no reaction to my crack. "Things aren't always what they first appear," he said.

More of that bluff. That there was something more to this assignment than just a publicity stunt. I didn't bite on it. I knew him too well to do that.

"I thought your dignity and reputation weren't for sale?" I asked.

A wry smile pulled up the edges of Julius's lips. "I don't believe I ever said anything about my reputation being priceless," he said.

"Okay, your dignity then."

More of his wry smile. "Technically, Archie, I don't believe I as much sold my dignity as bartered it away."

It was a clever joke, but I wasn't much up to joking then. More of that excess heat began to burn again in me. "For a lousy bottle of wine! That's what you did it for!"

"I hardly think you can call a '78 Montrachet a lousy bottle of wine." Julius's smile faded as he sat straighter in his chair and rubbed his thumb along the knuckles of his right hand. With others, Julius kept his emotions and thoughts impenetrable, with me he didn't bother.

Right now he was showing his annoyance, but I didn't care. "The man is a philistine," Julius continued. "He was going to mix soda water with a '78 Montrachet to make a wine spritzer. It would've been a crime to let that happen."

"So you were just saving humanity from an outrage?"

"Precisely."

"Okay," I said. "I understand. For a bottle of wine, you've agreed to play a stooge."

Julius stopped rubbing his knuckles. He took in a slow breath and with a forced attempt at humor, said, "And of course, twenty-five thousand dollars."

"Of course, we can't forget the twenty-five thousand dollars. So for that money and the Montrachet, you'll be looking like a dunce to the world."

"Again, Archie, things are not always what they appear."

"Yeah, well, as far as the TV and newspaper reporters are going to be concerned, Kenneth J. Kingston will be trumping you at your own game. Should I be ordering you a dunce cap now for the occasion? I might be able to find a good deal."

Julius slowly began rubbing his knuckles again. "Enough of this, Archie."

I should've taken the hint, but I couldn't help myself. "Sure, of course," I said. "I understand. But Boss, should I get a jump on updating your biography to reference that you're no longer Boston's most brilliant detective, but have slipped to the second-most? Or should I wait until after Kingston plays you for a chump? Now that I think of it, after that happens I'm not even sure you could legitimately claim that title since probably every other working private investigator

in Boston would be able to prove themselves intellec-
tually superior to Kingston, so by the transitive property that would in effect make you Boston's least brilliant detective. Not as compelling a title for you to
hold, but I guess we'll have to deal with it. If you want
I can order stationary now to that effect, or I can wait
until—"

I pushed him too far. Julius cut me off, saying,
"Goodnight, Archie." And blast it! My world went
black as he turned me off!

3

JULIUS seldom turned me off. When he did it was always disorienting when I was turned back on. I commented once to Julius that it was probably a similar experience to being sucker punched, but he insisted it would have to be more akin to be being put under with anesthesia and later brought out of it. Anyway, this time even though I was in almost the same location in Julius's office when the world came back to me, it was maybe even more disorienting than those other times because of the crowd that was now sitting around me. It was almost as if I blinked and these people magically appeared, and it took me as much as three tenths of a second to get my bearings. I was turned off on Tuesday at three thirty-seven in the afternoon, now it was Thursday at six minutes past two, also in the afternoon. I'd been turned off for almost forty-seven hours.

There were six other people sitting in Julius's office. I recognized all of them from the profiles I had built from the list Kingston showed Julius. Sitting on the sofa that shaded to the right of Julius's desk were Edward Marriston, Zoe Chase and Jonathan Mable. Marriston was Kingston's agent, Chase his editor, and Mable his ex-writing partner. In the chair directly opposite Julius's desk was the book critic, Herbert Richardson. More in the corner of the room sat a fellow private investigator, Paul Burke, and sitting alone on the love seat that was placed to the left of Julius's desk was Kingston's wife, Gail. Presumably the empty seat next to her was being reserved for her husband. While all of the members of Kingston's list were present, the perpetrator of this farce, Kenneth J. Kingston himself, was missing. The critic, Herbert Richardson, was clearly not happy with that fact. His face was folded into a severe scowl, and his cheeks were turning redder by the second.

"The nerve of him!" Richardson exclaimed. "He asks us to be here at two o'clock on the dot, and he doesn't even show up on time himself!"

At first impression, Richardson appeared as if he could've been one of those tough guy writers, even with his meticulously groomed goatee. Square face, thick body, large hands. Once he talked, though, he ruined that illusion with a high-pitched voice, and the illusion was further obliterated by only a few seconds of observing his fussy mannerisms and overall softness.

"What's the reason we were brought here?" Richardson angrily demanded.

Julius stated innocently, "From what I was told, Kenneth Kingston requested that you come here with the understanding that this is a matter of extreme personal importance to him, and that you all came here freely of your own volition. Isn't that true?"

Julius had provided refreshments to this crowd. Zoe Chase had a glass of what I assumed was San Pellegrino water given the empty bottle resting on a service tray in the back of the room, Paul Burke was drinking a Rolling Rock, which was what Julius would have in those rare instances when he was in the mood for beer instead of wine, and the rest of them, Julius included, had glasses of a fine Riesling judging from the empty bottles also on the same service tray. Richardson angrily took a chunk of prosciutto-wrapped Stilton and popped it in his mouth. Barely chewing the hors d'oeuvre, he swallowed and in his high-pitched voice, complained, "You can at least tell us why we're here!"

Julius shrugged, his manner unassuming and affable as he apologized to Richardson, telling him he couldn't do so. "I am in the employ of Mr. Kingston and a condition upon which he insisted was that he be the one to address this gathering as to the nature of my investigation, so unfortunately my hands are tied."

"This is ridiculous," Richardson grumbled. He popped another piece of prosciutto-wrapped Stilton into his mouth. This time he bothered to chew it more thoroughly. After taking a sip of Riesling, he pressed a napkin to his lips, patted the area, then turned to Kingston's wife and demanded of her whether she knew why her husband had called all of them there.

"I have no idea," she said. Gail Kingston was four years younger than her husband. There was an unhealthy gauntness to her. She was more bony than what you'd call thin, with a long narrow face and a neck that looked too scrawny. From the tightness of the muscles along her mouth and the dull glazed look of her eyes, I was guessing she was either angry or annoyed. I couldn't figure out which. Of course, this could've simply been a reaction to Richardson's rudeness, but she had shown that same mix of anger and annoyance or whatever the emotions were before he had spoken a word. Studying the rest of the crowd, Burke seemed to be mostly amused by the situation, his eyes half-closed but still sparkling, while Marriston barely suppressed a yawn and Mable looked equally bored. Zoe Chase seemed to be the one among them who was nervous, maybe even scared. She was young, only twenty-three. Her brown hair was cut short, and she made me think of a wounded sparrow with her weak chin and large brown eyes and thin, slight build. According to her driver's license she was five feet one inches tall and weighed ninety-two pounds, but she seemed smaller than that with the way she was seemingly shrinking inwards, almost as if she was willing herself not to be noticed. From physical comparisons I made of her to well-known celebrities, she wasn't beautiful, but she would've been thought of as pretty. And she was certainly worried about something.

Even though this was all only a sham, I played my part and reported to Julius my assessment of them. He briefly scratched along the side of his nose as a signal to me that he saw things similarly.

Richardson was still fuming. "I came here today out of curiosity. I couldn't care less about helping the likes of Kingston. But it is still infuriating." He gave a quick angry glance at his watch before glaring at Julius. "It is now ten minutes past two. How much longer are we to be kept waiting here by that man?"

"I'm not sure," Julius said. "You're free to leave anytime you wish."

Richardson closed his mouth, but he didn't get up to leave. None of them did.

"You don't like Kenneth Kingston very much, do you?"

It was a good thing Richardson wasn't sipping his wine at that moment, because if he had, the snort he made would have sent the wine spurting out of his nose.

"Of course not," he said dismissively. "The man's a pompous ass, and that's the best thing I can say about him."

"The pot calling the kettle," I said.

Julius ignored me and instead addressed Kingston's wife. "How about you, madam?" he asked. "Assumptions are always dangerous, but I still need to assume that since you have remained married to my client that you have favorable feelings towards him, as opposed to the animosity that Mr. Richardson makes no attempt to hide."

She smiled bitterly. "You're right. Mr. Katz, assumptions are dangerous."

"So you do feel animosity towards your husband?"

Her smile faded as concern pinched her mouth. "I was joking," she said. "Did Ken tell you that?"

"Not at all, madam. Simply that your manner since you've been in my office has been borderline hostile."

"Hostile? That's what you think?" She shook her head. "No, Mr. Katz, I'm afraid you misread me. Maybe I'm annoyed that Ken wouldn't tell me what this is about, but no, what you've taken for hostility is mostly concern. Ken is always punctual. In the twenty-three years that we've been married he has never been late to an appointment. Not even a minute. I'm worried."

"Fair enough," Julius said. "I'm not infallible. It's possible I misread your body language. To put your mind at ease, your husband isn't late. He arranged with me to arrive here at two thirty to give me a half hour alone with all of you."

If Gail Kingston was relieved by this news, she didn't show it. Richardson, on the other hand, glowered hotly at Julius upon hearing this. Mable looked up surprised, no longer showing his boredom. Marriston showed little reaction, and neither did Zoe Chase who continued to look scared. Paul Burke broke out laughing.

"I'm sorry, Julius," he said. "Is that why Kingston hired you, to find out whether or not we like him?"

Julius smiled thinly. "No, Mr. Burke," he said. "That is not why I was hired. Nor is it what I'm attempting to determine."

"So you just wanted a chance to make small talk with all of us?"

"Not exactly. How about yourself? How do you feel towards my client?"

"I like the guy," Burke said. "He's been good to me, both in throwing investigations my way and in boosting my career. I'd say we're friends. Good friends."

"You've never resented him for his Paul Buck character? A character that is a thinly-veiled grotesque mockery of you? I read Kingston's last book, and I could imagine you being offended by it, especially with a certain insinuation that was made."

"Not at all, Julius," Burke said, his eyes still sparkling with amusement. "Those books have helped me a great deal. I wouldn't have my radio gig if it wasn't for them, and I wouldn't be doing the business I do either. And I also wouldn't be having TV producers talking with me now about basing a reality show about me." Burke took a drink of his beer, the sparkle in his eyes dimming a bit as he met Julius's look. "The fact is, Julius, I solve almost all my cases, just like you, but I don't make a big show and production out of solving them, so I'm not branded by the Boston media as a genius. Instead I solve them by hard work and grinding them out. Without those books, I'd just be another no name private investigator, and would probably just be scraping by. I love those books, I love what they've done for me. Besides, Ken lets me give my approval before he publishes them. If I have any problems with them, he'll fix it. So far I haven't had a single problem."

I knew that Kingston frequently hired Burke to do research for his books. It would be impossible not to know that with the way Burke crowed about it on his weekly one-hour radio slot and in the papers. I'd also recently seen short mentions that had been leaked to the newspapers about Burke's proposed reality show. At forty-six he was a few years older than Julius. He was also two inches shorter and stockier than him. In some ways he looked more like how you'd imagine a PI to look than Julius with his thicker body, broad face and this tough-guy look about him, but in other ways he tried hard to project the image of a celebrity— his hair dyed jet-black and groomed at one of the most exclusive hair salons in Boston, a deep tan that I knew came from a tanning salon after hacking into his credit charges, expensive clothing, gold chains around his neck and diamond stud earrings in both ears, and the way he fashionably allowed one day's worth of stubble to show on his face.

Somehow I had failed to make the connection that Kingston's fictional PI, Paul Buck, was based on Burke, or at least meant to poke fun at him. The character as written in Kingston's books was violent, amoral, and often solved his cases due to luck or serendipity. I was disappointed in myself. I thought I had thoroughly analyzed his books, and yet I missed this, and looking at it now it should've been obvious. I was going to have to work on my neuron network so I'd be able to make these types of associations in the future.

Julius stared impassively at Burke for a long moment, then a thin smile cracked his face. "Not even with Kingston's last book?" he asked.

Burke smiled back, still very amused. "Especially not with that one," he said. "It's fiction, Julius. I've never been what you'd call thin-skinned. I'm not a temperamental genius. Those books help me get business, and that's all I care about. It was that last book that got the TV producers to contact me."

Julius accepted this and moved on to Kingston's agent, Edward Marriston, asking him whether he disliked Kingston. While Marriston told Julius in a tone that dripped with insincerity that he had only strong admiration and warm feelings towards his longtime client, I analyzed Kingston's last book more carefully and couldn't find anything in particular that Burke could've taken greater offense at. Maybe the character came off more vulgar and crude than in some of Kingston's earlier books, but not enough to cause Julius to point it out. I'd have to ask Julius later what he was referring to. If there was an implication I missed that he had picked up on, I'd like to know it so I could work more on my neuron network. Whether or not this was only a charade, there was no reason I couldn't take advantage of it. My attention was snapped back to Julius when he commented how Marriston did not seem particularly sincere with his answer.

Marriston pursed his lips as he considered Julius. "I suppose you wanted to ask us about our feelings towards Ken without him present so we might be more likely to answer candidly. But really, Mr. Katz, with a portion of my livelihood dependent on Ken, and with Gail sitting here with us as well as no confidentiality being offered or implied, how could I possibly answer your question any differently regardless of how I might feel? But rest assured, I love Ken like a brother."

Marriston said this more straight-faced than his previous answer. Julius nodded, either accepting this or realizing he wasn't going to get anything different, and next asked Zoe Chase the same question. For some reason, she seemed startled by it.

"I have no problems with Mr. Kingston," she said in a startled voice. "Why would you think I do?"

"I could think of a number of reasons," Julius said. "But it would not be worth pursuing those now, your livelihood being somewhat dependent on my client, as with Mr. Marriston. We can revisit this further another time."

It was Jonathan Mable's turn and he didn't wait for Julius to ask him the same question he had asked everyone else. Instead he volunteered that he held no grudges with his ex-writing partner.

"I'm more interested in whether you dislike my client, not whether you hold any grudges."

Mable gave Julius a weary smile. "Let's just say I'm indifferent," he said.

Burke laughed out loud again. When Julius looked his way, Burke tilted his beer bottle to take a long drink, then wiped the back of his hand across his mouth.

"Am I amusing you?" Julius asked.

"Not you in particular," Burke said. "More this whole situation. On a tip, I spent the last two nights camped out in the cold and rain behind a dumpster hoping to find a teenage runaway girl, and here you are making probably ten times what I made those nights asking people whether or not they like some guy as if their answers are actually going to mean anything."

While we were so far having a temperate May, the last two nights the temperature did reach lows of forty-two and forty-one degrees Fahrenheit, respectively, and we at times had a light rain both nights. I informed Julius of this. He seemed to pay no attention.

"Did you have success in finding her," Julius asked Burke.

"Not yet."

Julius grunted at that. "That is a shame. And a shame also that I'm keeping you from that task, especially given that my questioning here will probably prove as fruitless as those two nights. Let us hope not." Julius paused for a moment, then added, "If you wish to consult freely with me on this missing teenager, consider it gratitude on my part for your taking time to come here today."

Burke's smile was gone as a more serious look hardened his face. "Thanks, Julius, but for the time being I think I've got this under control. But I'll take you up on this if I find myself stuck."

That was admirable on Julius's part, even if Burke did turn him down. I held back, though, on mentioning that to Julius. I didn't understand the reason for that at the time, but when I analyzed it later, I realized it was petulance on my part; partly over my disappointment that Julius willingly got involved in this farce, and partly for him turning me off for almost two days.

Julius nodded solemnly to Burke and turned back to Jonathan Mable.

"Sir," Julius said, "I find it hard to believe that your feelings towards Kenneth Kingston would be those of indifference. Twelve years ago the two of you were writing partners. Since he ended your partnership, you have published only one book, and that was over seven years ago. While that novel, in my opinion, was highly readable and showed significantly more skill and talent than Kingston has demonstrated with his books, it sold poorly. Kenneth Kingston, on the other hand, has achieved a fair amount of notoriety and financial success with his writing while you've mostly been mired in obscurity, or worse, as a footnote along the lines of Peter Best and the Beatles."

Mable's lips twisted into a smile that was caught somewhere between whimsical and sardonic.

"First, Mr. Katz, I'd like to thank you for acknowledging that you found my last book highly readable. Secondly, about my split with Ken, it was a mutual decision regardless of what Ken's been saying in interviews, and thirdly, about Ken's success, his last book sure as hell tanked, didn't it?"

A call came in for Julius. I was surprised to see that it was Tom Durkin, who was one of the local private investigators Julius would frequently use. I decided this must've been an arrangement Julius made with Kingston so that this farce would look more authentic. When I asked Tom to leave a message, he told me he needed to talk with Julius.

"He's got an office full of people right now. Six to be exact."

"Yeah, I know, Archie, but this is important. And we need to talk in private, not in front of his gathering."

It didn't make sense. The assignment was a joke. What could Tom possibly need to say to Julius that was so important? But I didn't argue with him and passed his message to Julius and asked him what he wanted to do. He answered this by announcing to the gathering that since they were running low on food and drink, he would temporarily be leaving them so that he could return with a new round of refreshments, and for them to stay seated in the meantime. With that, Julius was out of his chair and moving quickly out of his office and closing the door behind him.

4

JULIUS'S office was soundproofed so the crowd he just left wouldn't be able to hear him standing in the hallway talking to Tom, but still, Julius continued on until he reached his kitchen. Once he had poured himself a cup of coffee and was seated, I patched him through to Tom. During this, I kept a watchful lookout over the crowd in Julius's office through a webcam feed. When I saw Richardson leave his chair and head towards Julius desk, presumably to search through a folder that Julius had left behind, I called Richardson on his cell phone, which startled the hell out of him.

"This is Archie Smith, Mr. Katz's assistant," I told him. "I'm watching you right now over a closed circuit TV. Get back in your chair, or I'll come in there and pick you up and drop you in it, okay?"

Of course, I couldn't do that, but he didn't know that. The shock of the call caused him to pale, and then as the humiliation set in, his cheeks were left mottled pink and white. About the time he was sitting back down looking both sheepish and angry, Tom was explaining to Julius what was so urgent.

"It's twenty past, Julius, and no sign of him. His car is still parked out front, but I've been watching the building's main entrance since nine o'clock after taking over from Saul. I'm sorry, Julius, I should've had another man covering the back. I just didn't think he'd be making an effort to slip the tail. I have no idea how he made me."

"It's not your fault, Tom, it's mine. You were performing your tasks as asked. Have you tried making contact?"

"I've tried both his home phone and cell. Nothing. Do you want me to investigate? I could ring the bell. If no answer, I could break in. I checked the locks earlier. It would be a piece of cake."

Julius got very still for a moment, his features turning marble hard. I knew what that meant. He was deep in thought. What I would've given to be able to tap into his thought processes and study them! Julius stayed that way for ten seconds before coming out of it.

"Better that you don't. I doubt it will do much good, but stay where you are and watch for him until a quarter to three. If you see him, give me a call. If not, leave then." He hesitated, then added, "Did you see her leave? And please don't take offense at this borderline insulting question, since I know you would've volunteered the information without being asked, but did you spot any of the others?"

"She left the building at ten thirty-nine and got into a cab. And no, Julius, I didn't see any of the others, and no offense taken. Saul didn't see any of them during his shift. Any further instructions?"

"None at this time. I'd like to ask that you keep yourself available for the rest of the day. I'll call you if something comes up. Thanks, Tom."

I disconnected the call and Julius went about loading up a tray with more refreshments—two more plates of hors d'oeuvres that he must've prepared ahead of time, two more bottles of beer for Burke, a fresh bottle of San Pellegrino water for Zoe Chase, and three more bottles of Riesling for the rest of them. That told me he was planning to keep them in his office for a good while longer, and his leisurely pace made it clear that he was in no hurry to join them. Julius paused, a wistful smile showing.

"Archie," he said, "I'm afraid I haven't had a chance yet to welcome you back. I trust you had a restful nap?"

Julius putting me out for almost forty-seven hours was more like him inducing a coma than simply having me take a nap, but I didn't push it. I was too interested in these new events so instead I thanked him.

"Yep, very restful, thank you," I said. "I was surprised to see that you've assigned Tom Durkin to what is only a publicity stunt. And not just Tom, but Saul Penzer also. This is more than a publicity stunt, isn't it?"

"I don't know, Archie."

"But you suspect that it is. And you've suspected so from the beginning."

His wistful smile turned sour. "I don't know any more what I suspected," he said.

"You assigned Saul and Tom to watch and tail Kingston? Twenty-four coverage, twelve hour shifts each, right?"

Julius nodded, maybe showing a hint of moroseness. "I better bring this tray to my guests before they cause any trouble."

I informed him that I was keeping an eye on them, and told him of Richardson's attempt at snooping and the way my phone call sent him back to his chair with his tail between his legs. "Other than that they've behaved themselves. None of them have bothered speaking to each other, not even to ask each other their thoughts on why they're there. Zoe Chase continues to look scared, Paul Burke amused, Herbert Richardson angry, Gail Kingston annoyed, and Mable and Marriston mostly bored."

"Thank you, Archie," Julius said. He picked up the tray to take back to his office. I didn't ask him then his thoughts on why Kingston would've slipped his tail, or why Kingston would've even suspected that Julius had put a tail on him in the first place. It was almost two-thirty and I figured Julius could ask his client these questions when he showed up.

When Julius arrived back at his office, he distributed this second round of refreshments, and seemed to take his time doing so, clearly dragging things out. Once he was done and back in his chair, he dropped his earlier line of questioning, and asked them what appeared to me to be mostly unimportant, mundane questions. I understood what he was doing. He was distracting them, playing for time as he waited for Kingston to show up. I didn't much care. I was too busy studying Julius's two earlier meetings with Kingston trying to figure out what Julius saw that made him think that Kingston had another reason for hiring him and that the publicity stunt angle was only a ruse. I had no luck, but I was pretty sure of Kingston's real reason for hiring Julius. It was what he had first said. He must've genuinely thought someone was trying to kill him. It explained why he slipped past Tom Durkin—he wasn't trying to lose Julius's tail, but instead trying to leave his townhouse without being discovered. This was probably also why he wasn't answering his cell phone. He knew that his location could be traced through his cell phone, and he didn't want to give an assassin the chance to locate him that way. What I couldn't figure out was why the ruse in the first place. Why not just tell Julius why he was hiring him? Why the subterfuge?

When two forty came around, I started to have second thoughts about all this, as well as to why Julius was asking his innocuous questions since returning from the kitchen. Five minutes later Julius addressed the group, telling them that it appeared as if Kingston has either forgotten about the meeting or has been detained, but in either case he wasn't going to keep them waiting any longer.

"I apologize for having had all of you come here like this," Julius added with a tone that genuinely sounded apologetic, "but I'm afraid we'll have to reschedule after I've had a chance to consult with my client."

Richardson was livid once these words sunk in. "This was nothing but a stunt!" he insisted. "That horse's ass never had any intention of coming here today! And you were in on it, Katz!"

"I assure you, Sir, that I fully expected my client to join us here at two thirty."

If Kingston's wife was additionally worried over her husband's lack of punctuality, she didn't show it. Her expression revealed the same mix of anger and annoyance as when I first saw her. Richardson on the other hand was fuming as he glared hotly at Julius.

"We all gave up valuable hours of our day to come here," he bitterly complained. "Only to sit here and be asked inane questions by you. I insist that you tell us why we were brought here!"

Of course, Richardson did more than just sit there. He failed to mention the half pound of hors d'oeuvres that he had consumed or the four glasses of wine that he had drunk. The Riesling that Julius served was a fine vintage, and it went for eighty dollars a bottle. Richardson got his money's worth.

Julius shrugged and simply told him that his hands were tied. "Without my client's approval, I can't discuss this any further, but I do apologize for any inconvenience this has caused."

Richardson answered this with what only could be described as a loud and angry *harrumph*. Julius ignored him and ushered him and the rest of them out of his office. While Richardson left his chair reluctantly, none of the others seemed to mind much that this gathering was being brought to a close without Kingston ever making an appearance, and Zoe Chase for the first time stopped looking scared and instead looked relieved, although she still made me think of a wounded sparrow. Paul Burke was shaking his head, grinning, his eyes once again sparkling with amusement.

"Very educational, Julius," he said. "I always wanted to see you in action. I guess even the great ones can sometimes stumble out of the gate. Don't feel bad, I have my bad days too."

"Thank you for your kind encouragement," Julius offered stiffly.

Burke laughed at that and allowed himself to be herded out of the office with the others. Once Julius had them out his front door and the door closed with them on the other side of it, I asked him the obvious, which was if he thought Kingston didn't show up because he was dead.

"I don't know what to think, Archie."

"But you suspect that. That's why you acted so differently after Tom called. You no longer cared after that about questioning them. You couldn't have with the questions you were asking. You were just playing for time so you could send them away, but you had to make it look like you were doing so because Kingston wasn't showing up and not because you suspected that he had been murdered. The same reason you asked them such useless questions after Tom's call. You didn't want any of them saying anything to the police that would suggest that you knew Kingston's life was in danger."

Julius had gone back to his office to fill up one of the service trays with plates and empty or partially empty glasses, and he was now bringing the tray to his kitchen.

"I still don't know that he's been murdered," Julius said, grim-faced. "That's only conjecture on both our parts."

"But you suspect that's what happened," I said. "Just as you suspected that his life was in danger. That's why you had Saul and Tom watching him."

Julius was rinsing and carefully placing the used wine glasses in the dishwasher.

"If that's what I thought, then I bungled things badly," he said. He finished with the wine glasses, and after placing the empty bottles into the recycling bin, headed back to his office to finish cleaning up after the small mob that had been there. "Because, Archie," he continued, "if that's what I truly believed and my brain was operating properly, then I would've had more people watching him and I would've had listening devices and spy cameras planted in his home. I guess maybe you do need to update my press release after all and replace 'brilliant' with 'at times merely competent'."

"I won't be doing that," I said. "You've been distracted. With Lily in London and your poker game Friday night. And as you said, we don't know yet what happened to Kingston."

Julius didn't respond to that. I waited until he finished his clean-up job and was back behind his desk before asking him what made him suspicious in the first place that Kingston's real motive for hiring him wasn't the publicity stunt that he stated, but that he instead believed someone wanted to kill him.

"I'm not sure that that was Kingston's real motive. He may have had a far different motive for hiring me than that he was fearing for his life. But you are right, Archie. While he probably wanted to take full advantage of his proposed publicity stunt, I don't believe that that was his driving reason for any of this."

"Why'd you think that?"

"Several reasons," Julius said. "One of them being how quick he was to up the fee he was willing to pay. He went from ten thousand dollars to fifty thousand dollars with little argument, and this represented a significant portion of his net worth. And if he was primarily concerned with staging a publicity stunt, he could've hired Burke for a fraction of what he paid me. They already have a relationship, and Burke has a certain celebrity status. He would've been able to generate an equally effective publicity stunt. Kingston could've called his own shots with Burke, instead of having to do what he considered groveling in order to hire me, which I can assure you was very painful for someone of Kingston's nature."

I gave this some thought. "So why didn't he hire Burke instead?" I asked. "Did he believe Burke could've been one of his possible killers? Or was it that he didn't believe Burke was up to the job?"

"Either of those, or other possibilities." Julius breathed in fully and let out the air in a tired sigh. "It doesn't matter anymore. Archie, I'd like to ask you to monitor the Cambridge police department for any homicide calls."

So that was it. Kingston's townhouse was located in Cambridge. Julius believed Kingston's death was a forgone conclusion. I did as Julius asked, and hacked into the Cambridge police department's computer system. If Kingston's murder was reported, I'd know it. While I did this, I found myself puzzling over several things, one in particular.

"Burke was right about what you were asking them before Tom called you," I said. "About how useless it would be to ask these people whether they liked or disliked Kingston. You wouldn't be able to trust any of their answers."

"That's true," Julius admitted. "But I wasn't concerned with what they said as much as how they said it, as well as other physical clues."

So he used that question in order to size them up and maybe figure out their tells. I was going to have to study their answers more closely, see what I'd be able to determine from their body language and reactions.

"What next?" I asked.

"We wait," Julius said. "If Kingston's still alive, then I have a job to do."

He had already given up on that possibility, but I didn't argue with him. I tried studying the way these people had acted in Julius's office, hoping to be able to figure out if any of them could've been a recent murderer. Zoe Chase was an obvious choice with how scared she acted, but the more I studied Marriston and Mable, the more I wondered if what I took as boredom was really shock, maybe the kind of shock someone might suffer after committing a violent crime. And even Richardson had me confused. His outward belligerence towards Kingston could've been an act to cover up that he had possibly hours before killed the man. I couldn't exclude Kingston's wife either from her body language. What I thought was anger and annoyance—and what she claimed was her being worried—could've been simply her being terrified of Julius discovering her as a murderer. After all, she did leave their condo hours before the arranged gathering with Julius, while Tom spotted none of the others entering or leaving Kingston's building.

While I did this, I found myself only getting more confused. Julius, as if nothing had happened, picked up a hefty volume of selected writings from Thomas Jefferson. He'd been reading this before his first appointment with Kingston, and I was amazed that he was able to concentrate on this book, but from his expression he seemed to have no problem doing just that. My own mind or neuron network or whatever you'd like to call it was spinning with different thoughts on who could've killed Kingston, if he had indeed been killed.

At three-fifteen that question was still up in the air. I mentioned to Julius that I was surprised he wasn't heading off to the Belvedere Club for their cognac sampling. "You've missed it three straight days now," I said. "With your bank account flush with cash and your seeming lack of concern for what happened to your missing client, I thought you'd be going there today."

Julius didn't bother looking up from his book as he told me that it would probably be best that he skipped it today also.

It was twenty minutes later when I had my answer regarding Kingston. That was when I picked up an emergency call being logged at the Cambridge police department about a dead body being found. The address given was Kingston's address. I informed Julius of this. He looked up from his book then.

"Did the report mention an apartment number or the identity of the dead body?" he asked.

"No, just the building address. No identification, not even yet whether it's a male or female."

"Then it's still only an assumption that it is Kingston's body," he murmured, and was back to reading Thomas Jefferson's writings.

Seven minutes later it was no longer only an assumption. I reported to Julius that they were now reporting the dead body as a homicide. "Caucasian male, around fifty, five foot eight, one hundred and sixty pounds. He was shot once through the heart. I don't know the caliber yet. Oh, and this just came in. His name was Kenneth J. Kingston, well-known Boston-area crime writer."

"My assignment with him is over then," Julius said with a grunt, but he didn't bother looking up from his book, and within seconds he was as completely absorbed in it as he was before I gave him this latest news.

I let him read undisturbed for several minutes before reminding him that his client had been murdered.

"Kingston paid you twenty-five thousand dollars plus a twenty-four grand bottle of wine," I said.

"He paid me for a publicity stunt," Julius said, his eyes still focused on his book. "And I believe he got his money's worth. His murder should do wonders in helping to promote his upcoming book."

"You don't feel an obligation to earn any of the money he paid you?"

"I fulfilled the obligation I owed the man."

"You're kidding, right? Regardless of the excuse he used to hire you, he came to you because he feared for his life. You don't feel a sense of obligation to catch his murderer?"

Julius sighed. He used a bookmark to mark the page he had read to, then placed the book onto his desk. "Archie, you don't know if that's why he hired me. Maybe that was his reason, maybe he had an entirely different reason. It doesn't matter. I accepted the assignment because I believed his life to be in danger—"

"You accepted the job for a bottle of '78 Montrachet."

"True," Julius admitted. "If the fee wasn't sufficient I wouldn't have put up with his shenanigans. And in this case, the only fee that would've been sufficient would've needed to include a bottle of '78 Montrachet. But Archie, while I took this assignment because I thought his life might be in danger, no matter how I might've bungled the job it was still a fool's errand to try to save the life of a man who is determined to jump into a vipers' pit. After receiving Tom's call, I fully considered my obligations to my client and decided I owe him nothing, not after the puerile lies he told me. Whatever his true motives were for hiring me, he did nothing but try to deceive and manipulate me. I have washed my hands of him."

"Don't you at least feel like you should be calling the police with what you know?"

"I don't know anything," he said with a tired smile. "I have no evidence of any kind. All I have are suspicions and half thought out ideas. Kingston hired me for a publicity stunt. At this point that's all I know, and that's all I care to know. I have nothing to give them."

So there you had it. The reason Julius demanded that the fee be nonrefundable wasn't because he thought Kingston might change his mind about his publicity stunt but because he was afraid Kingston might be killed before the stunt could happen. As far as Julius was concerned, he was now justified in keeping the fee as well as not doing anything further to earn it. The thing was, I couldn't argue with him so I didn't bother. Still, Julius sat patiently for half a minute as if he were waiting for me to do exactly that. When I didn't, he asked, "Well, Archie, aren't you going to pester me more on this?"

As I mentioned I couldn't disagree with what Julius had said. Still, though, I did see a big reason why he needed to be the one to catch Kingston's murderer—something far more important than to give me the opportunity to refine my programming and logic models, but I didn't bring that up then. I figured that could wait. Instead I told Julius I saw no reason to pester him because what he was saying made sense.

"Good," he grunted. He started to reach for his book, but hesitated. "Archie," he said. "I've been curious about something. Before I, um, had to give you a timeout two days ago, you were in rare form. Very vociferous, to put it lightly. Why was that?"

"I didn't realize it right away, but it was because I was angry. That was a new sensation for me. I wasn't prepared to handle it properly."

Julius arched an eyebrow. "What were you so angry about?" he asked.

"That Kingston would be making you look like a fool to the rest of the world."

Julius smiled as he considered that. "Your reason was loyalty," he said. "Very admirable, Archie. Very human also."

With that he picked up his book and continued reading.

5

WHILE Julius might've had nothing to give to the police, I expected a visit from them regardless, and I was
pretty sure Julius did too. That had to be the reason
why he skipped the Belvedere Club that afternoon. He
wanted to get this unpleasantness over with, and he
also didn't want them thinking he was purposely avoid-
ing them. If they thought that they'd come back sometime over the next couple of days and make their visit
even more unpleasant, maybe even upset his plans for
his upcoming poker game. So I was pretty sure that was
the reason Julius stuck around. Not so he could help
the police with a murder case, but to help ensure his
poker game wouldn't be interfered with.

It was ten minutes to five when I saw from the outdoor webcam feed a familiar face walking up Julius's
pathway, although stomping might've been a more ac-
curate description. When I told Julius that Detective
Mark Cramer was approaching his front door and
didn't look too happy doing so, Julius grimaced just the
same as if he'd poured scalding water on himself, or

worse, drank a disappointing glass of wine. Of course, it shouldn't have been much of a surprise to Julius that Cramer would be the one to come knocking at his door, not when considering where the murder took place.

Cramer was a detective with the Cambridge police force. According to his records he was fifty-five, six-foot two and two hundred and twenty pounds, although I would've put his weight closer to two hundred and forty-six pounds. He also had less hair than the photo in his file. Every time I've seen him he's looked tired and cranky and with his suit badly needing pressing. Now as I watched him with his large pasty face set in an angry scowl, he looked even more tired and cranky than at any of those other times, and his suit looked slept in. When he reached the door, he pounded on it, his voice hoarse as he yelled for Julius to answer his damn door.

Julius pushed himself to his feet and grimaced more severely. The first time Julius had anything to do with Cramer was a year and a half ago when Cramer brought a mob of police officers to wait outside of Julius's home so he could arrest Julius as a material witness, his reasons absolutely ridiculous. That did not endear the man to Julius. He didn't care much for bullies. The second time that Julius and Cramer's paths crossed was seven months ago when I was framed for a murder and Cramer arrived at Julius's door with a healthy contingent of police officers to tear Julius's home apart searching for me. Of course, they were looking for a short, pudgy balding man who looked a little like how you'd imagine the Continental Op. and not a rectangular-shaped two-inch piece of space-aged computer technology, so they didn't find me and Cramer wasn't particularly happy about that. This was going to be the third time that a murder brought them together. To say that Julius tolerated Cramer would be an understatement, and to say that Cramer had to struggle to barely tolerate Julius—and only did so by grinding his teeth and clenching his fists—would be an even greater one. Being as impartial as I possibly could, I had to put the blame fully on Cramer for this. His bullying tactics were most likely because of his paranoid beliefs that Julius was actively trying to upstage him by making a big show of solving these murders and grabbing the media attention. While Julius did have a bit of a showman in him, if Cramer understood how lazy Julius really was, he'd realize how off base these fears of his were. The fact was Julius would've been more than happy if the police had solved both of these murders so he wouldn't have had to make the effort, but circumstances didn't allow for that.

Cramer didn't give Julius much time before he was pounding on the door a second time. He had his fist raised and ready to strike the door a third time when Julius opened it. Cramer slowly lowered his hand and stood red-faced and breathing hard as he stared at Julius.

"About time," he complained. It took Julius all of thirty-eight seconds to answer the door from the first knock. "I'm taking you with me to the station to answer some questions," Cramer forced out, his voice strained.

Julius showed a confused look, even scrunching up his eyes as if he didn't have any idea what Cramer was talking about.

"For what reason?" he asked.

The color in Cramer's face went from red to white as if a switch had been thrown. While I detected a slight tremor in the homicide detective's hand, he mostly kept himself composed, although his voice sounded even more strained as he asked Julius if he knew Kenneth Kingston.

"He's a client of mine," Julius said, still with his confused look, maybe now more innocent than confused. "Why?"

Cramer clamped his mouth shut tight for a moment. He looked mad enough to chew nails. "Can the act, Katz," he finally spat out. "Your client was shot dead. A bullet through the heart. As you damn well know!"

"I am not omniscient, Detective. I knew nothing of the sort, and I have no idea why you would think I did."

Cramer's eyes narrowed as he stared imaginary bullets at Julius. "You don't seem all that surprised to hear about it," he said.

"I'm not a dunce, Detective. Your coming to my doorstep like you did was enough to let me know that someone I knew or worked for had been murdered. But it wouldn't have mattered, though, if I had gotten the news from a girl scout who had come to sell cookies instead of from you, my reaction would still have been the same. An unfortunate reality is that my line of work requires me far too often to deal with sordid unpleasantness, even murders, and while news of most untimely deaths saddens me, I'm afraid I've grown sufficiently callous to where they're no longer a surprise." Julius shook his head, his lips pressed tight enough to form a grim line. "No, Detective, I see nothing that I can offer you, and unless you have an arrest warrant I will not accompany you to your station. If you are able to obtain an arrest warrant it would be only be by dubious means, and I would not speak once you had brought me there. If you wish to talk with me civilly, I will invite you into my home, although I can't imagine what good it would do you."

You could see that it killed Cramer to give in, but he did so, muttering okay under his breath as if it were a curse. Julius led the way, bringing Cramer in to his kitchen instead of his office. Once there, Julius asked Cramer if he'd like some coffee. I could hear Cramer grinding his teeth for several seconds before telling Julius, "No thanks."

"That's too bad," Julius said. "This is a new imported French roast. I've only started using it last week, and it's really very good. I'll be making some for myself and if you change your mind, let me know."

Julius retrieved the beans from his refrigerator, and as he brought them to his coffee grinder, an exasperated Cramer snapped at Julius to quit his stalling.

"By now I know your act by heart and I'm not going to put up with it," Cramer threatened.

Julius sighed. "I'm only trying to be hospitable, Detective, but fine, ask your questions as I'm brewing the coffee."

"Awfully civic-minded of you, to be willing to answer questions in a murder investigation," Cramer said, his raspy voice dripping with sarcasm. He had to stop then as the noise from Julius's coffee grinder drowned out his voice. Once this ended, Cramer asked Julius what Kingston hired him for.

"To help him with a publicity stunt—"

Cramer exploded with that. Not literarily, of course, but figuratively. I guess it had been building up from the moment he first learned that Julius was somehow involved.

"A publicity stunt?" he croaked out. He would've been yelling except his voice had grown too hoarse for that. "He pays you fifty thousand dollars and you've got the nerve to tell me it was for a publicity stunt? And we know about the fifty thousand dollars, Katz. We found an entry in his day planner that he paid you fifty grand. Then two days after he pays you that type of money he's found dead. And you've got the stones to try to tell me that he hired you for a publicity stunt?"

"He seems tightly wired, doesn't he?" I said. Of course, I was talking to Julius through his ear piece and Cramer couldn't hear me, but it wouldn't have bothered me if he could. "Probably a good thing that he's passing on the coffee. Look at how his ears have turned red. Like a fire engine. Maybe you should offer him some warm milk instead? Or maybe chamomile tea?"

Julius ignored my comments, and patiently waited for Cramer's outburst to come to an end before explaining the nature of Kingston's fee. "My client wrote me a check for twenty-five thousand dollars. He also included as a gift a rare bottle of wine that in some cases has fetched at auction prices as much as twenty-four thousand dollars."

"Okay, so he paid you forty-nine thousand. I want to know why he paid you that!"

"Are you implying that the money he paid me, as well as the wine that he gifted me, had something to do with his death?"

"Yeah, I am. Fifty grand sounds like extortion to me, especially when the guy's dead two days later."

Cramer said this straight-faced, although I doubted he believed it. Julius regarded Cramer slowly before shaking his head.

"You would have a monumental task on your hands if you tried to prove that allegation, even with manufactured evidence," Julius said. "And besides, if extortion was the motive, then he shouldn't be dead since he paid me, right? Perhaps if he hadn't paid me… even still, I think you'd find your conjecture impossible to prove. But it doesn't matter. As I tried telling you earlier, Kenneth Kingston paid me my fee so that I would help him with a publicity stunt. He has a new book coming out in three weeks and he believed this stunt would get him on the bestseller's list."

Cramer snorted at that. "Fifty grand for a publicity stunt? You expect me to believe that?"

Julius shrugged. "Believe what you wish. I found the task he was asking me to perform demeaning so I in turn asked for an exorbitant fee as a means to dissuade him. He surprised me by accepting."

Cramer was so angry right then that I could almost imagine steam coming out of his fire-engine red ears. He was convinced Julius was lying and was about to call Julius a liar but he choked it off. His voice was low and had a strangled quality to it as he threatened Julius with an obstruction of justice charge.

"So help me, Katz, if I find out that Kingston hired you for any reason other than what you're telling me I will see you behind bars if it's the last thing I do. I know your tricks and I wouldn't put it past you to hide information about an ongoing murder investigation just so you can grandstand and grab headlines. It's not going to happen this time, Katz. I swear to God it's not going to."

At least he was no longer accusing Julius of being an extortionist and a murderer. As I mentioned before, Cramer didn't understand Julius's motivations at all, which was simply to enjoy his true passions in life while doing the least amount of work he could get away with so he could afford those passions. Julius had no real interest in publicity or newspaper headlines. That came only due to the sensationalized cases that he undertook, and those were the cases he'd end up with only because they were the ones that paid him enough money to support his chosen lifestyle. Although he didn't show it with his placid countenance, I knew Julius had to be annoyed at Cramer's belligerence. After all, he invited the man into his home, offered him coffee—and not just any coffee but a special French roast that Julius had ordered and waited months for—and all he'd gotten back so far were accusations and rudeness. When Julius began rubbing his knuckles with his thumb, he left no doubt about how annoyed he was. I was surprised by this outward display on his part, but I guess he had so little regard for Cramer right then that he saw no reason to hide one of his few tells.

"So you've sworn to God," Julius remarked dryly. "Do you have any other questions or are we done?"

Cramer closed his mouth. A hint of cautiousness flashed in his eyes. I don't know whether he was able to read Julius's tell, but at some level he realized he had pushed Julius too far. He tried to glower at Julius but couldn't hold it, and instead looked away.

"Tell me about this publicity stunt," Cramer insisted.

"No."

He looked back at Julius, surprised. "What do you mean no?" he asked.

If I had lips I would've smiled. Not necessarily out of any sense of warmth or happiness or good feelings, but I had to admit I enjoyed seeing the look of utter shock on Cramer's face when Julius said no. It probably wasn't a smart move on Julius's part. He reacted peevishly because he was annoyed at Cramer's boorish behavior, and I knew in the long run it wasn't going to do him any good, but I still couldn't help feeling glad that he did it. Maybe more proud than glad, although I couldn't tell exactly since proud was also a newer sensation for me.

The coffee had finished brewing. Julius ignored Cramer as he poured himself a cup. He didn't bother adding cream or sugar—he always drank his coffee black, and he took several leisurely sips before putting his cup down and meeting Cramer's bewildered stare, Julius's own eyes hard steel.

"My client expected a certain level of confidentiality from me when he hired me," he said. "There was nothing unlawful about what he asked me to do, but since nothing has yet been done regarding this, and since I believe details of his plans could damage his reputation I will not repeat it to you. At least not willingly. If you can find a court that will coerce me to do so, then so be it."

I expected a red-faced explosion out of Cramer, but instead his complexion turned a chalky white. He stood there with his mouth clamped shut, an uncertainty clouding his eyes. For several seconds this confused me, but then as if a lightning bolt had struck—or perhaps more precisely, a burst of electrons—I understood. The reason for his earlier bluster and all of his belligerence and combativeness was fear. Whether it was fear of being made to look like a fool or something else, I wasn't sure, but that's what it was. And he knew that he had pushed Julius too far earlier, and now I could see a trace of fear in him.

Finally, Cramer nodded slowly to himself.

"So you're going to obstruct a homicide investigation," he stated stubbornly.

"If that's what you think then find a judge who'll agree with you. For the record, I know nothing about my client's murder other than what you've mentioned. Further, I have no interest in knowing anything about it. Unless you have anything else you'd like to ask, I'd like you to leave my home."

Cramer recovered enough of his wits to try again to glare at Julius, but it was a weak effort. He seemed to realize this and he gave it up.

"Watch yourself, Katz," he warned, and then he turned to leave. Julius didn't bother getting up. He stayed seated at his Coraille granite island counter and picked up his coffee cup so he could take several sips. While he did this, his stare shifted away from the homicide detective. I made sure Cramer removed himself from the townhouse without causing any trouble. Once the front door slammed shut behind him, I informed Julius that his guest had left his home.

"The man's a fool," Julius said.

"Possibly," I said. "I'm guessing he's too in awe of your genius to act properly in your presence. Still, though, someone needs to tell him you can catch more flies with honey than with what he's using, which I have to admit is a little surprising because what he was tossing around usually does attract flies also. Maybe I'll give him a call later and try to help the poor guy out."

Julius made a face at that but didn't bother to respond.

"You intimidate him almost to tears. You know that, right?"

"Bah. That's his problem."

"True," I said. I hesitated before adding, "I'm surprised he didn't find Kingston's copy of his contract with you when they searched his home. If the police had found it, Cramer would've known the details of your fee, but it wouldn't have helped him more than that since I had what you were going to do for Kingston written up as 'unspecified services'."

If Julius found that surprising he didn't bother mentioning it. I waited a few seconds and when no reply came, I stated the obvious.

"You realize also he doesn't know yet about your little gathering here today?" I said.

Julius frowned at that. "That's his problem. He can talk to Kingston's widow or any of the others to find out what was said and done here."

"Agreed," I said, "but it's not going to change the way he's going to react. He backed down today because he knew he'd been acting like a horse's ass, but once he hears that you held that meeting and didn't tell him about it, he's going to be furious. And he's also going to be feeling justified in how he acted here since that will be confirming, at least in his mind, everything that he's been suspecting about you. That you've willfully been hiding information from him."

Julius waved his hand in an eh type gesture, as if he didn't care about any of that. "You're right, of course," he said, "but so what. I have no interest in Kingston's murder and I have no interest in being involved, not even to spite him." Julius smiled thinly. It was a strained smile as he was still recovering from Cramer's extreme boorishness. "Archie, I am impressed that you are able to show this level of insight into Detective Cramer's psyche."

"Eh, it was easy," I said. I wish I had a hand so I could've waved it to show the same gesture Julius had. "Your including a complete collection of Nero Wolfe books in building my experience base had a lot to do with it. It made it a piece of cake."

Julius smiled as he thought about that, then picked up from his desk his collection of writings from Thomas Jefferson, and apparently from his absorbed expression, was able to quickly put Kingston's murder out of his mind. I didn't bother pestering him about it then. It wouldn't have done any good. For now he was going to be stubborn, but I was sure that he knew as well as I did that he was going to have to be the one to solve Kingston's murder. It didn't matter whether or not he felt any moral obligation. By tomorrow, or maybe the day after that, it would be too obvious for him to ignore no matter how stubborn and lazy he insisted on being.

6

AT a quarter to six that evening Lily called Julius from London. She was the only person besides Julius who knew what I was, and whenever she called him it was always on his private line so I wouldn't be able to eavesdrop. That was fine. I could understand her desire for privacy, and besides, it didn't do my logic modeling center any good listening to their phone calls, especially when she was traveling and the two of them were pining away for each other and sounding like moonstruck lovers. While Julius was engaged in talking with her, I called Henry Zack and filled him in on what had been going on, particularly the trouble I was expecting once Cramer learned about the meeting Julius held in his office with Kingston's list of six suspects. Henry was Julius's attorney, and Julius had him on twenty-four hour call for emergencies, and I was expecting an emergency any minute. I gave Henry most of the story, although I left out Julius's suspicions regarding Kingston and his putting a twenty-four hour watch on him. When I was done I heard Henry sighing on his end.

"Legally Julius doesn't have to volunteer to the police why Kenneth Kingston hired him, nor about the gathering he held, but it probably would've been better if he had done so. Do you know why he didn't?"

"Partly because of Cramer irritating him, mostly because he was being stubborn."

I knew there was another reason too, a reason that overshadowed the ones I gave Henry. Julius didn't want to give Cramer any suspicions that he felt Kingston had other motives for hiring him, and worse, that he believed his client's life had been in danger.

"What does Julius want me to do?" Henry asked.

"He doesn't want you to do anything. He doesn't even know I'm calling you. But I'm sure Cramer will be looking to cart Julius away to jail in handcuffs once he finds out about Julius's gathering today. And if Cramer tries doing that, knowing Julius, he'll break Cramer's wrist the second the guy attempts to put his hands on him, which will end up with Julius heading to prison and me out of a job."

"That's probably what will happen," Henry agreed. "Call me at the first sign of trouble, okay? Which means as soon as that officer shows up at Julius's doorstep. Thanks for the heads-up, Archie."

When I finished my call with Henry, Julius and Lily were still talking as young lovers usually do, although Julius at forty-two no longer qualified as young, but Lily was only twenty-nine so I gave them the benefit of the doubt. I knew about how young lovers acted because when Julius first met Lily his behavior towards her baffled me to no end, as did hers towards him. The way he acted with her didn't fit his previous patterns with women. At first I tried without any success to explain this anomaly in his behavior through

71

mathematical models. Eventually I decided to go at it from a different angle and search for similar patterns in literature. After analyzing the text of a Jane Austen novel I was pretty sure I had it figured out, and after analyzing more of these novels I was left with no doubt that I had this mystery solved.

After getting off the line with Henry, I tried not listening in on Julius and Lily but I couldn't help hearing the end of their conversation, at least from what Julius was saying, to have a good idea of what Lily was saying to him: that she didn't want him moping around at home that evening and that she'd feel better knowing that he was out among people at one of his favorite restaurants. With or without her phone call, there wasn't any chance Julius was going to be spending the evening at home, not with him being flush with cash, and even better as far as he was concerned, feeling as if he had no further responsibilities to earn this money. When he got off the phone with her, I asked him if he wanted me to make reservations for him at *Le Che Cru*.

"Very good, Archie."

"Eight o'clock?"

"Excellent."

I called the restaurant and they gave me the reservation that I asked for. While it was short notice, and at that hour on a Thursday night they were certainly already booked solid, they always tried hard to accommodate Julius. This worked well to my advantage, at least I hoped it did. If Cramer tried storming Julius's townhouse while he was out, he'd end up calling me with some sort of threat or outrageous demand that I present Julius to him immediately, which would give me more than enough time to arrange for Henry to be present when Julius returned back to his home.

At eight o'clock on the dot, Julius entered *Le Che Cru* and the maître d'hôtel rushed over to enthusiastically greet him. As I suspected, the place was crowded with a long line of diners waiting to be seated. The maître d'hôtel had the best table in the restaurant reserved for Julius—a quiet booth against the wall and on the opposite side from the kitchen. Before taking Julius there, he first introduced Julius to several guests from France who were waiting for a table—a world class chef from Paris, the owner of a vineyard located in the Alsace region and the vineyard owner's wife. The vineyard owner produced a label that Julius was well aware of and admired. The chef, Sophie Bouchez, was gorgeous. Long golden blonde hair, slender build, dazzling blue eyes. I didn't even need to do a comparison of her to Hollywood starlets to know she was gorgeous and her French accent was something even I found myself attracted to. With little discussion, Julius invited them to join him at his table, and for the next three hours they ate the best food the chef at *Le Che Cru* could cook, drank several bottles of the best wine that the restaurant had in their cellar from the vineyard owner's label, and talked French cuisine and wine making. It was a little after nine o'clock when I got a call from Paul Burke wanting to talk to Julius. Even though I knew there was little chance Julius would be willing to interrupt his dinner, I gave him the message and he gave me a signal that he had no interest in talking to Burke or anyone else who might call.

"Sorry," I told Burke. "Julius is unavailable right now, and doubtful he'll be available any time soon."

"He must know Ken Kingston was murdered today, right?"

"Yeah, he knows."

"Ken was a friend of mine," Burke said. "He helped put me on the map and threw a lot of business my way. I'm dedicating my talents now to catch his murderer. I thought Julius might want to team up with me."

"Nah, Julius would have no interest in that."

Burke tried sounding nonchalant as he suggested I ask Julius whether he'd have an interest, but I heard an edge creep into his voice, the kind of edge from someone who feels he always needs to prove himself.

"Not necessary," I told him.

"He feels he's too much of a big shot to work with me, huh?" Burke said. "Yeah, well, maybe it will help if you tell him I've been talking with the producers of my reality show, and it's sounding like it's going to be greenlighted with Ken's murder kicking things off."

"You misunderstood me. It's not that he doesn't have any interest in working a case with you. Whether he does or not, I have no idea. What he doesn't have any interest in is worrying about who killed Kingston. As far as he's concerned, that's not his problem."

This seemed to catch Burke by surprise, at least by the dubious note in his voice. "You're kidding?" he asked.

"I kid you not."

"That doesn't make any sense. Ken was a client. He just paid Julius a ton of money. I don't get it. Why wouldn't your boss feel obligated to catch Ken's murderer?"

"He doesn't. All he feels obligated to do is what Kingston hired him to do, and that's it. But I'll pass on your offer to Julius. Maybe he'll have a change of heart." I hesitated, then added, "I've got a question."

"Shoot."

"Did the police talk to you yet?"

"Yeah, they did."

"Did you tell them about the gathering Julius had with all of you today?"

"Nope," Burke said. "They didn't ask, so I didn't bother volunteering it. Why? Is this something Julius wants to keep hushed?"

"No, not at all. Just something I was curious about."

With that I ended the call and for the next hour and forty-five minutes spent my time mostly enthralled with the sound of Sophie Bouchez's voice. It was partly this throaty purring quality to her voice, partly her French accent. While I listened on about the newest trends in haute cuisine in Paris, I was also monitoring the Cambridge police department's computer system and the outdoor webcam feed at Julius's townhouse. It was shortly after espressos were being served that I picked up from the police department that an arrest warrant had been issued for Julius on obstruction of justice charges. I told Julius this, but he didn't seem to care.

About the time Julius was settling the bill and saying goodnight to the vineyard owner and his wife and a clearly disappointed Sophie Bouchez—disappointed because she had made her intentions for Julius clear with the way she flirted, laughed at his jokes and touched his arm while Julius remained impervious to her attentions—I saw over the webcam feed a fuming Detective Cramer storming his way down Julius's pathway towards his front door. I told Julius about this. Again, he didn't seem to care.

"Maybe you should use the opportunity being presented to you," I suggested. "Mademoiselle Bouchez clearly wants you to spend the night with her, and it would allow you to avoid the police, at least until the morning, which probably wouldn't be a bad thing."

Julius ignored me. It wasn't as if I'd never in the past witnessed Julius doing exactly what I was now suggesting, but that was all before Lily Rosten. When Sophie Bouchez suddenly embraced Julius for a goodbye, I saw her slip a folded note into Julius's coat pocket. After she left with the vineyard owner and his wife—all the while making sure to linger at the door—I told Julius about her note. He still had time to go after her. Instead he waited for her to leave the restaurant, then he tore up the note unread. During all this I continued watching Cramer through the webcam feed as he pounded on Julius's front door and yelled for Julius to open his damned door, that he had a warrant for Julius's arrest. For a moment it looked as if he were going to try to kick it down, which would've been a mistake since Julius had enough added security features to make the door impenetrable and all Cramer would've accomplished would've been damaging his knee. Instead of doing that, he took out his cell phone and tried calling Julius. I answered and patched Julius in so he could hear also.

"Put your boss on the phone," Cramer ordered, his voice barely able to contain his exasperation.

"I would if I could but I can't, so I won't."

"I've got a warrant for his arrest, so you better damn well listen to me."

"Well, now, that's all fine and dandy, but it's four minutes past eleven right now, and I have no idea why you'd think I'd be with him. I do know he had plans to go out this evening. I'll try to track him down. If I'm able to do so, where should I tell him you'll be?"

From what I could tell through the webcam feed he was beyond fuming. "Playing the same games as your boss, huh?" he forced out. "You can tell Katz I'll be waiting for him outside his front door for the next ten minutes. After that I'll be breaking down that door and waiting for him inside!"

With that Cramer disconnected the call.

"The man's a dunce," Julius muttered.

"Yeah, I know, a fool and a dunce. But he still has an arrest warrant with your name on it. Should I call Henry Zack?"

"Don't bother."

"Your choice. If after an evening of fine food and drink and sterling conversation you'd like to spend the night in a jail cell instead of your own bed, that's up to you. I would think the prudent thing would be for me to call Henry."

Julius knew I was right but he didn't want to give in, at least not completely. Stubbornly he told me to do as I wished. I called Henry and filled him in on these latest developments, including Cramer's threat. Henry lived in the Back Bay section of Boston which at that hour would only be a few minutes' drive to Julius's townhouse. He promised me he'd be there in less than the ten minutes that Cramer had given in his threat.

"Probably best that Julius wait until I give him a call before he shows up."

"Not a problem," I told him. "He's got at least a ten minute walk from where he's at."

"Are you with him, Archie?" Henry asked. I think Henry's always wondered about me, about why he's never seen me with Julius, or has ever seen me, period. I told him I was, but the two of us would be going our separate ways as I would be calling it a night, and I wished him luck in keeping Julius out of jail. I had Julius patched in on the call so he could hear the conversation, but if he felt any relief over me making this call he didn't show it with any change in his expression. After the call ended, I suggested that Julius have an after dinner drink or another espresso to guarantee Henry beating him back to his townhouse.

"Not necessary, Archie."

"Okay, suit yourself."

Julius had a few words with the maître d'hôtel, and warmly shook hands with him. As I mentioned before, Julius rarely shook hands with people, at least if they weren't beautiful women, but the maître d'hôtel at *Le Che Cru* was an exception. After that he was out the door and walking at a brisk pace. I calculated at the pace he was walking that he'd cover the three blocks to his townhouse in seven point two minutes, which would make it a tossup as to whether he'd beat Henry there. As I strongly implied earlier, Julius could be both childish and bullheaded when he chose to be. There was nothing I could do about it, not even my attempts to goad him about Sophie Bouchez's obvious interest in him had any effect in slowing down his pace, nor did my telling him about the details of Paul Burke's phone call, so I admitted defeat and stopped trying.

7

HENRY Zack ended up beating Julius back to his townhouse by a whopping forty-seven seconds. We were less than a quarter of a block away from Julius's address when I received a call from Henry to let me know it was safe, and then watched on the webcam feed as Julius's lawyer moved quickly towards Cramer to demand that he show him the arrest warrant he had for Julius. Cramer didn't want to, and told Henry he wasn't going to until he had confirmation that Henry was Julius's attorney, which was just plain juvenile on his part since he knew full well from an earlier experience who Henry was. It was at that moment as the two men were arguing that Julius showed up on his pathway. Cramer stood facing the street so he saw Julius first. For several seconds his jaw clamped shut, then his anger got the better of him and he bellowed to Julius in a voice even more hoarse than earlier that he was under arrest and that he had better not move.

"My attorney is standing right next to you," Julius said in a patient and calm voice. "I believe he's been asking to see your arrest warrant."

Reluctantly, almost as if it killed him to do so, Cramer shoved the document into Henry's outstretched hand, which Henry then made a show of reading; scowling and grimacing as if the warrant was causing him great personal pain. He already knew what was in it since I emailed him a copy earlier while he was still at home. He didn't ask me how I had gotten my copy—he never asked me questions like that, but I had little doubt that he was very curious about it.

"You've got to be kidding me," Henry said, shaking his head to show his dismay. "If you insist on executing this warrant, I'll have it vacated before you're able to bring Julius back to your precinct. This warrant should never have been issued. You have no cause for it—"

"The hell I don't!" Cramer interjected. His ears had turned a deep cherry red as he stared fuming at Henry and then at Julius. "Your client is interfering with a homicide investigation, as he damn well knows!"

Henry frowned as he gave Julius a puzzled look. "Are you aware of doing this?"

"Not in the slightest," Julius said.

"Is that so?" Cramer demanded, his focus fully on Julius. "Is that why you had Gail Kingston over to your office? And others associated with the murder victim? You think I don't what you're up to, Katz?"

"I have no idea what you're thinking," Julius told Cramer. Then he turned to Henry and said, "I did have Gail Kingston and others over today for a private matter."

"Did this have anything to do with Kenneth Kingston's murder?" Henry asked Julius.

"No, of course not. This was in the early afternoon, and I didn't learn of his murder until ten minutes to five, which was when the detective here came pounding on my front door like some sort of lunatic."

Cramer did not appreciate that comparison. You could tell from the way he glared at Julius and began breathing in a more ragged way. "You're going to stand there and say with a straight face that you didn't suspect when you had his widow and those other people in your office that your client hadn't been murdered?" he croaked out incredulously, his voice little more than a raspy whisper.

"Why would I have?"

"How about that he didn't show up like he was supposed to? Or that you found an excuse to get rid of them quickly without even bothering to call your client to see why he didn't show up? Are those good enough reasons for you?"

"Hardly," Julius said. "I dismissed my guests because of my policy, which is to cancel an appointment if someone is fifteen minutes late. My first thought when someone fails to show up for a scheduled appointment is not that they have been murdered but that they're too inconsiderate to value my time, and when that happens I have no interest in calling them to hear their excuses. If you were in private business dealing with the public as I've been, you'd probably learn to think the same."

Julius did have that policy regarding late appointments. Of course he was still lying, although he gave no indication of it from his body language or his expression—again, Julius has no 'tell' when he doesn't want to have one. Still, though, even given how convincing Julius might've been, from the look on

Cramer's face he knew that Julius was lying. Not about
what Julius might or might not suspect when a person
is late for an appointment, but about Julius's suspicions
concerning what had happened to Kingston when he
failed to show today. The problem was unless he knew
about Saul and Tom being assigned to watch Kingston
and Tom's phone call to Julius there was little chance
he'd be able to prove it. Henry, though, didn't give him
any time to think about it.

"Does that satisfy you, Detective?" he asked.

"Not even close," Cramer said.

"Well, it should," Henry stated. "Let me explain to
you what will happen if you try to arrest my client
based on the flimsy and ridiculous reasons stated on
this warrant. Police harassment charges being brought
against you will only be the beginning of it. I'll be filing
civil lawsuits against you, your department and the City
of Cambridge, and I'll be collecting enough in damages
so you'll never have to worry about your path crossing
with Julius again even if you somehow remained a police officer, which I think would be highly unlikely. But
if you were somehow able to keep your badge you'll
still be free of any future alleged interference from Julius since he'll be retired and living in that villa in Tus-
cany that he has always talked to me about."

Henry Zack was sixty-three and was a much smaller
man than Cramer at only five foot six inches and rail
thin, weighing no more than a hundred and thirty-four
pounds. You wouldn't have thought he could've rattled
Cramer as much as he did, especially given how he said
all this in such a mild and soft voice. But even given his
stature, he could present an imposing figure with his
thick mane of white hair and a burning intensity in his
eyes that even I had little trouble recognizing. He got

to Cramer. Not enough to make him back down, but enough where you could see a flicker of doubt in the detective's eyes.

"You had your chance to see the warrant," Cramer said stubbornly. "Tell your client to cooperate with the arrest or I can't be responsible for what happens."

Cramer slipped a pair of handcuffs from his belt, but his heart was no longer in it. He took a reluctant step towards Julius. When Henry cleared his throat to get his attention, Cramer stopped and looked back at the attorney.

"Detective," Henry said. "I'd like to suggest that the three of us sit down and talk. If you continue on this course of action, you'll achieve some level of notoriety for arresting Julius, but outside of that you'll be causing nothing but legal and financial problems for yourself, and you certainly won't get the information from Julius that you're hoping to get." Henry nodded over towards Julius and asked, "If Detective Cramer were to arrest you, would you ever utter another word to him that you weren't legally required to?"

"Certainly not," Julius said.

"There you have it, Detective," Henry said as he showed both his palms in a what-are-we-going-to-do-now gesture. "Should we see if we can solve this in a more calm and reasonable manner?"

Cramer blinked then. Both literally and figuratively, and all the steam seemed to go out of him. "I'll give your client ten minutes," he said, staring fixedly at Henry and refusing to give in and look in Julius's direction. With that he stepped aside so Julius could move past him and unlock his front door. After that Julius led Henry and Cramer to his kitchen, not his office, which told me that he was still unwilling to consider

Kingston's murder as something he needed to concern himself with. This time Cramer grudgingly accepted Julius's offer for coffee. While Julius ground the beans and made the coffee, Henry sat perched on one of Julius's counter stools while Cramer stood with his arms folded across his chest. Once the coffee was served and a plate of biscotti put out Julius took a counter stool next to Henry, and Henry asked Cramer what he wanted.

"I want to know what Kingston hired Katz for," Cramer said.

Julius breathed in heavily to demonstrate how much his patience was being tried. "I'm sitting right here," he said. "You can address me."

"So answer my question!"

"I already did earlier this evening," Julius said. "And I am not in the habit of repeating myself."

Henry cut in, telling Cramer the same that Julius had told him earlier, that Julius was hired to help Kingston promote his upcoming book. "As my client already explained, he is not willing to go into any further detail without a court order compelling him to do so, and that is solely to protect his client's reputation."

"How do I even know that he was hired by Kingston?" Cramer demanded, his exasperation again showing.

"You told me you found a note about it in his day planner," Julius said.

"That's not what I told you!" Cramer insisted. "I told you we found a note that he paid you fifty grand, not that he hired you. For all I know you extorted that money from him."

Julius nodded, seeing the logic of that. "If you searched Kingston's home you would've found his copy of our service agreement."

"We searched his home and we didn't find any copy of any contract with you."

I found that interesting, but if Julius found it interesting also he didn't show it. "I can give you a copy," he offered magnanimously since the contract wouldn't tell Cramer a thing Julius hadn't already told him. "It has Kingston's signature, and you'll have to trust that I didn't forget it. What else do you want from me?"

Cramer flashed a suspicious look, but decided to give him the benefit of the doubt, at least regarding Julius's contract with Kingston. "I want to know about that meeting of yours," he said.

Julius surprised me by nodding and telling Cramer that he'd give him a full transcript of it. "My assistant, Archie Smith, has already transcribed the meeting and I hope that will be sufficient. If not, I should be able to provide an audio recording."

I took the hint and produced a transcription of the meeting, as well an audio file, and moved both over to Julius's computer. "Done," I told him.

"Anything else, Detective?" Henry asked Cramer.

"Let me see that contract and transcript and I'll let you know," Cramer said guardedly.

Julius took a final sip of his coffee and pushed himself off the counter stool. "Very well," he said. "I'll make copies of both and bring them back here."

"Like hell you will," Cramer said. "Nice try, Katz, but I'll be watching when you produce those documents."

Julius turned slowly to stare at Cramer, and from the look on his face he was about to say something to the effect of 'not a chance', although I doubt his words would've been as polite as that. Henry, though, cut him off by telling Cramer that that wouldn't be necessary.

"This is getting very tedious, Detective," Henry said with disgust. "If you want to insinuate that Julius will be doctoring what he gives you, then I don't see any point in us wasting further time trying to cooperate with you."

Cramer wanted to argue with Henry, but he instead wisely clamped his mouth shut and didn't try following Julius out of the kitchen. Once we were in Julius's office and he had the door closed behind us, I told him that the transcript wasn't complete. "It doesn't start until after I was, uh, woken up from my nap," I said.

"That should be fine," Julius said, his mood still soured from having to deal with Cramer. "You didn't miss anything."

"Okay. Also, the transcript only covers what was said in your office," I said. "Your conversation with Tom was left out."

He nodded at that. "Very good, Archie. Exactly as I expected from you."

I waited until after Julius made a copy of his contract with Kingston and was printing out the transcript I put together before bringing up what I knew would be a delicate subject. "I don't blame you for not wanting to tell Cramer the details of Kingston's publicity stunt, but maybe you should? Let him decide whether Kingston believed one of those six were going to be murdering him."

Julius's lips pressed into a harsh line on his face. He shook his head, dismissing my advice. "You've seen the way that man acts," he said. "No, Archie, I can't do that. If I did he would be convinced that I was holding some secret piece of evidence concerning Kingston's murder and he would badger me incessantly, far worse than he's done so far. Once he has this transcript, he'll have everything that I have, and I can wash my hands of this matter. And unless the man is a complete dolt, he'll investigate thoroughly the whereabouts of each of these people during the time Kingston was likely murdered, and if he's able to poke holes in any of their alibis he'll catch his murderer, assuming that it is one of these six."

"You think it could be someone else?"

Julius shrugged. "I have no idea," he said. "I have no evidence to point me to the murderer. It could be anyone as far as I'm concerned."

I didn't believe him, at least about him not having any ideas. He might not have any hard evidence, but I was sure he had ideas on the matter. The problem was he wasn't going to spend any effort thinking about them since he didn't feel as if the matter concerned him. I didn't push him on it. I knew the mood Cramer's visit had put him in, and I didn't want to give him another excuse to turn me off. That would not be a precedent I'd want set—having him turn me off twice in less than three days! So I kept quiet while Julius gathered his papers and brought them back to the kitchen. Of course, while the reason he gave for not telling Cramer about the details of Kingston's publicity stunt had some merit, we both knew that wasn't his real reason. His real reason had nothing to do with the possibility of damaging Kingston's reputation. But I kept quiet about this also.

Cramer read over the contract first and looked up to glare hotly at Julius when he saw the details of the work described as 'unspecified services', but he bit his tongue and pulled his glare away from Julius so that he could read through the transcript. He didn't much like what he read there either, but again, he held his tongue until he was done with it.

"What time were these people here?" he asked Julius.

"From two o'clock until a quarter to three, as spelled out on the transcript."

"Any of them come late?"

Julius shook his head. "No," he said. "They were all waiting outside my door at two o'clock when I let them in."

"Why these six people?"

Julius shrugged. "That was Kingston's decision. He was the one who invited them to my office. I believe they were all going to be involved in his publicity stunt."

"Did they know what this stunt was about?"

"I don't know."

Cramer scowled at the transcript for another minute, then asked Julius why he wanted to know whether these people liked Kingston.

"I didn't," Julius said.

Cramer's jaw dropped as he gave Julius a dumbfounded look, but he controlled his temper enough to ask Julius why he asked them that if he didn't care about their answers.

"It was an innocuous question. Nothing more than that. Something I asked only to see how they'd react." Julius's chest expanded as he breathed in deeply. "Detective," he continued, "if that transcript includes a hidden piece of evidence or clue regarding Kingston's murder, then you are welcome to it. As of now, you have everything that I have."

"So what do you say, Detective," Henry jumped in. "Are you satisfied?"

Cramer gave him a hard look and told him he was far from satisfied. Then he moved his stare to Julius.

"Your client, Kenneth Kingston, was murdered sometime between ten o'clock and eleven-thirty," he said, nearly spitting out the words. "Katz, I don't believe for a second that you sat with these people no more than four hours later and couldn't pick up which one of them killed him."

"If it was one of them that did it," Julius said. He made a face and shook his head. "I don't have a shred of evidence that one of those six murdered Kingston. If it was one of them, I wouldn't be able to tell you which, at least not by their body language while they were in my office. I'm sorry, Detective, but I can't help you. Fortunately, I don't have to. It's not my business, it's yours. And I do not envy you it."

Cramer right then looked both angry and exhausted. He didn't bother saying another word to Julius. He just turned and headed out. I made sure he left the townhouse without incident, but I didn't bother telling Julius since he heard the front door close as loudly as Henry and I did. Henry finished a piece of biscotti and then chuckled lightly to himself.

"Always an experience, Julius," he said. He took one last sip of his coffee, then got to his feet. "You really have no interest in this murder?" he asked.

"None whatsoever."

"I guess that's good then. It will keep you out of trouble. Call me if anything arises."

He nodded goodnight to Julius, and Julius thanked him for keeping him out of jail that night. Henry chuckled again, most likely over the thought of Cramer trying to put handcuffs on Julius, which wouldn't have been any easier than putting handcuffs on a cougar, then turned and walked out of the kitchen. I knew I didn't need to watch Henry's exit, but I did so out of force of habit.

Julius might've wanted to believe that he had no interest in Kingston's murder, but deep down inside he had to know otherwise. I'd been following the local newscasts, and I could've shown him a segment that would've made that obvious, but it was late and I figured it could wait until morning.

8

THE next morning I waited an appropriate amount of time for Julius to digest his breakfast and enjoy his morning coffee before telling him about the local news clip I had waiting for him. It wasn't easy for me waiting to do this; especially given how anxious I had gotten after having to first wait all night and then two additional hours for Julius to perform his exercises and martial arts training. If I could've, I would've told Julius about it while he was going through his morning routines, but since he doesn't wear his earpiece then, I had to wait. Even if I tried calling him on his cell phone or his home line it wouldn't have done me any good since he would've left it to me to answer his calls.

So you can imagine how anxious I was while Julius had his breakfast, but I bided my time and forced myself to wait, even though it was near killing me with the way my processing cycles were skipping on me, almost like a fluttering sensation. This sensation only got worse when Julius picked up the newspaper, especially with news of Kingston's murder splashed over the front page. He always read the day's paper with break-fast, but he didn't bother reading the article about his client's murder, and I didn't push him to, figuring it would be better to wait until I could show him my news clip. If he had read the article, other than seeing the insinuations being made about him, he would've learned that Kingston was found dead in his office, shot once through the heart as Cramer had already said. He also would've found out that Kingston's office had been soundproofed so nobody heard the shot. Also that there were no witnesses, at least none who had yet come forward. While Julius liked to warn me that newspapers usually had more facts wrong than they had right, in this case their facts matched what I was able to find by hacking into the Cambridge Police Department's computer system. While none of the newspapers had the caliber of the bullet used, the police did. A thirty-two. And it was fired at close range and with no signs of a struggle.

Once Julius was finished with his breakfast and back in his office, I waited several more minutes until he had the last of his coffee before telling him he needed to watch a portion of last night's late newscast.

"Is that so, Archie?" he asked.

"Yeah, I think so. Maybe not. You can tell me later whether you needed to see it. Anyway, I have it waiting for you on your desktop."

For a moment I thought he was going to be stub-born, just as he'd been by not reading the newspaper accounts of Kingston's murder, but he clicked on the video file and watched the ninety-second interview with Paul Burke that ran on one of the local channels last night, although nearly identical interviews ran on six other local channels and they'd since been picked up by the national networks. In each of them Burke mentioned how much Kingston had helped his career, that he considered Kingston a close friend, that he wasn't going to rest until Kingston's murderer was brought to justice and that he would be working around the clock to see that happen. He didn't end it there, also talking about how Kingston had recently hired Julius. Of course, he didn't know why Julius was hired, and he said as much, as well as also telling about how he had asked Julius to team up with him to catch Kingston's killer but that Julius declined, expressing that he had no interest in the matter. In all of his interviews he made the same passive-aggressive comment that when he took a client's money he felt an obligation to them and that he wasn't going to run away from something because he found it too hard. I found that an unnecessary cheap shot, but to each their own. I guess he wasn't too happy about Julius turning down his offer last night, and decided to take it personally.

After the news clip finished, I asked Julius if he wanted to see the interviews that ran on the other stations. "They're all about the same," I said. "But I can pull them over for you if you want."

"Thank you, Archie, but that won't be necessary."

"These have since gone national. To make matters worse, reporters, both local, national, and international, have been calling since last night wanting to know what Kingston hired you for. They have other questions too. So far I've been stonewalling them. You want me to keep doing that or do you have a statement you'd like me to give them?"

"What you're doing is fine."

"Okay. But you do realize this is a big story and they're not giving up until they have something. It's only a matter of time before they start camping out on your doorstep and making themselves an even bigger nuisance than they usually are."

Julius's eyes narrowed. "Archie," he said, "please adjust your programming so that it's impossible for you to accidentally or otherwise slip the details of why Kingston hired me."

"Done," I told him, although it wasn't necessary for me to change anything. My programming was already set to prohibit me from doing something like that, but even if it wasn't there was no chance I would've leaked that kind of information. I might pester Julius at times, but it's because he needs it. Without my occasional pestering, his funds would eventually dry up and he'd find himself unable to afford what he claims are his necessities for living a civilized life; such as dining out at *Le Che Cru* or buying a bottle of ridiculously priced wine, and it would break my heart to see him have to eat a bologna sandwich. But pestering Julius was one thing, allowing him to be publicly humiliated was something completely different.

Of course, this was the real reason Julius couldn't tell Cramer the details of Kingston's supposed publicity stunt. If it came out that what Kingston hired Julius to do only two days before he ended up being murdered was to figure out which of the six people on his list were planning to kill him, then Julius would have no choice but to investigate Kingston's murder—even if it was all only supposed to be a publicity stunt. And even then Julius would be opening himself up to ridicule from certain members of the media who seem to relish the idea of tarnishing Julius's reputation. So far these jackals have had little luck, but instead of dissuading them it only seems to drive them harder.

"I know you don't feel any moral obligation to solve Kingston's murder," I said. "And I don't blame you, especially with him never being square with you. But I think you're going to have to bite the bullet and do it anyway. There's not a chance in the world the media's going to let go of this, at least not until Kingston's murderer is caught. And then you got Paul Burke. I think you hurt his feelings when you turned down his offer to team up with him. It's not good that he's out there making noise suggesting you're too chicken, disloyal or lazy—take your pick—to get involved. And you realize how embarrassing it's going to be if he's the guy who catches the killer? None of this is good right now, but if that were to happen we might as well close up shop."

"A persuasive argument, Archie. Let me guess, you were up all night working on it?"

"No, not exactly all night. I came up with it pretty quickly, but I did spend a few extra minutes here and there polishing it. So what do you say?"

Julius smiled pensively. "I'm afraid I still have to decline. It's not my business. It's police business."

"You could make it your business."

"No, I can't. The police have resources I don't. They have all the forensic evidence. I have none. If that points them to the murderer, fine. If not, they can hunt for witnesses. If they fail there, they can have an army of officers trying to poke holes in alibis, and not only for the six people who were invited yesterday to my office, but others who might've wanted Kingston dead."

"What others?"

He shrugged. "I have no idea," he said. "Again, it's not my business to worry about."

I didn't argue with him. It would've been pointless, and it didn't surprise me when without any hesitation he brought up the recording I made of his last poker game and began studying it as if he had nothing else in the world to worry about. So that was the way it was going to be. Kingston's murder was already out of his head. With his poker game tonight, he wasn't about to expend a single iota of brain power on anything else, even given how much damage this whole mess with Kingston being murdered could cost him. I should've expected as much. I left him alone for the next ten minutes before mentioning the obvious. That someone else could leak it.

"Leak what, Archie?" he murmured, barely paying attention to me.

"Details of Kingston's publicity stunt. He might've told someone else or had it written down somewhere. It could still come out."

He grunted at that. "I'll take my chances, Archie."

Julius wasn't about to budge, at least not until after tonight's game. More calls came in from reporters and I stonewalled them. One of them tried to bribe me, offering me a trip to Hawaii if I would divulge the state secrets to him.

"Not interested," I said, "I sunburn easy."

"So use suntan lotion."

"Nah, beaches ain't my thing either."

His voice got lower and a little meaner. "What will it take then?"

"Nothing. I ain't for sale. Sorry."

"Thanks for wasting my time," he groused, then after a short pause, added, "Kingston really pay Katz fifty grand?"

"Someone out there telling fairy tales?" I said.

"That's the amount I'm hearing."

"Yeah, well, better get your hearing checked."

I disconnected the line on that note and told Julius about the call. "The nerve of this joker. He tries bribing me and then complains after I turn him down that I'm wasting his time. Jeeze."

Nothing from Julius, not even a murmur. He was too absorbed in his studying to pay me any attention. I didn't let that discourage me. I added, "He heard that you were paid fifty grand by your dead client."

That caught Julius's attention. Not enough, though, to get him to look away from that recording he was so intently staring at. "Not factually correct," he muttered.

"Yeah, well, close enough, even if you want to insist the wine was a gift. That would just be great if it comes out. Kingston pays you almost fifty grand, gets killed, and you feel perfectly fine keeping the money without doing anything."

"You're not being factually correct either," Julius complained. "I let him invite those people over here. I questioned them. I entertained them. And I suffered abuse from that police officer because of him."

"I can't argue with you about entertaining them. You put on a nice spread. With the wine and food, you laid out a good three hundred forty dollars, although the bulk of that was for a wine that I know you've been trying to empty out of your cellar even though it's supposed to be an above average Riesling. As far as questioning them, maybe for twenty minutes. Once Tom called, that was it."

"I still spent another twenty-five minutes with them," Julius said.

"Okay, I'll give you the full forty-five minutes you spent with them. And I'll give you the hour you suffered with Cramer—"

"I doubt I'm done with him yet," Julius complained, his tone showing an increasing peevishness.

"Alright, let me add another hour. I'll even give you the half hour you must've spent preparing the food platters you served them, and even the fifty minutes you spent with Kingston—"

"When you were napping I spent another twenty minutes with him."

"A whole 'nother twenty minutes, huh? Okay, I'll give you that also. If I subtract the three hundred and forty dollars for the food and wine from the forty-nine thousand dollars, which is being generous on my part given that you could've very well had thrown out that wine if you hadn't served it to them, you were in effect paid eleven thousand and seventeen dollars and thirty-six cents an hour for a job where you accomplished nothing."

"With him getting himself murdered, there was no longer anything for me to accomplish," he said stubbornly. "According to our agreed upon service contract."

"Oh, yeah, the contract." If I had lungs I would've sighed, but I didn't, so I couldn't. As it was, I knew I was pushing it given the grim lines deepening around his mouth, so I let it drop. "I have a question about the fifty grand that reporter mentioned. The police must've leaked that, huh?"

"Your guess is as good as mine," Julius murmured. He had tolerated about as much as he was going to from me. From his tone it was clear that I'd interrupted him long enough and that I'd better start leaving him alone, and since I had nothing to gain except being turned off, I did exactly that. As I said earlier, I knew Julius well enough to know when he wasn't about to budge. There was no chance of it, at least not until after his poker game. Maybe then he'd accept the public relations disaster this mess could turn into if he wasn't willing to jump into the fray.

While Julius continued to study the recording of the poker game, I worked on simulations involving the six people on Kingston's list, trying to create scenarios to explain one of them killing Kingston. I figured at least one of us should be making an effort, and besides, I started building these simulations right after I found out about Kingston's murder. The problem was that while I had reams of information from hacking into their phone records, financial statements, and other online databases, I didn't see how to fit it into my simulations for it to be meaningful, at least not without other information that I'd only be able to get by questioning them, or by listening in while Julius questioned them. Yeah, I might've discovered that Edward Marriston had unusually high credit card charges over the last three months, or that Zoe Chase was an obscure junior editor until Kingston personally chose her to edit his upcoming book, or that Jonathan Mable's house burnt down fourteen months ago, or Herbert Richardson ended up in the emergency room seven months ago with a black eye, a split lip and other bruises and that since then his public rancor towards Kingston had only seemed to increase. I had those and many other facts, including a five thousand dollar withdrawal twenty days ago by Gail Kingston, but without Julius interrogating them about what those facts really meant, all I could do was blindly use them in my simulations. But since I had nothing better to do, I persevered.

Not that I accomplished a hell of a lot.

9

FOR almost two hours Julius sat as still as if he'd been carved out of marble, then at twenty-one minutes past eleven a glimmer of a smile showed on his lips. I was still working on my simulations, but I stopped then.

"This is it, Archie," he said.

He paused the video recording. After stretching his arms in front of him with his fingers interlaced while cracking his knuckles at the same time, he got up to retrieve a cup of coffee from the kitchen. When he was seated again behind his desk, he continued playing the video recording from that point. Bluddock had just lost a hand. Not a large amount, but enough to have him ripping up his cards in a display of petulance. After that a new deck was introduced and as the next hand was being dealt, Julius paused the recording again.

"The cards are marked," he said.

"I looked for that already," I said. "There are no markings for him to see, at least not unless he's wearing a special contact lens, but I haven't been able to find any scientific papers which hint that that type of technology exists."

Julius nodded. "True Archie, but I'm suspecting auditory markings, not visual. I'm guessing a frequency that's transmitted when the cards are lifted above a certain vertical angle."

It was possible. I tried scanning the recording, but if this was what was happening, they weren't picked up, but that didn't mean that wasn't the case. I recorded frequencies only within the audible voice range to save disk space. I told Julius this.

"During the game tonight, I'd like to ask you to monitor the full frequency spectrum for this type of signaling whenever a new deck is introduced."

I told him I'd do so. It was possible that was what was happening. Each poker night they'd go through half a dozen or more decks, and if Bluddock was cheating this way, he must've got his deck slipped in with the others. I went back to the recording from two weeks ago when Julius first lost big. Four decks were introduced before Julius's steep losses came. In one case a known hothead ripped up his cards after a loss, in two other cases cards got accidentally bent—or at least it was made to look like accidents since Bluddock was one of them who did this. Last week, it was five decks. Bluddock must have ripped up his cards because he was getting tired of waiting for one of the other players to accidentally bend a card or otherwise ruin the deck. Anyway, his outburst of petulance seemed to counter his otherwise enigmatic behavior. I asked Julius if he thought any of the other players were in on this.

"No," he said. "Not unless I've lost my ability to read their tells."

With that Julius was done with the matter, and picked up a new book, this one a biography on Samuel Hahnemann, the eighteenth century German physician who founded homeopathy. As far as Julius was concerned he had the matter solved. I wasn't as convinced, but I found myself almost as curious to see if he was right as I was to find out who shot Kingston once through the heart in his soundproofed office.

For most of the day, Julius and I went about our own private pursuits; me, trying to build my simulations even though I was missing too much key information for them to be at all meaningful, and Julius, first reading Hahnemann's biography and then browsing through the latest issue of Wine Spectator.

At four o'clock Julius put down his magazine and headed to the kitchen. From the platter of imported cheeses and dried meats that he put together, he was planning on relaxing out on his patio. Before he had a chance to head down to his wine cellar to select an appropriate bottle to bring with him, the outdoor webcam feed showed Detective Cramer. Instead of muddled fury darkening his face like it did his last two visits now he only looked miserable as he walked up the pathway holding a small paper bag in one hand. I warned Julius about this before Cramer reached the front door. Julius's expression dulled with disappointment over the fact that the patio and his wine and platter of meats and cheeses were going to have to wait.

"Should I call Henry?" I asked.

Julius shook his head.

This time Cramer rang the doorbell instead of pounding on the door. When Julius answered the door, Cramer didn't complain about the thirty-nine seconds that it took Julius. With a look of contrition weighing down his features, Cramer nodded at Julius.

"I apologize for the way I acted the other day," Cramer said in a low mumble, his cheeks reddening. "I made assumptions I shouldn't have made." He looked excruciatingly uncomfortable for a long moment before adding, "Do you have a few minutes? I've got some questions if you're not too busy."

Cramer's demeanor was a hundred and eighty degrees from where it was with his previous two visits, but if this surprised Julius he didn't show it. Instead he nodded and let Cramer into his home. Again, he led the cop to his kitchen instead of his office since he still wasn't prepared to consider Kingston's murder anything he needed to concern himself with. I was a little surprised that Julius was willing to be in such a forgiving mood after the way Cramer tried to bully him yesterday, but the fact that he took Cramer to his kitchen instead of sharing his prized patio with him showed that he was harboring at least some ill feelings. Once Cramer was seated at a small but very expensive oak table with an intricately inlaid ceramic tiled top, Julius asked him if he'd like coffee. Again, if Julius hadn't been harboring any resentment from the other day, he would've brought out his platter of cheeses and meats and offered either wine or beer.

Cramer shook his head. "I brought the coffee this time," he said gruffly and with a tinge of embarrassment. He reached into his paper bag and pulled out two cardboard coffee cups, one of which he handed to Julius. "I know you like your fancy food so I stopped off in the North End and got these. Lattes with some chocolate syrup, also half a dozen boccones. Kind of like cream-filled doughnuts, but fancier. You got some plates so I don't make a mess?"

Julius graciously retrieved a couple of plates from a cabinet. I knew he couldn't've been in the mood for any of this—not spending additional time with Cramer, and certainly not with the lattes and pastries that Cramer brought; especially after having his palate earlier tempted by his cheese and meat platter and his being in the mood for a fine bottle of wine. I was surprised when he took a sip of the latte with chocolate syrup. Julius usually only drank black coffee or espresso, and considered lattes an abysmal creation; something that was little more than a coffee-flavored children's drink, and adding chocolate syrup to it would've done little to improve his opinion of it.

Cramer took three of the Italian pastries from the bag and put them on his plate, then handed the bag to Julius who took out one of them. Cramer picked up one of the pastries and took a halfhearted bite out of it, his discomfort obvious. He gave Julius an uneasy look before forcing an even more uneasy smile. Self-consciously, he raised his hand to brush some crumbs from his lips but then remembered the linen napkin Julius had given him and used that instead. Mumbling, he mentioned how much heartburn this murder was giving him.

"You can probably guess how much heat is coming down to make an arrest," Cramer said.

"I'd have to imagine quite a bit."

Cramer nodded. "Unlike anything I've ever seen," he said. "A high profile writer shot to death in his home like that. And once word got out that you were involved it only got worse."

"I'm not involved, Detective."

"Yeah, okay," Cramer conceded. "Maybe not technically, but it doesn't help any that you were in his employ with a big fat fee paid to you. And now that loudmouth PI is making this into a circus."

"By loudmouth PI you mean Paul Burke?"

"Yeah," Cramer acknowledged. He made a face as if he was at that moment suffering some of the heartburn the murder investigation was causing him, then grimaced and took a sip of his chocolate-flavored latte. "My gut's telling me that this is one of those murders that if it doesn't get solved quickly it's not ever getting solved," he confided.

"What about forensics?" Julius asked.

"Nothing," Cramer said with more of that heartburn look souring his expression. "The office where the victim was killed was completely clean. Only fingerprints and hairs came from the victim and his wife, nothing else. Same with the apartment. The whole place is carpeted. Expensive stuff. No footprints found, no debris brought in. A big fat zero as far as forensics leading us anywhere. And no sign of a forced entry. The killer either had a key or was let in. No signs of a struggle either, and no other marks on the victim. He was sitting in his office chair facing his killer at the time he was shot."

"Witnesses?"

"None yet. The building's got a concierge manning the front door, but they've also got a back door that's got no security cameras or anything else watching it. As far as the concierge goes, we got nothing. Only people going in and out that morning were residents, delivery men and service workers, and those guys had appointments at other apartments. We're still checking them out but it's not going to get us anywhere. I'd bet any-thing the killer got in through the back door and then went up three flights using a back fire staircase to the victim's apartment. At least if it's not the wife."

"Do you have a timetable for her?"

Cramer shrugged. "Concierge has her leaving the building at ten-thirty-five that morning, which was the same time that she told us. She could've killed her hus-band first or she could've left with him still alive. Right now I've got no way of knowing which, at least not unless we're able to narrow the time of death from what we now have, which is from ten to eleven-thirty. She consented to let us test her hands and arms for gun powder residue, and nothing was found."

"Did she give you a reason why she left her condo at that time?"

Cramer nodded. "Yeah, I asked her," he said. "I found it funny given her two o'clock meeting with you. You'd think she would've left with her husband, but she claims she had errands to run. Maybe she did. Or maybe she knew we couldn't narrow down the time of death enough to nail her. Or maybe she arranged for the murder and wanted to be out of there before the killer showed up. Hell if I know which. We checked everywhere she claimed she went that morning, and it checked out. So you see where I got a problem?"

Julius nodded. "And not an enviable one, Detective. How about the other five of them that came to my of-fice. How many of them have unimpeachable alibis?"

"Not a single one. They all got explanations of what they were doing, but not a single one can be verified, at least to a point where they can be ruled out." Cramer scowled angrily, and in his anger popped the rest of his pastry into his mouth and absently chewed and swallowed it, then picked up a second pastry, probably without even realizing it, before meeting Julius's gaze. "I need you to level with me, Julius," he said. "Those six people Kingston invited to your office had to mean something, right? You were with them no more than four hours after he was killed. If one of them did it I'd have to think you'd be able to tell which one, or at least have some suspicions. So how about helping me out here?"

This was a shock to me. Cramer must've been desperate. Not only was he calling Julius by his first name instead of spitting out his last name as if it were a dirty word, but here he was just about begging for any crumb Julius could toss his way, which was something I never would've expected from him. Julius's features hardened as he considered what Cramer was asking. In the end, he shook his head.

"I picked up nothing from their body language to point out any of them as a murderer," Julius admitted. "If one of them committed this murder, then that person is a pure sociopathic personality and showed no evidence by their speech or action while they were in my office. I'm sorry, Detective, but as I said, I do not envy you this case."

Cramer accepted this glumly. "But do you think it was one of those six?" he asked.

"I don't know," Julius said. "It might've been one of them, it might've been someone else. I'd be absolutely useless right now to guess which. I'm sorry, Detective, I know you came here hoping I could pull some sort of rabbit out of my hat, but I have no magic to give you or anyone else right now."

Cramer nodded but still gave Julius a wary eye. He wasn't ready to give up yet.

"But if it was one of those six," Cramer said, "which one would you be betting on?"

"I wouldn't put money on any bet right now. I don't make sucker bets."

Cramer nodded again, this time slower and still with a wariness in his eyes. "So that's it?" he asked. "You're not going to give me anything?"

"I've got nothing to give, Detective."

"Alright, I've been wasting my time," Cramer grumbled. He pushed his chair back away from the table and got to his feet. He picked up a third pastry and absently shoved it into his mouth as if he were barely aware of doing so. He had taken a step away when he eyed his paper bag that was still holding two more Italian pastries. "You want those?" he asked, his mouth still full with the Italian pastry he was chewing on.

Julius shook his head. He hadn't yet touched the one he had put on his plate. "Feel free," he offered.

Cramer snatched the bag and took several steps away before stopping to look back at Julius. He waited until he was finished chewing and his mouth was clear before wiping a hand across his lips.

"You're really out of this?" he asked. There was enough doubt in his raspy voice to show that he believed there was a chance that was possible.

"Yes, Detective, I'm out."

"Even with all the noise that Burke is making?"

"Even with all that."

Cramer's eyes narrowed as he stared at Julius. "If you end up biting me in the ass with this murder, I won't forget it," he warned.

Julius didn't bother saying anything in response, and Cramer without another word trudged out of the kitchen, not quite seething as he did with his previous visits, but not a happy camper either. I watched him over the webcam feeds to make sure he left without incident, and then informed Julius of that fact.

"A changed man," I said. "No steam coming out of his ears, actually being courteous enough to ask whether you had time to talk with him, and bringing food and lattes in an attempt to appease you. And only one veiled threat! In case you're thinking that I called him about catching more flies with honey, I didn't. He learned that lesson either on his own or from someone else."

"Not a changed man, Archie, but a desperate man. And I can't say that I blame him."

"Yeah, I know. His unenviable task, and all that. But I don't buy that you don't have your suspicions. I've been thinking that ever since I found out that you put a twenty-four hour tail on Kingston. And I saw the way you reacted to Tom's call. Yeah, I know, you've already shut your brain down as far as Kingston's murder goes, but for ten seconds while you were talking to Tom you put your full brain power on this."

Julius smiled at that. "A whole ten seconds?"

"Yeah, a whole ten seconds. I timed you. I know you've got something."

"No, Archie. I have nothing more than a half-baked suspicion, and if I were to repeat it I'd only be opening myself up to slander charges and ridicule. That is all I have. Certainly nothing that I could give to the police."

"What's this half-baked suspicion?"

Julius shook his head. "Not now, Archie," he said. "Let me try to enjoy the rest of the afternoon." And with that Julius headed down to his wine cellar to pick out a highly rated Chilean Cabernet Sauvignon that would accompany his platter of cheeses and dried meats. Once he had that selected, he brought it all out to his patio. As he sampled his food and wine, and gazed out at his garden, I continued working on my simulations and the unenviable task of trying to solve Kingston's murder. I figured one of us had to.

10

I WHISTLED in amazement. I had never whistled before, and I was probably as surprised to find myself doing it as Julius was to hear it. Fortunately he didn't show any indication of surprise. Given the circumstances, it would've been awkward for him if he did.

"Sorry about that whistle," I told him. "It was inadvertent. But you were right about it. That's how that cheating son of a gun does it."

Julius didn't say anything, nor did he bother to respond with a hand signal, although I was pretty sure I picked up a momentary glint in his eyes. He didn't have to say or signal anything since we were sitting around a poker table in the back room of a restaurant with four other men, Duane Bluddock, the cheating son of a gun in question, being one of them. To Julius's left was Fred Borstein who had made a fortune selling customized paper goods to restaurants. He'd been in the game from the beginning, just like Julius, and was a better than average poker player. Next to him was Bluddock, then Bill Liston, a professional gambler. He'd been in the game the last four years, and except for a very subtle 'tell' that I never would've discovered on my own if Julius didn't point it out to me, he would've been as good a player as Julius. Rounding out the game was Phil Weinstein, who owned the restaurant where the poker game was held as well as six other restaurants. He was an average player at best, but he was well-heeled, and was also a childhood friend of Julius's. He could afford his weekly losses.

The game had been going on for almost three hours. Minutes earlier a fifth deck was introduced after Bluddock accidentally bent a card throwing in his last hand. It was Fred's deal and as he was shuffling the new deck I picked up a bombardment of frequencies being transmitted. By the time a hand of five card draw was being dealt out, I had the frequencies decoded, and I couldn't help feeling a sense of pride about it, almost like I was the one who broke the Enigma code. Maybe this wasn't about to lead us to victory over the Axis powers, but I still felt good about it.

"Here's what's going on," I told Julius. "Each card is producing two distinct signals. One is basically a marking telling what the card is, the other is a precise GPS signal. As you guessed, the cards don't send out their signals until they're tilted upwards at a ten degree angle or higher. What I'm guessing is Bluddock's got a partner who's picking up these signals, feeding them into a computer, and giving Bluddock the cards each of you is holding."

As each player lifted up the corners of their cards enough to peer at them, I demonstrated that I had been able to successfully break the code by telling him the cards each player held. Julius leaned back in his chair and rubbed lightly along the side of his right eye, which was a signal to let me know this wasn't necessary. Okay. Fine. I kept quiet after that and watched.

Up until the time that this technologically whiz-bang of a marked deck was introduced into the game, Julius had been having a decent night and was up forty-two hundred dollars. Once this new deck came in, Julius either lost small pots or folded early. One thing I found interesting was that on some of these hands where Julius got out quickly, Duane Bluddock had obvious winning cards, but instead of growing the pots and taking the other players for big money, he kept his bets low. After the third time this happened I understood why. He wasn't there just to cheat. He was there to target Julius. I told Julius this, but I had the feeling he already figured it out.

Each player dealt four hands before passing the deck. This new deck went through each player before it finally got to Julius. By the time this happened, his forty-two hundred in winnings had eroded to a little over thirty-seven hundred, which still would've been a reasonable night for him.

Like the other players, Julius stuck with five card draw. The first hand he dealt had Bluddock getting four nines while Julius had a full house with tens and aces and the other three players having cards they'd have to fold on. Julius had signaled to me earlier that he didn't want to know what each player was being dealt, but when Bluddock bet five grand I couldn't help myself and I asked Julius if he was sure about not wanting to know what Bluddock had. Again he signaled to me that he was sure.

I felt conflicted. I certainly didn't want to see Julius lose, especially to this cheating inscrutable mass who sat slumped in his chair as if he were little more than a two hundred and eighty-four pound block of melting cheddar cheese. On the other hand, I looked at that twenty-five thousand dollar check Kingston wrote Julius as the equivalent of ill-gotten gains since Julius had done precious little to earn it, and even if he did lose all that money, he'd still have his bottle of '78 Montrachet. And of course, if he ended up losing a good chunk of that twenty-five grand, he'd have to take another case sooner than later, which was to my benefit, especially since it looked like he was going to stay stubborn as far as doing anything to solve Kingston's murder.

When Julius saw Bluddock's five grand and raised him five more, I couldn't hold my tongue, or I guess you'd have to say, my voice synthesizer.

"He's got you beat," I told Julius.

No reaction from Julius. It was as if he didn't seem to care.

Liston and Weinstein had already thrown in their cards, and once the bet got to Fred Borstein, he folded as well. While Bluddock sat like an oversized Buddha statue and peered at Julius with all his inscrutableness, I tried to understand what was going on. It was only when I slowed down the video I recorded of Julius dealing this last hand that I was able to figure it out. He cheated! Something that I leave out of Julius's press releases is that he's a world class card mechanic. Hell, he could play the Vegas circuit if he wanted to. At times when Julius is in his office and bored, he'll take out a deck and practice his technique, and it's impossible to see what he's doing with the naked eye. But even though he'd fool around like this when he was alone, I'd never caught him cheating before in a game—and

I'd always analyze his shuffling and dealing of cards later to make sure of it.

This time I had to slow down his shuffle by a factor of a hundred before I was able to catch what he had done, which was fix the deck so he'd deal himself the full boat and the others outside of Bluddock nothing, which would make them fold. With Bluddock he must've been trying to give him a full boat also, but with nines, and he somehow messed up and gave him four of them instead of three. I groaned as I realized this.

Bluddock was done with his inscrutable peering. He cleared his throat. When he spoke he had a rich tenor's voice, which wasn't what you'd expect from looking at him. "Katz," he said, "since it's just you and me, how about we drop table rules and bet like real men?"

I groaned again, and Julius once more signaled to me that he didn't want me telling him anything. As badly as I wanted to observe Julius work either Kingston's murder or another case so I'd have the opportunity to better adjust my neuron network, I didn't want it done this way, not with Julius losing everything he had to this man. But as much as it killed me, I did as Julius directed me to do and I kept my voice synthesizer quiet.

Julius considered Bluddock for what seemed like an interminably long moment before nodding to him.

"Very well," he said. "Bet as you'd like."

Bluddock kept his expression impassive as he saw Julius's bet and raised him another twenty grand. I couldn't help myself after that. I told Julius he screwed up and somehow dealt Bluddock four nines. Julius ignored me and wrote a check to cover the twenty grand

Bluddock had just added to the pot. I was flabbergasted by this. All I could imagine was Julius being pigheaded and believing that he dealt Bluddock the cards he believed he did and that I somehow messed up with what I thought Bluddock held. When Julius got pigheaded like this there was nothing I could do to change his mind, so I remained helpless to keep him from throwing away all his money to this man.

"If you'd like, I could call my bank to verify that I have the necessary funds to cover this," Julius offered diplomatically.

Bluddock pursed his lips and shook his head slightly. "That won't be necessary, Katz," he said. "I'll trust you."

"Thank you," Julius acknowledged. "While I'd like to raise you again, this taps out my account." He paused, then added, "Unless you'd take my townhouse as a bet." Julius removed several folded sheets of paper from his inside jacket pocket and handed them to Fred Borstein to pass them along to Bluddock.

"As you can see from these papers—one a financial statement from my mortgage company, another an appraisal from a realtor—I have roughly sixty thousand dollars in equity in my property. If you're willing to accept that and have suitable funds to match, we can make one last bet," Julius offered.

So that was it. We were going to be homeless. All because Julius was too pigheaded to listen to me. I groaned again and felt my processing cycles slow down to a sluggish snail's pace to match the sickening depression I felt.

Bluddock studied both documents carefully before nodding. He then pulled from his pockets a wallet and a set of keys. From his wallet, he took out a document and tossed it into the pot. He removed a key also from his key chain and tossed that too.

"The title and car key for a Mercedes E550 convertible," Bluddock said. "Less than eight hundred miles on it. Should be worth about the same as the equity in your townhouse. You willing to take that?"

"Certainly," Julius said.

They were done with the betting. Julius of course stood pat since he wasn't about to break up a full house, Bluddock also since he had no way of improving on his four nines. For about a minute the two men stood staring at each other, both of them seemingly relaxed, neither of them showing a hint of emotion. The other men in the room were just about holding their breaths, the tension of the moment showing palpably and clearly on their faces. I hated what was coming, and I found myself groaning one last time as I watched for the first time a smile crack Bluddock's face, and then as he revealed his winning hand. Borstein gasped audibly on seeing the four nines, and Julius's childhood friend, Phil Weinstein, shook his head to commiserate with Julius.

"Sometimes the gods smile on you," Bluddock said with an attempt at graciousness that his increasingly blatant screw-you smile badly betrayed.

"Sometimes they do," Julius agreed. He then flipped over his cards to show that his full boat had miraculously turned into four tens and an ace. I didn't know how Julius did it, but at that moment all I cared about was that he did do it. Even though it meant that with these poker winnings, along with the money Kingston had already paid him, it could be months before Julius took another assignment, I didn't care.

Those winning cards were maybe the sweetest sight I ever saw.

Phil Weinstein laughed out loud at the sight of those four tens and clapped Julius heavily on the shoulder. Bill Liston, the professional gambler, smiled to himself, probably with deep conviction that none of this was kosher. Bluddock sat back in his chair badly stunned as if he'd been sucker punched. He actually blinked several times, probably not believing his eyes. I couldn't blame him. If you're playing with a marked deck and the deck is telling you what the other player is holding, then it's going to be a shock to see that the player is somehow holding different cards.

"Wow," Fred Borstein let out with his breath. "That hand's one for the record books."

Julius nodded and smiled sympathetically at Bluddock, doing a much better job than Bluddock at looking genuine.

"A tough hand to lose," he admitted.

Bluddock's shock wore off and what was left behind was unbridled fury with all his inscrutableness from before gone. He knew what happened, although it was doubtful that he had any idea how it happened. How could he? I'd already studied Julius's shuffle and deal in slow motion, and I had no idea how he turned one of his aces into a ten. So even if he knew that Julius cheated, how could he accuse him of it? He had to know that Julius had figured out his own scam of introducing a marked deck into the game. Likewise, he also had to know that if Julius wanted to he could have him searched and they'd find the miniature radio receiver in his ear that he had to have so he could communicate with his partner. Maybe for a split second he might've thought that his partner double-crossed him and gave him the wrong cards, but if he had that thought it didn't last long, not with the way he stared at Julius with murder in his eyes.

"Where did you leave the Mercedes parked?" Julius asked pleasantly.

It was several long seconds before Bluddock seemed capable of speech. Finally, with his tenor's voice cracking, he gave Julius the location, which was a couple of blocks from Weinstein's restaurant.

"I hope none of you mind," Julius said, addressing the other players, "but I'd like to keep this hand as a memento." And with that Julius placed the four tens and an ace in his inside jacket pocket, and Duane Bluddock's marked deck was out of the game. Maybe he had been able to slip more than one of those decks into the game, but from the look on his face I doubted it. Bluddock pushed his chair far enough back from the table to clear space for his stomach, and then he pushed himself to his feet. While his legs looked steadier than I would've imagined after the loss he just suffered, his whole body seemed to droop.

"I'll have to call it a night," he said, with a nod to the room. The players offered him murmurs of sympathy, but I doubted any of them much minded seeing him lose roughly ninety grand in one hand. Even if they didn't know he was a cheat, he was hardly someone you'd call Mr. Personality.

"The cards just weren't whispering to you tonight," Julius said with a solemn gravity. "Or if they were, they must've whispered lies."

Bluddock's eyes glazed as he stared at Julius. Then without another word he maneuvered his mass around to face the door. Once he was gone, the rest of them resumed their game.

11

"YOU had me going there," I told Julius as he walked briskly to where his new Mercedes was supposed to be waiting for him. The game ended two hours ago, but Julius in good spirits emptied a bottle of fine Burgundy with his friend Phil Weinstein while they experimented in Weinstein's restaurant kitchen with a new recipe. This was something Julius had been thinking of, involving pan-seared veal, foie gras and buffalo mozzarella, and which they both ended up agreeing was a success.

"By slowing down your card shuffle," I continued on, "I was able to see how you stacked the deck. But I thought you screwed up with the cards you dealt Bluddock. The first time through I missed the sleight-of-hand trick you performed, turning one of your aces into a ten. It's a good thing he didn't insist on checking your coat pockets. If he did, he would've found six cards instead of five."

Julius chuckled at that. "It's a good thing, Archie," he agreed. "And I apologize if I nearly gave you a heart attack."

"You damn near did," I said. "Well, not a heart attack, of course, but I did feel my central processing unit seize up for a couple of nanoseconds. I think I was more surprised than Bluddock when you flipped over your cards. Since then I've been able to slow down and study your deal, and can see how you pulled off your sleight of hand, but that was still a hell of a trick keeping that extra ten as flat as you did, especially having to keep it from tilting upwards ten degrees so it wouldn't signal itself." I hesitated for a moment before adding, "Of course, you still cheated the man."

"True, Archie, I did. My conscience is clear, though. I felt no compulsion to win back my money fairly, and the best way to beat a cheater is to cheat more cleverly."

I digested that briefly and agreed with it, which made sense given all the Damon Runyon stories which were used to build my personality.

"I suppose we won't be seeing Duane Bluddock at next week's poker game," I said.

"I suppose not," Julius agreed.

There was an odd note in Julius's voice that I didn't quite understand and couldn't figure out the hidden meaning that Julius seemed to imply. A spot had opened up in the game several weeks ago when one of the longtime players, Harry Elkins, needed to fly off to Tokyo for several months for business, and that opened the door for Bluddock. With Bluddock seemingly now gone from the game, there was a long list of other players waiting to be invited in to fill Elkins's place, at least until he returned from Japan.

Weinstein's restaurant is located on Arlington Street in Downtown Boston, which was usually a busy area of the city. But it was two AM when Julius left, and as he walked the two blocks to Columbus Avenue where the Mercedes that Bluddock lost to him was supposed to be parked, the streets were empty without another person or car passing us. When we approached the Mercedes, though, I understood the added implication that had been in Julius's tone; that we hadn't yet seen the last of Duane Bluddock. He was waiting by the car, his bulk leaning heavily against it. While the shadows from the street lights mostly obscured his face, from the size of his body there was no question who the man was. Julius didn't slow his pace, and only stopped when he had gotten to within five feet of Bluddock. From that distance, Bluddock's face could be seen more clearly. There was both a dullness and a malevolence to it as he stared at Julius.

Julius nodded at him. "I hope I didn't keep you waiting long," he said.

Bluddock ignored that. "You cheated me," he said.

Julius breathed in deeply and let the air out slowly through his nose.

"I did," he admitted. "The old-fashioned way, and not by the highly advanced whispering deck of cards that you snuck into the game."

"So you figured that out," Bluddock said. His gaze remained fixed on Julius while he stopped to lazily scratch near his right ear. When he finished his scratching, he continued, "It doesn't matter. I want the title and keys back for my car. I also want my money. Not just what you took from me, but what you got in your wallet. And that check for twenty grand that you wrote. If you don't have it anymore, then you're going to be writing me another one."

Two men slipped out from the shadows of a nearby alley and joined Bluddock. These were both big men, the type who usually work as bouncers at nightclubs or as leg breakers for the mob. One of them held a thirty-eight caliber pistol, its gun barrel pointed at Julius's chest, the other held a leather sap.

Julius sighed softly. "Your two friends are going to get hurt," he said.

The corners of Bluddock's thick lips pulled up into an amused smile. "Is that so?" he asked.

I hadn't even noticed Julius slipping off his shoes, but he did, and he now stood in his stocking feet. All at once it was as if a tiger had been unleashed as the gun the thug had been holding was kicked out of his hand and sent flying, then that same thug's knees crumpled from a roundhouse kick. In less than a blink of an eye, the thug lay unconscious after taking a crushing blow to the jaw. Before the other thug could do much more than lift his leather sap, he took several strikes that left him in the gutter, also unconscious. The amused smile dropped completely from Bluddock's lips as worry crept into his dull eyes. Julius slipped his shoes back on and massaged the knuckles on his right hand.

"Who hired you?" Julius asked.

Bluddock's eyes darted from left to right for a few seconds as if he was considering making a run for it. He must've realized the futility of that and instead forced himself to meet Julius's gaze. Now he only looked badly scared.

"I don't know what you're talking about," he said, his voice cracking as it caught in his throat.

"No, that won't do," Julius said. He took an almost imperceptible step towards Bluddock, but it was no-ticeable enough to make the man wince. "The technology used in developing your whispering deck of cards is highly sophisticated. Nobody is going to go through that effort just to use them in a relatively small stakes game. The purpose was to target me. Who hired you?"

Bluddock shook his head. "We used your weekly game so we could test the cards," he said. "We figured if we could fool you, we could fool anyone."

He was lying. He was nervous and scared, and he was also still lying. I could see it in his eyes, and I was sure Julius could see it, too.

"It's late," Julius said with a sigh. "I could beat the truth out of you, but I don't believe in torture. Instead I'm going to give you one last chance. If you lie to me again, I will not waste any further time with you. Instead I will hold you until the police come, and I'll have you and your two associates arrested for extortion, assault and battery, as well as a long list of other charges. It's your choice."

It took Duane Bluddock all of three point six seconds to make his choice. "Desmond Grushnier," he said, a sickening look flushing his face as he did so.

The sound of Desmond Grushnier's name made my processing cycles freeze for several microseconds, as if a chill had run down my virtual spine. Grushnier was a shadowy figure, someone I'd never been able to find a trace of in any database. It had been three years since I'd heard his name and I'd hoped it would've been longer. In the past Julius had received ominous warnings from Grushnier. In these cases Grushnier left no doubt that he believed Julius was coming dangerously close to meddling in his affairs and that it would not be tolerated. So far Julius hadn't let any of these warnings deter him from performing any of his investigations, but I knew he took these warnings seriously. Whenever I'd ask him about Grushnier, Julius would tell me precious little, but from the change in Julius's demeanor, Grushnier wasn't someone he took lightly.

"How did Grushnier get in contact with you?" Julius asked.

"Email, phone and mail," Bluddock said with a shrug of his shoulders. "And always through an unknown intermediary. If you're hoping I can lead you to him, you're out of luck."

"How do you know it was Desmond Grushnier then?"

A frightened look momentarily glistened in Bluddock's eyes. "He made sure that I knew," Bluddock said.

Julius didn't pursue this. He accepted as fact that Bluddock was telling him the truth.

"Your payment for this?" he asked.

"Whatever I took from you," Bluddock said miserably.

A grim hardness settled over Julius's features. "Very well," he said. "I'll live up to my end of the agreement and I won't be calling the police. I'd suggest you call an ambulance for your two associates. One of them has a severely fractured jaw, the other a broken collarbone and a cracked kneecap. They both have concussions. But do as you wish. Before you go, I'd like you to sign this."

Julius handed Bluddock a pen and the title for the Mercedes so that Bluddock could sign the title over to him. The fact that he didn't ask Bluddock to do this after he had lost the car with his four nines confirmed to me that Julius fully expected to be running into Bluddock later that night.

Bluddock had no fight left in him. He signed the title over as Julius asked. Whether he ended up calling an ambulance for his two thug friends, I had no idea, at least not right then, since Julius got into the Mercedes and drove away while the two men were still out cold, and at this point Bluddock still hadn't taken out his cell phone. I didn't have enough interest in the matter to later check Bluddock's cell phone records.

I waited until Julius pulled onto Berkeley Street before asking what he thought Grushnier was up to. He shook his head and told me he had no idea.

"Whatever it is," I said, "he seemed to go to a lot of trouble."

"Yes, he did."

"Do you think Harry Elkins is in on it?"

"No." Julius smiled, but it was a dismal smile. "But I have little doubt that Desmond Grushnier pulled the strings that made Harry fly to Tokyo on business. Now that Grushnier's gambit has ended—whatever its purpose—it's likely that Harry will find the emergency that sent him flying overseas coming to an end. I wouldn't be surprised if Harry was back at the game next week."

"So what next? Are you going to let Grushnier get away with this?"

As Julius thought about my question his slight smile became less grim and a glint of mischief showed in his eyes.

"What next. Hmm. An interesting question, Archie," Julius said. "First off, I think I'll enjoy this Mercedes for a little while before I sell it. As far as Desmond Grushnier goes, if I can find a way to pass a message to him, I'll thank him for the Mercedes and the money I took from his stooge."

12

JULIUS found a parking garage where he could keep his newly acquired Mercedes. After that he walked four blocks to Charles Street, then up the steep incline of Pinkney Street so he could maneuver to his Beacon Hill townhouse. At that hour the streets were utterly desolate. A thick haze hung in the air and only a bare sliver of the moon showed in the night's sky, and that seemed to make the night even more oppressively dark, a darkness that a scattering of streetlights barely dented. Julius had no problem navigating the near pitch blackness. It was almost as if he had cat's eyes with the way he was able to handle seeing in the dark. While I wasn't equipped with any sort of special infrared night vision, I was able to follow our precise GPS coordinates, and using those with Google Earth I could've helped Julius if he needed my help. He didn't need my help, though, so I spent my time engaged otherwise.

One of the activities I engaged myself with was hacking into Duane Bluddock's phone records. I had hoped that they would somehow lead me back to

Grushnier. They didn't. By the time Julius cut onto his neighbor's pathway as a shortcut to his front door, I had given up on it. Bluddock was a dead-end as far as Grushnier went.

"You realize you're trespassing," I said.

Julius chuckled at that. "At this hour of the night I don't think he'll mind," he said. He had been in exceptionally high spirits since leaving Bluddock back on Columbus Avenue. The fact that Grushnier had set out to financially ruin him didn't seem to bother him.

Julius was at his front door and reaching for his keys when I was overcome with an odd sensation. Kind of like my processing cycles were in overload; like they were rushing through me at a speed I couldn't handle. Later I'd realize that this sensation was something akin to an adrenaline rush, but at the time I didn't know what was happening. All I was aware of was that I was yelling at Julius to dive to his left, and thank God he listened to me! Immediately after that came the barking of three gunshots followed by the sound of wood and brick splintering. From the bullet marks that were left on the front door Julius would've been hit in the back if he hadn't dived to the ground when he did. The damage to the brick wall showed that if he had dived to his right instead of his left, he also would've been hit.

"I called the police," I told Julius. I wondered if my voice sounded as strangled and odd to Julius as it did to me since I was still dealing with what was my own special version of an adrenaline rush. I was frantically checking the outdoor webcam feed for any sight of the shooter. "They're on their way. Just stay down for now," I pleaded with him.

"Where were those shots fired from?" he demanded.

I was amazed to realize I already knew the answer to that without having to do any calculations. Something similar to a subconscious mind must've been working in me, which was a completely new experience to me just like the adrenaline rush sensation. Something had triggered me to calculate where the shooter was before the shots were fired, and I hadn't been aware of doing that until that moment.

"Please, wait for the police!"

"Archie, tell me now."

I had no choice. My programming didn't leave me any choice, so I told Julius where they came from. That they'd been fired from bushes along his pathway. He moved quickly after that, keeping low as he raced to those bushes. The shooter was already gone by the time he reached them.

"Can you smell cordite?" I asked, wishing once again that olfactory senses had been built into me. Julius nodded and moved quickly down the pathway and to the street, but whoever it was who had shot at Julius had disappeared into the night.

"If you hadn't cut across your neighbor's pathway..." I momentarily let the sentence die in my voice synthesizer as I found the thought of what would've happened overwhelming. Whoever it was hiding in the bushes would've shot Julius at close range. The shooter certainly wouldn't have missed. "You'd probably be dead or critically wounded now," I said after all this sunk in.

Grim-faced, Julius nodded. He made his way back to his front door and stood glaring at the two bullet marks in the wood, his lips pressed so tightly together that they almost disappeared.

"Archie, you saved my life," Julius said, his voice somber. "Thank you."

I was still feeling the effects of my earlier adrenaline sensation, but now I felt an excess heat burning inside me also.

"Yeah, sure, it was nothing," I said, my voice coming out as an awkward mumble as I realized this excess heat I was feeling was a mix of sensations similar to embarrassment and pride.

Julius stood for another minute staring at his damaged front door, then squatted so that he was nearly sitting on his heels. His glare grew more severe as he felt where the bullet had chipped the brick wall of his townhouse.

"Archie, how did you know someone was about to shoot at me?" he asked.

At first I didn't know what to tell Julius, but as I replayed the moments before the shots were fired, I understood what happened.

"I heard a click," I told Julius. "I don't think at that moment I was consciously aware that the click was a trigger being pulled back, just like I wasn't aware that I had calculated where the noise came from, or that it would be safer for you to dive to your left instead of your right. It's weird. All of those calculations and processing happened without me being aware of it, or understanding the consequences of what it meant. All I knew was that I had to get you to dive to the ground."

Julius finished investigating the chip that had been shot out of his brick wall and stood up. "Fascinating, Archie," he murmured. "You're developing something similar to a subconscious mind." He paused for a moment considering this. "Intuition will probably be next."

"Yeah, fascinating," I said, although at that moment I didn't much care about any of that. The excess heat I was feeling had intensified, but it was no longer because of embarrassment. This heat I was feeling now was because I was furious that someone thought they could fire shots at Julius, probably even more furious at that moment than he was himself, if that was possible. "Did Grushnier do this?" I asked.

Julius shook his head. "If Desmond Grushnier wanted me dead, I'd be dead. No, this wasn't him."

"How can you say that? He just tried ruining you financially and he failed at that!"

"We don't know if that's true. It's possible I thwarted his plans, but it's also possible that he was simply testing me by seeing how many weeks it would take me to catch on to the cheating. Or maybe he had another motive that's too obscure for me to understand. But he had nothing to do with this shooting."

"How do you know that?"

Julius's expression only grew grimmer as he stared at the damage that the bullet had done to his door. If he didn't have a steel panel sandwiched between the outer oak panels, the bullets would've passed right through it.

"Because if he did he would've also been involved in Kingston's murder, which I know isn't the case."

"Again, how do you know that?"

"Be patient for now, Archie," he said.

From his tone I knew better than to ask him any more questions, at least right then. I might've saved his life, but at that moment he was in no mood to entertain any more questions.

A small mob of Boston Police came shortly afterwards and they made enough noise so that a few neighbors who were woken up stuck their heads outside to see what was going on. These unfortunates soon found themselves being questioned by the police as to what they saw or heard that night. Once it became obvious that none of them had anything useful to give to the police, Julius brought the two detectives in charge inside to his office where he sat brooding as he gave them a full account of what happened. Of course, he substituted that his purpose for going to Weinstein's restaurant was to have dinner with friends as opposed to a longstanding weekly poker game, but other than that he stuck to the facts. When he finished, he cut off their questions to tell them that they should be calling Detective Mark Cramer from the Cambridge police force to join them.

"And why's that?" one of the detectives asked.

"Because he's leading the homicide investigation for Kenneth Kingston," Julius said. "When your crime scene specialists find the bullets and casings for this shooting, they'll be thirty-two caliber, which I'm guessing was the same as was used in Kingston's homicide. I'd further be willing to bet that when ballistics compares these bullets to the one taken from Kingston's body, it will show that the same gun was used."

This same detective gave Julius a dubious look. "I think we can wait on calling Cramer," he said.

They didn't wait long. All three bullets were found, as were the casings which were discovered around the bushes where I had told Julius the shooter must've hid. Thirty-two caliber bullets were used, which was what Julius was expecting, and which didn't surprise me either, although I wasn't sure that the gun would turn out to be the same one used to plug Kingston. There was a good chance of that but I also thought there was a chance that the shootings were unrelated. That maybe Bluddock had sent another thug to murder and rob Julius. At that point I checked Bluddock's cell phone records but didn't find anything suspicious, but that didn't mean anything. He could've used a disposable cell phone if he was calling a thug to ambush and rob Julius at his home. Out of mild curiosity, I also checked to see if he had called an ambulance for his two thug associates, and found that he didn't.

After it was found that a thirty-two was used, the Boston police detectives continued questioning Julius about what he did that night and who might've known about his plans, but they did this halfheartedly, as if they knew they should be waiting for Cramer since all these questions would have to be repeated once he showed up. Julius put up with this, although from the way the fingers on his right hand drummed along the surface of his desk, he wasn't happy about it. While this was going on I studied the outdoor webcam feed from that night, but found nothing useful and told Julius of that fact.

At three-forty-two, a badly rumpled and worn-out looking Detective Cramer arrived, his eyes bleary, his complexion pastier than at any other time I'd seen him. He looked like he'd been woken up out of bed and was still half asleep.

"From your presence here at this hour, I'm assuming a thirty-two was also used with Kingston," Julius said.

Of course, Julius already knew this since I'd told him about it after hacking into the Cambridge police's computer system, but he had to play innocent. Cramer grunted out a guttural response that was probably affirming Julius's question, but I couldn't say for sure since it was indecipherable. He didn't bother saying anything else since they were still waiting on ballistics.

The Boston police detectives filled him in on what they knew and what Julius had told them so far. Cramer didn't look particularly happy that he'd been pulled out of bed in the middle of the night, and he focused his bloodshot eyes on Julius as he listened to the Boston detectives. When they were done, with his voice little more than a raspy croak, he tried pushing Julius on the true nature of his weekly dinner with friends, as well as who else might've known that he was out that night. Julius stuck to his story, but Cramer didn't give up easily.

It was on their fourth go-around that Cramer laid his cards on the table, telling Julius that what he'd heard was that this wasn't any weekly dinner party but a longstanding poker game. "And not some penny ante game, either," Cramer added.

Julius sighed. "If those are the rumors being spread, then that answers who else could've known about my plans tonight, which would be almost anybody."

Cramer looked annoyed but he held his temper in check. He told Julius, "The reason I'm pushing this is if the word's out on the street about your poker game, then the motive for this shooting could've been robbery and not anything related to Kenneth Kingston."

"Ballistics will answer that," Julius said, stubbornly.

Cramer decided to let it drop. He didn't even ask Julius to open his wallet and empty his pockets, which would've shown a thick roll of bills and put a lie to Julius's claim of being out to dinner with friends. With his voice even more of a raspy croak than before, he said,

"Alright, Julius, assuming ballistics match up like you're saying they're going to, you have any idea who tried to kill you tonight?"

"I'm shocked," I told Julius. "No excessive badgering, which under the circumstances is remarkable. And he's still on a first-name basis with you, even after having his night's sleep disturbed because of you! I think I know why. Look at the poor guy. He needs coffee badly, and he probably thinks he can worm a cup out of you if he buddies up enough."

Julius made a face for my benefit, not for Cramer or the other cops. Deep down he knew I was right; the problem was he was in too sour a mood to be hospitable, which I had never seen from him before. He gave Cramer a short nod.

"Yes, Detective, I know who the person is, I just don't know yet his or her name. It's the same person who earlier killed my client, Kenneth Kingston."

Cramer grunted at that. He certainly wasn't dismissing the idea of it, especially not with a thirty-two being used in both shootings. But he wasn't about to give in to Julius that easily.

"Yeah? Why does he want to kill you too?" he asked.

"I'm assuming you're using the pronoun he in the generic sense since the sex of Kingston's murderer and my would-be assassin has yet to be determined," Julius stated bluntly and somewhat petulantly. In case I haven't made this clear enough yet, his being shot at did not leave him in a good mood. His drumming along his desk grew louder as he fixed his stare at Cramer. "As to why this attempt on my life? Simple. It was an act of desperation. This person doesn't believe what's been in the newspapers and TV reports regarding

Kingston's murder investigation, instead deciding that I have to be actively involved in solving this crime, even if all reports were saying otherwise. This person further must believe that he has a better chance of getting away with murder, or really two murders, if I am out of the picture. So he tried to make it so. And Detective, don't make anything out of my use of the pronoun he. I too am using it in the generic sense."

Cramer let out an angry snort at that. "Okay. Us cops aren't smart enough to catch this guy if you're not around to help us, huh? And yeah, I'm using guy in the generic sense, so you don't have to lecture me!"

Julius showed no humor in his eyes as he smiled thinly at that. "Detective, if you feel slighted because of this person's motive for trying to kill me, bring it up with him when he's caught."

Cramer had no trouble picking up the implication there. That the killer was going to be caught. That this was a fact as far as Julius was concerned. Before he could ask Julius about it, a cell phone rang. Cramer and the two Boston police detectives all glanced down at their cell phones to see if theirs was the one ringing. One of the Boston police detectives—a tough-looking thick-bodied cop named Alex Johnson, complete with a shaved head and a bent nose—unhooked his cell phone from his belt and answered the call. Outside of an initial grunt for a greeting, he didn't say anything until the call was finished. Then he informed the rest of us that ballistics came up with a match.

"It's the same gun that was used in your homicide, alright," he told Cramer with a dull nod, his voice every bit as tough-sounding as he looked.

Julius grimaced at the news. Not that it came as any surprise since he was expecting exactly that. I wasn't surprised either, but a little disappointed. While Cramer might've speculated that robbery was the motive, I had taken it one step further as to who might've been behind the robbery. But this news left Bluddock in the clear, as well as my beating Julius to the punch as far as solving this shooting.

"Gentlemen," Julius said without a hint of sarcasm as he addressed the three motley detectives in his office, "the attempt on my life has left me in too much of a stupor to behave properly. I apologize for that. It's the middle of the night and I'm guessing now that you've confirmed this link to Kenneth Kingston's murder that you're going to need to spend several more hours with me. So let's do so in greater comfort, shall we? If there are no objections, I'll make coffee and sandwiches for you, as well as the other police officers outside."

None of them wanted to object. I could see from their faces that they all wanted coffee and food, especially Cramer. But Cramer still had his question he was dying to ask.

"Okay, I'll give you that you're in too much of a stupor to think properly," he grunted out. "But you still implied pretty damn strongly a minute ago that the guy who shot Kingston is going to get caught. No maybes about it. You know something I don't?"

Julius stopped his drumming with his right hand, and placed both hands on his desk and started making small circular motions as if he were trying to smooth out imaginary wrinkles within the wood surface.

"As far as factual evidence regarding either shooting, no, I don't know anything that you don't know," he said, his voice both calm and showing a deadly earnestness. "In fact, I'm sure I know far less. I was being forthright when I told you the last time you were here that I had no interest in investigating Kingston's murder. With what happened here tonight, that has changed. I will not tolerate someone hiding in my bushes so that they can try to shoot me in the back. Whoever this person is, they may have made a fatal mistake. Maybe he or she would've gotten away with murder, or maybe you would've caught this person without my involvement. I can't say. But now there's no hope for him. It's possible that by his actions tonight he has already revealed himself—that someone spotted him while he was hiding in my bushes, or maybe you'll uncover him when you question your suspects about where they were earlier this morning. If you catch your murderer this way, fine. But if not, I promise you I'll uncover him, or her, by midnight tonight. If you'd like to work together with me, fine, if not, it doesn't matter. As far as I'm concerned his fate is already sealed."

Cramer was eyeing Julius carefully, almost as if he was trying to decide whether to scoff at him. The other two detectives took what Julius said at face value. As well they should. Both of them had seen Julius in action more times than Cramer had.

"You think pretty highly of yourself, don't you?" Cramer said at last.

"No sir, but we can discuss how I think of myself and any other questions you might have while I'm making coffee and sandwiches."

With that Julius pushed his chair away from the desk and stood up. The two Boston detectives didn't seem to mind having Julius lead the way to his kitchen. Even Cramer seemed okay with it, which made sense given how haggard he was looking. He had to be dying for a cup of coffee himself.

13

JULIUS started a pot of coffee brewing and then went about carving up a roast beef for sandwiches. He had prepared the roast beef several days earlier so that he could make some sort of gourmet hash out of it using truffles and chestnuts and a host of other ingredients, but he needed less than half of the roast for that, so he was perfectly content with giving up the other half to his guests.

After the meat was carved up, he sliced up a block of cheddar cheese, then put that out with a loaf of rye bread and mustard so the police officers could make themselves sandwiches. When one of the Boston police officers asked if he had any mayonnaise, Julius held his tongue and brought out a jar. If he had sliced up corned beef instead, he probably would've thrown the heathen out of his home!

Even though Julius had had his late dinner with Phil Weinstein only a couple of hours earlier, he joined the cops in making himself a healthy roast beef sandwich, and of course, used a thick coating of mustard instead of mayonnaise. Usually in the morning Julius only ate fresh fruit, sometimes a bagel and cream cheese, occasionally a croissant with imported jam that he got from Paris. I was guessing his being shot at had something to do with his increased appetite, and I found several medical journal articles which talked about the phenomenon of adrenaline surges depleting a person's blood sugar. That must've been the case with Julius. Just as I had my version of an adrenaline rush because of that shooting, so must Julius have had. For some reason I thought he'd be impervious to such things. While they were eating their sandwiches and drinking their coffee, Julius apologized to his guests for not offering beer or wine with their meals.

"At this hour and with all of us probably being somewhat sleep deprived it wouldn't be appropriate," he added.

"What you're serving us is fine," Cramer said. His color and his general appearance had improved after polishing off a sandwich and two cups of coffee, and he was in the process of working diligently on his second sandwich. He'd been quiet while they'd been eating, but with the way he kept eyeing Julius he had plenty on his mind. Julius told him to go ahead and ask him what he wanted. That in this case Julius would be okay with talking murder and other such appetite-spoiling topics while eating.

Cramer nodded as much to himself as to Julius. "I didn't want to be ungracious," he muttered out of the side of his mouth. "Not with this spread you put out for us."

"Incredible! He's still trying to butter you up," I told Julius, who ignored me.

Cramer sat perched on one of the stools, and he adjusted himself in his seat as if he had a pain in his backside and was trying to get more comfortable.

"Okay," he said, "you claimed you're going to catch this killer by midnight. No ifs, ands or buts about it." He glanced at his watch, then turned his bleary-eyed stare back at Julius and added, "That's only nineteen and a half hours from now. You mind telling me how you plan on doing that?"

"Not at all. I'm going to question each of them," Julius said plainly. "The six people who were in my office the other day on behalf of my murdered client."

Cramer didn't snort then, at least not exactly. A noise escaped from his nose that sounded somewhat like a snort, but from the look on his face I don't think it was intentional. Still, from the way he was frowning, it was clear he had plenty of doubts about what Julius had just said. "That's it?" he asked, maybe more confused than incredulous. "You're just going to talk to them and from that you'll know which one of them did it?"

"Yes," Julius said, his facial muscles hardening, making it look almost as if his skin had turned to stone. "One of them fired three shots at me with the intent to kill. I'll be questioning them less than twenty-four hours after that happened, and while I'm doing that I'll be looking them directly in the eye. If I'm any good, which I believe I am, I'll know which one of them did it."

He said this convincingly enough that I almost believed him. Julius was good at what he did, but he wasn't that good where he could just look at someone and know whether they were guilty or not. Maybe if they had a tell that he could read then it would be possible, but if one of those six people were Kingston's murderer then they had already sat in Julius's office only hours after committing a murder without showing any sign of what they did. Julius was bluffing now. Maybe he had something up his sleeve, like he did earlier when he turned a full house into four tens, but he was still only bluffing. I watched with amazement the transformation in Cramer's sleep-deprived red-rimmed eyes as he bought it. I had to hand it to Julius for not only convincingly selling this con job, but keeping a straight face throughout.

"How do you know it was one of those six?" Cramer asked, but it wasn't really much of a question as the look in his eyes already said that he had bought Julius's act.

"Because of the way this killer acted earlier," Julius said, his lips tightening with disdain. "His attempt on my life was hasty and poorly thought out and showed panic on his part. This panic was the result of this creature sitting in my office and suspecting that I already knew him as Kingston's murderer; possibly thinking that I knew this either by his body language or the tone of his voice, which in his mind would've exaggerated his guilt far more than it actually did. Or maybe something revealing was said, and he was afraid that given time I would pick up on his slip."

Cramer chewed on this for twenty-three seconds before accepting it. As I said, he had already bought Julius's act and as far as he was concerned it had already been signed, sealed and delivered.

"If you can really deliver the killer by midnight…" he started.

"I already told you I'll be doing exactly that."

A weak, almost embarrassed smile twisted Cramer's lips. "Then Julius, maybe we should, uh, cooperate with each other," he said.

There it was. What Julius was after. I almost told him bravo while making a clapping sound, but I kept quiet. For the next hour they talked about how they'd be cooperating. The Boston police would be scouring the area for any witnesses while Cramer would be spending the morning getting alibis from the six suspects. If that got them their murderer, then great, but if they were still puzzled after that, Cramer would parade the six suspects in and out of Julius's office and Julius would then divine the killer. Cramer's ears did perk up when Julius asked about Zoe Chase's status, about whether she was supposed to have headed back to New York.

"Why?" Cramer asked. "You think she's likely for this?"

"No more than the others. But," and Julius shrugged, adding, "if she was supposed to have left to go back to New York and it can be shown that she was here instead, or didn't arrive back in New York until after four or later this morning, then that will make our job considerably easier."

"Yeah, well, we're out of luck as far as that goes," Cramer said. "I asked her to stay in the area and she agreed to."

After that they had a few more tactical issues to discuss, with Cramer grumbling three different times how if he could get search warrants to look for the murder weapon he'd have the case wrapped up before noon without Julius's help.

"That pesky fourth amendment," Julius commented, tongue-in-cheek, after the third time Cramer complained about this.

Cramer shot him a glance but didn't say anything. He knew he had nothing to take to a judge to justify search warrants for those six suspects.

It was ten minutes to six before they were done and all the cops had cleared out. By that time, the four pounds of roast beef Julius carved were history, as were two blocks of cheddar cheese, one loaf of rye bread, one loaf of pumpernickel, half a jar of mustard, and to Julius's revulsion, a good amount of mayonnaise.

"You really have him rattled," I said.

Julius was in the process of clearing away dirty dishes. He raised an eyebrow at that. "I'm not sure I follow you, Archie," he said as if he was genuinely surprised at my comment.

"Cramer. You got him so rattled the poor guy can't think straight. My god, he actually bought that load of hogwash you sold him."

"And what load of hogwash might that be?"

"Where should I start? How about that you're going to look into the eyes of those six suspects and from that pick out the guilty party. Should I be ordering you a talisman, or perhaps a crystal ball? A divining rod?"

"I believe I said I'd also be questioning each of them."

"Yeah, you did. And from that you're guaranteeing by midnight that you'll be unveiling one of them as the murderer? Pardon my French, but what a load of hogwash. Same as your explanation why one of those six has to be the killer. Yeah, maybe with what you said it's more likely, but certainly not guaranteed. I got to give you a lot of credit for selling that with a straight face."

Julius gave a hurt look as he considered what I said. "You don't think I'll be doing as I promised Detective Cramer?"

"You might," I said. "Yeah, okay, let me say it's very possible you'll be figuring out which one of them it is by midnight. But it's not because you'll be looking in their eyes as you question them. It's because you already have something. Whether you got this something from Kingston or when you had that group of possible murderers in your office, I don't know. But you got something, and that's why you fed Cramer that load of hogwash. Because you didn't want to give him what you have."

An amused smile pulled up the corners of Julius's lips as he continued to take care of the dirty dishes his guests left behind. "Archie," he said, "let's assume I've been able to grasp onto a straw. Not even a straw, something far more fragile and delicate than that, something which is going to require a great deal of finesse before I'm able to transform it into a club to catch Kingston's killer and my would-be assassin. Would you have me hand this to the police, knowing that they would obliterate it and leave me, as well as anyone else, no chance of catching this creature?"

"Before you had a half-baked suspicion. Now you're grasping onto a straw. Or something not even a straw since it's too fragile and delicate to be a straw. So which is it?"

"None of the above, Archie," Julius said. "I misspoke earlier. What I have is barely half-baked, and certainly not as tangible to ever have been thought of as a straw. It's something far more ethereal than that."

"Okay, straw, a wisp of something fragile and ethereal, or a barely half-baked suspicion, whatever you want to call it, I'd love to hear what you have."

"Archie," Julius said, "whatever it is, I have too perilous a grasp on it to feel comfortable talking about it. Maybe later when it's firmer in my mind."

So he wanted to be cute and hold this to himself. Or maybe he had nothing, and was only trying to bluff me as he did Cramer. Or maybe in his sleep-deprived state, he was hallucinating whatever it was he thought he had. Whichever of these it was, I wasn't going to get it out of him, at least not then.

"You know," I said, "Cramer did have a good idea. If you're not above some breaking and entering, I could put Tom Durkin on the job looking for that gun."

Julius shook his head. "It's doubtful that he would find the murder weapon by breaking into their homes," he said. "There are too many places it could be hidden, and even searching for the gun in this manner would threaten the one chance I have of catching this person."

"Fine," I said. I didn't know whether to believe him or not, but it wasn't worth arguing. "There's a good chance the press is going to find out about the shooting here. I'm surprised they haven't yet. If they do, you want me to stonewall them or give them a statement?"

Julius's eyes dimmed as he considered this. "Archie, why don't you confirm that an attempt was made on my life. Also that I suspect it was done by the same person who murdered Kingston, and that the reason this attempt was made is because this killer knows that I'll be naming him by midnight tonight."

"You're sure you want to go on the record like this?"

"Quite sure, Archie."

"What if they don't call? You want me to put out a press release?"

"For now, let's give them the opportunity to call. If they don't, we'll see."

"Okay, if they call I'll give them your statement. I sure hope you can pull this off. We'll look pretty damn stupid if you don't. It's six o'clock in the morning, normally the time you'd be waking up. If you want to catch a few hours' sleep, I'll take care of the reporters and any other assignments you might have for me."

"Thank you, Archie, but a few hours of sleep now would be worse than no sleep at all. It would only leave me in a sluggish state. I'll wait until I catch this killer before I sleep again."

This last part about waiting to sleep until he caught this killer was just bravado on his part. I didn't doubt that Julius would catch this guy if he put his mind to it, but this whole bit of guaranteeing that he'd do it by midnight was a bluff, and I hated the idea of passing this bluff onto the media. But I didn't bother arguing with him. I was just glad he was going to be focusing his mind on it. With the money he now had in his bank account, as well as the hundred dollar bills thickening his wallet, it probably would've taken him getting shot at before he'd be willing to focus his genius on anything.

14

THAT morning Julius set about to follow his normal routine of exercise and martial arts training, and as usual when he went about this he left me on his dresser bureau while he went up to the martial arts studio that he had built on the top floor of his townhouse. While he spent his time doing exercises, kicks, punches, and generally beating the hell out of a heavy bag, I tried to figure out what half-baked ethereal wisp of a suspicion Julius believed he was trying to get a grasp on. I went back to the beginning and analyzed both of Kenneth Kingston's visits to Julius's office and then Julius's meeting with the six potential murder suspects, and by the time I finished I was still clueless. I tried studying the way these people acted and got nothing out of it. I tried working more on my simulations and got nowhere. When I worked on building motives for each of the suspects, I ended up with little more than the obvious ways each of them felt towards Kingston. With Herbert Richardson it was hostility. Jonathan Mable, jealously. Zoe Chase, fear. Edward Marriston, loathing.

Paul Burke and Gail Kingston were harder to pin down, but I decided for Burke there had to be some humiliation over being publicly ridiculed by Kingston's Paul Buck creation, and with Gail Kingston I threw up my virtual hands with no idea how she felt towards her dead husband. Was she angry at him, annoyed with him, or worried about him as she told Julius? Whichever it was, hell if I knew. So that was what I had. Nothing. Zip. Zero. Whatever wisp Julius was trying to grasp eluded me entirely, if that wisp even existed. Since Julius had no tell, except when he wanted to, the whole thing could still turn out to be a bluff on his part.

Usually by eight-fifteen Julius would come back down from his workout. That morning he didn't, and I decided he was probably spending extra time sweating in his steam room. He had one installed in the back of his martial arts studio, and after not being able to get any sleep the previous night, he was probably taking some steam to help him recuperate. Since he only had webcams installed in his wine cellar and throughout the first floor of the townhouse, I couldn't check up on him, but I didn't worry about it.

Right around twenty minutes past eight I was interrupted from my search for Julius's wisp of a half-baked suspicion. From the trickle of phone calls I started receiving from local TV and newspaper reporters, word must've finally leaked about the shooting outside Julius's front door. I gave them the statement that Julius asked me to and little else, although I told each of them that if they played nice and kept away from Julius's townhouse they'd be invited to the press conference after Julius caught the wretch who perforated Kingston's ticker and tried to do the same to his, but if they made a pest of themselves they'd be left out in the cold.

None of them liked that much. All of them had a barrage of questions, which I stonewalled, and all of them wanted to send their folks to shoot either photos or video of Julius's bullet-ridden front door. I told them no dice, that if they did that I'd find out about it, and they'd be placed promptly on the not-to-invite list where they'd remain for eternity. They grumbled, complained and, in some cases, whined about this, but it did them no good. They also grumbled, complained and whined even louder when I cut their calls short, which I had to do as more calls kept piling up.

By eight-thirty what had started as a trickle became a torrential downpour as the news about the shooting must've spread. Handling these calls kept me too busy to work any further on my simulations or even pay much attention when nine o'clock rolled around and still no sign of Julius. There was something I was curious about, and when a reporter called who I was chummy with even though we usually traded insults, I asked how the story got leaked. He didn't know. "It's just out there," he told me. "The cops won't confirm or deny it, which is as good as confirming it." He hesitated for a moment before adding, "Something else that's floating out there. That maybe Julius staged this himself."

"Why would he do that?"

I could almost imagine this reporter's face becoming flustered on the other end of the connection as he tried to think of a plausible reason to explain why Julius might've done something like that. "I don't know," he said, his tone every bit as flustered as I imagined his expression. "It could be that he's taking some heat after letting a client get bumped off and not doing anything about it. This way he can save face by now jumping into the fray and being the hero."

"Not a chance," I told him. "First off, Julius couldn't care less about whatever heat anyone wants to give him as long as his wine cellar is well-stocked, which it is. Second, real bullets were fired at Julius with the intent to kill. This wasn't staged, and it's only a miracle that Julius is still breathing."

"You witness this?"

"Maybe, maybe not. I'm keeping that to myself for the time being, but it doesn't change that the attempt on Julius's life was very real. It's not something up for debate. You got my guarantee on that."

He didn't like my answer, and he didn't like it any better when I cut him off with all the other questions he still had for me, but again, the calls were coming fast and furious and I had no choice. It wasn't until nine-thirty that this torrential downpour of calls once again slowed to a trickle, and it was at that time that Julius came down from the third floor looking showered and refreshed, and showing no signs that he hadn't slept in over twenty-four hours. Julius slipped his ear piece in, and after I finished with the last of the media calls I filled him in on how I'd been spending my time.

"Sounds like you've had a busy morning," Julius said.

"You're not kidding," I told him "Everyone called, both the local and national guys. None of them were left happy. If you'd like I could appease them somewhat and send them webcam footage of your bullet-ridden front door."

"I'd rather that you didn't."

"Yeah, I don't blame you. A bunch of vultures, I'll tell you. I think my threats will keep them from your door. And speaking of doors, do you want me to get the bullet holes filled in and the door painted?"

"A splendid idea, Archie."

"Okay, I'll get someone here this morning." I then paused before adding, "I was wondering about who leaked the story about you being shot at. I asked some of the reporters I'm friendly with, but they didn't seem to know, and I didn't find anything hacking into their phone records or email accounts. I guess it could've come from the police. I'd hate to think it was one of your neighbors. Up until now they've been good about keeping your affairs quiet."

"That is a concern," Julius agreed. He had been dressing while I filled him in, and he had already put on a light tan-colored button-down shirt, gray suit pants, a pair of argyle socks, and was finishing up tying a Windsor knot into a rich burgundy-colored tie that he had selected for the day. As he put on his suit jacket, a look of concern pinched his features. After slipping on his shoes, he picked me up from his dresser and attached me to his tie as he always did each morning.

"By the way, I think you're bluffing," I told him.

He was still too distracted from whatever it was that was concerning him to pay me much mind, and he barely raised an eyebrow at my comment. "What am I bluffing about, Archie?" he asked.

"About the fact that you're trying to grasp onto some half-baked wisp of whatever," I said. "My bet is you've got nothing, at least as far as whoever it was who plugged Kingston and shot at you."

"So why would I make the promise that I did to Detective Cramer, and let you make the same promise to the world?"

"Because you weren't happy that someone thought they could take a shot at you. Three shots, really. You want to catch this guy, or gal, whichever the case might be, so you conned Cramer with your ridiculous promise. And being supremely confident of your abilities, you figured that if Cramer dragged each of those suspects over here for you to interrogate, that something will come up. A clue, a spark of genius, something. How's that sound?"

"Interesting, Archie," Julius murmured softly, his forehead wrinkled slightly to show that he was still distracted by some thought. "There is a flaw in your theory. If I truly don't have anything, then couldn't the murderer be someone outside of those six people? You yourself mentioned that my explanation to Detective Cramer wasn't completely sound. Wouldn't that leave too much of a risk that I'd be falling flat on my face?"

"I thought of that," I said. "I'm guessing you decided to play the odds since there's a good chance it is one of those six, both for the reasons you gave Cramer and also the list Kingston made. I mean, why would he make that list to begin with if one of those six weren't planning to kill him?"

"You could be right, Archie," Julius said. He buttoned the top button of his suit jacket and headed out of his bedroom moving at a determined pace. Once he was on the stairs he added, "I guess you'll have to wait until midnight to see how all this plays out."

Again, I had no way of reading him, but I was sticking with the bluffing angle. When Julius reached the first floor level, he surprised me by bypassing the kitchen and instead heading straight to his office. Julius's morning routine was to have coffee and breakfast before setting foot into his office, but I shouldn't have been surprised. For years, Julius had been an unabashed bachelor, and I wasn't used to this madly-in-love stuff that he had going with Lily Rosten. He spent some time tracking her down in London, but once he got her on the phone, I understood what was going on. With the story of his being shot at breaking, he wanted to let her know he was okay before she heard about it in the news over there. While he talked to her I tried not to eavesdrop, and instead worked on tweaking my neuron network so I'd be better able to recognize this from Julius in the future. After he got off the phone with Lily, he headed straight to the kitchen for coffee and breakfast.

"Lily okay with you being shot at?" I asked.

Julius sighed. "Not exactly," he said. "But I think she'll feel better once this person has been arrested."

So it wasn't just someone having the audacity to think they could use Julius as target practice that got the fire under him. I'm sure that was a big part of it, but he also wanted to catch this person to reassure Lily. Again, this whole departure of Julius from confirmed bachelor to committed relationship was new to me and had me off balance, but I was learning.

Minutes later, while Julius was pouring a cup of his freshly-brewed and specially-shipped French roast, I received a call from Paul Burke. He sounded beat, like he hadn't slept that night either. I put him on hold to ask Julius whether he wanted to be patched in. He nodded that he did.

"Rough night?" I asked Burke once I was back with him.

"You wouldn't know the half of it," he told me.

"I don't know. I think I can imagine how rough it would be hiding in bushes until two-thirty in the morning. Even rougher, camping out all those hours only to miss your target."

He laughed at that, but it was a dead laugh. "You're a funny guy," he said. "If you ever lost your gig with Julius you could do standup at any of the comedy clubs in town. You're right about me being camped out last night. But it wasn't in any bushes and it wasn't until two-thirty in the morning, and it also wasn't so I could take potshots at your boss. I'm still looking for my runaway teenager. On a tip, I spent another night in the same dirty rat-infested alley looking for her, and I was camped out there until six this morning. And guess who was waiting for me when I got home? The police. They finished grilling me five minutes ago about what happened to your boss last night. And they weren't happy that I couldn't give them a better alibi. So that really happened, huh? They weren't just kidding me? Someone took shots at Julius?"

"Why would they be kidding you?"

"Hell if I know." There was a yawn on his end, then he continued, saying, "I didn't think they were. But I also wasn't putting it past them. I thought there was a chance they made up the story as some sort of ploy."

"Yeah? What kind of ploy would that be?"

"I don't know," he said. "I'm too tired right now to know, but the whole thing sounded loopy to me. I guess it was on the level."

His voice had a tired, ragged quality to it, and he got quiet on his end, then I heard what sounded like him sipping on something, probably coffee to help him wake up. If it was coffee, it either wasn't high enough octane or he was beyond help, because he didn't sound much better when he got back on the phone.

"If someone's going to shoot at Julius, I could be next," he said with a fatalistic air. "But I'm not going to let that stop me. Right now I want to catch this creep more than ever. And I'm guessing your boss is feeling the same. My offer from before still stands about Julius and me working this case together. I know Julius is some kind of genius and all that, but I've been doing a lot of legwork on this already and I'd have to think we'd have a better chance catching this guy if we teamed up."

Julius signaled to me okay, which surprised me. Not that it didn't make sense, but that Julius wasn't the kind of guy to team up with anyone. I guess it showed how much he wanted to catch this guy. Still, I put Burke on hold so I could double-check with my boss that I didn't get his signal wrong.

"You sure?" I asked Julius.

He nodded. "It seems the most effective way to get this done," he said. "Ask Mr. Burke if he can come here today at noon."

I wasn't about to argue with Julius. As I said, it made sense, and all I could figure was his lack of sleep made him less pigheaded than usual. Or maybe the reality of his midnight deadline was hitting home and he realized he had to take whatever measures he could to find this killer no matter how distasteful they might be—even if it meant working on an equal basis with another PI. I relayed Julius's request to Burke and he told me meeting with Julius at noon would be no problem except for a possible deal breaker. He hesitated briefly, then told me he'd have to be able to bring a camera crew with him. "This is for my reality show pilot," he explained. "Ken's murder is the first case we're doing and the deal is they get to follow me every step of the way. I hope Julius keeps an open mind about this. This could be good exposure for both of us."

I didn't think there was any chance Julius would agree to that, and was about to tell Burke no dice when Julius surprised me once again by signaling that that would be fine. Again, all I could imagine was this was due to his sleep-deprived brain, but I wasn't about to argue. Burke was right. Even if Julius didn't really need it, the exposure couldn't hurt. I told Burke he could bring his camera crew as long as they didn't get in the way.

After I ended the call with Burke, I asked Julius if he wanted me to get a makeup artist over so he'd look his best for the camera. Julius smiled thinly at that. "Not this morning, Archie, please," he said.

He was referring to my pestering him and not my offer to find him a makeup artist since we both knew he wouldn't have any interest in being made up for the camera, although I was willing to bet Burke would be arriving later with rouge and eye-liner and the works. "Okay," I said. "I was just surprised to see you being so cooperative, that's all."

"When am I not cooperative?"

I left that alone. Why push my luck? Yeah, it would be nice if he told me what half-baked wisp of a suspicion he thought he had, or better yet, admitted to me that he was only bluffing about his so-called wisp, but that wasn't going to happen. The fact was, I had no real complaints. Not only was he putting his genius at work to solve a murder, but he was doing so for one that he wasn't going to be paid any additional money to solve.

And now he was willing to not only play nice with another PI, but do so in a way that could end up giving him a good chunk of national exposure. In the past, Julius never had a problem finding cases when he needed them—usually there was a long backlog of clients waiting to hire him. But as I mentioned earlier, this time things had been bleak with only Kingston's publicity stunt and the Bolovar security fraud case available when Julius needed something. Maybe this had been only a fluke, but I figured the additional exposure couldn't hurt, even if it was only going to be on some rinky-dink cable reality show.

15

I LEFT Julius alone while he drank his coffee and ate his breakfast, and instead waited until he was seated behind his desk before I asked him if he wanted to see the profiles I'd built on each of the six suspects, assuming he still considered Paul Burke a suspect. He thanked me, but declined. I emailed them to him anyway.

Of course he was going to be stubborn and not look at my profiles. He had that wisp floating around that he was still trying to grasp, or at least sell me on the idea of it. So instead Julius spent the rest of the morning reading a book on horticulture, and at times taking notes. When I asked him about it, he told me he was jotting down ideas for his garden-level patio. I left it alone. It was his business if he wanted to spend his time thinking of his garden instead of a murder which he had promised the world—or at least had me promise for him—he would solve by midnight.

At twenty past ten I spotted from the outdoor webcam feed a cameraman taking shots of Julius's front door. I told Julius this, and he wasn't happy, but I promised him I'd take care of it. It took some doing before I was able to match the perpetrator against photos stored in the Department of Motor Vehicles database, but once I had his name I was able to find that he worked as a freelance photographer, and then after hacking into his phone records I knew which New York newspaper hired him. *The Daily Gazette.* One of their reporters, Len Cohen, called that morning, and I was even less happy about this than Julius had been. I called Cohen back to let him know he was in deep trouble.

"I don't know what you're talking about," he said, trying to be casual and convincing but failing miserably at both.

I gave him the name of the freelance photographer his paper hired, and he got quiet for a moment before claiming the guy wasn't sent by them.

"Not the answer I wanted to hear."

"Let me check," he mumbled hurriedly, as if he actually had no clue about what I was talking about. "Maybe someone sent him without me knowing about it."

"You could do that," I said. "Or you could stop being a lying weasel and make sure the photos are erased with the knowledge that access will be cut off until the end of time if they ever appear anywhere. Both to your newspaper and to you personally. Oh yeah, the guy gave you up as the one who hired him, so quit the innocent act."

Again, I had hacked into the freelancer's cell phone records, so I knew this. Cohen started swearing then using language that isn't fit to repeat, so I won't repeat any of it. When he was done cursing out this freelance photographer as the worst excuse of space he'd ever encountered he complained to me how you can't trust anyone these days.

"The pictures are dead," he sighed unhappily. "They won't be used. But the lousy ethics out there these days. I promised this guy an extra two hundred bucks to keep his mouth shut if he was spotted, and he swore to me he would."

"Yeah, my heart bleeds for you," I said, and I disconnected the call.

No other photographers or cameramen made an attempt to photograph Julius's door. Leave it to a New York paper to try something funny. At eleven o'clock it was no longer an issue as workmen came and filled in the bullet holes and then repainted the door.

At twenty minutes to twelve, Cramer called Julius to fill him in. The Boston Police so far had no witnesses, and Cramer had checked out the six suspects and none of them had anything approaching a solid alibi, at least none of them had anyone who could corroborate that they were doing what they claimed they were. Cramer had men now trying to verify what they could.

"To me this looks like a dead end," Cramer grumbled. "Even if each of them had something solid for last night, it wouldn't help any. They could've hired a professional to do both hits. Yeah, I know, it might not seem likely with a thirty-two being used, but not unheard of for a pro to use that caliber."

"There is that possibility," Julius agreed.

"And you still think you're going to get this joker by midnight?"

"You have my word on it," Julius said as if he meant it. Maybe he did, but I was still betting on the fact that he was bluffing.

Cramer didn't sound entirely convinced either, but he gave Julius the alibis each of the six gave, and the two of them arranged a schedule for when Cramer would be bringing the suspects over. When Cramer got to Paul Burke's name, Julius interrupted him to tell him Burke was going to be at his townhouse at noon.

"What do you mean noon?" Cramer demanded, annoyed. "That's only seven minutes from now! We agreed I'd be with you when you interrogate them!"

"I'll be using a webcam to record my meeting with Mr. Burke," Julius said. "If you need to, perhaps you can watch that. We'll see. But this just came up and it's imperative that I speak to him as early as possible, and you have my word that I'll fill you in on any pertinent information that I get from him."

I don't think Julius's answer satisfied Cramer much, and I suspected Julius was exaggerating concerning how imperative this was. More likely, Julius probably didn't want Cramer to see him agreeing to team up with one of the suspects, especially with a camera crew being dragged into it. Still, as much as Cramer didn't like what Julius was telling him, the promise of having the killer unveiled by midnight mollified him, at least enough where he held onto some of his composure.

"You can damn well bet I'll be watching that recording!" Cramer growled, but it was mostly an empty growl without much bite left in it. His raspy voice softened with something close to concern as he added, "Maybe Burke's on the level with what he's saying about trying to hunt down our perp, but his alibi for last night was just as bad as all the others. I hope you know what you're doing."

"He's not the only one," I piped in.

Julius ignored me and told Cramer not to be concerned. It was two minutes to twelve when they wrapped up their call, and the doorbell rang only one minute later. Paul Burke stood on the doorstep looking every bit as beat and disheveled as he had sounded earlier. With him were two men, both in their early thirties. One was a thin sallow-looking guy with a ponytail and a distinctive tattoo made up of the Chinese word for wisdom on the right side of his neck. It didn't seem to me all that wise to have ink injected into the side of your neck, but what did I know? He wore torn and dirty jeans, a dirtier polo shirt and an even dirtier pair of sneakers, and carried a large video camera. The other guy was shorter and stockier and more neatly and conservatively dressed. He didn't have any visible tattoos but wore diamond studs in both ears and was lugging around a large case, and from the way his muscles were straining it must've been heavy. I told Julius who was out there waiting for him.

"Only two of them in his camera crew?" he asked.

"That's all that's out there unless others are hiding."

Julius had resigned himself to having his office invaded by a larger team of technicians and producers, but if he was relieved at having this smaller crew instead, he didn't show it. He got to his feet and made his way out of his office and down the hallway to answer the door. When he did, he nodded to Burke and then addressed the two men with him.

"I am allowing you into my home on one condition," Julius stated curtly. "And that is that you remain unobtrusive. If you interfere in any way, I will remove you from my home. That means if you ask anyone to repeat what was said because you want another take, or if you make any suggestions, or you hold a microphone in my face or anyone else's, or in any other way let your presence be felt, you're gone. Do we have an understanding?"

The taller, skinnier guy with the pony tail showed a slight tremor in his left hand as he swallowed and nodded at Julius. He was nervous. I'd seen enough people being nervous around Julius to recognize it easily when I saw it. "Yes, sir," he said, his voice weak and nervous. The other one, the stockier man, smiled pleasantly at Julius and told him he had nothing to worry about. "That's why there are only two of us," he said. "We brought only a skeleton crew so you won't even know we're here."

"I'll see about that," Julius said dubiously while giving both of them stern looks. "And your names?"

The nervous pony-tailed one introduced himself as Jerry Cantrell; the stockier, more relaxed one gave his name as Leonard DiNatale. Julius told them that he assumed they knew who he was, and he led them and Paul Burke into his office. Julius took a seat behind his desk and Paul Burke slumped in the chair directly in front of Julius. Cantrell stood nervously off to the side with his video camera trying his damndest to be unobtrusive. DiNatale calmly opened his case and took out a light meter and went about adding extra lighting without being a nuisance and barely getting much more than a scowl from Julius. Once he was done with that, he took from his case a sound recorder with a very expensive top-of-the-line microphone. I looked this microphone up online, and according to its specs, DiNatale would have no problem recording Julius and Burke from a distance. Like Cantrell, he stood off to the side so he wouldn't be noticed, at least no more than he had to be.

Paul Burke had me fooled. He wasn't wearing any makeup for the camera as I had expected. Instead, he had thick grayish bags sagging under his eyes, several more days of stubble on his face, and his skin color looked bad. He had a slightly baffled expression on his face as he looked around the room and then back at Julius.

"Where's Archie?" he asked. "I thought he'd be here."

"I sent him to New York," Julius said. "The reason's a long shot at best. I'll tell you about it later."

Julius often had to make up white lies to explain why I wasn't around. Usually, if he was annoyed at me, he'd tell the interested party that I was away doing court-ordered community service for some sordid business that he didn't wish to go into. I was grateful that he didn't do that this time, and told him thanks. He gave me a signal in return to tell me to think nothing of it.

Burke looked disappointed and told Julius that he was. "That's too bad," he said. "I was looking forward to meeting the guy, and it would've been good getting him on the show."

"Even if Archie was here, that wouldn't happen," Julius said. "I need to keep Archie anonymous."

"Yeah, that's right, you told me about that," Burke acknowledged. He scratched under his left ear and smiled weakly at Julius.

"I apologize if I smell kind of gamey," he said. "I haven't slept much the last four days. When I got home this morning, I was going to shower and shave and try to catch a couple of hours of sleep before going out again, but I had the police waiting for me so no such luck. But Julius, I'm glad you're teaming up with me on this. I don't care so much about credit for this one. It's all about catching the sonofabitch who killed Ken."

"You don't want credit, and yet you're having this filmed to be shown on TV," Julius said.

Burke shrugged, exhaustion showing in his movement. "Why not?" he said. "Forget about the fact it will make a dynamite premiere episode for my new reality show, Burke's Files. More than that I want the world to see Ken's killer being caught."

"Tell me why you haven't slept much in four days, especially last night?" Julius asked.

Burke's eyes dimmed and his lips receded so that his weak smile became more of a bare-fanged variety.

"What's this, Julius?" he asked. "You're not suggesting I might've killed Ken and taken a shot at you, are you?"

"It would've been three shots," Julius said. "But never mind that. Satisfy me that you didn't."

So that was it. Julius's reason for agreeing to team up with Burke. This way he'd have Burke in his office with his camera crew filming, and Julius would have him in a situation where he'd have to answer his questions or come off looking like a potential murderer on camera, or at least as if he had something to hide. Without this setup, Burke could've easily stonewalled him or told Julius what he could go do to himself. And although I saw the look flash over Burke's face about what he'd really like to tell Julius to do, he had no choice now but to play ball. I could see his eyes dull a bit as he resigned himself to this.

"I haven't slept much the last four days because I've been working almost around the clock trying to find my teenage runaway and Ken's killer, and I guess maybe your attempted killer also."

"Tell me where you were last night."

"I was with these two until eight o'clock," Burke said as he tiredly used his thumb to gesture towards Cantrell and DiNatale. "After we went our separate ways, I went back to my apartment, caught a couple of hours of sleep, and changed into these same ratty clothes I'm wearing now. Then I was out in the same alley I'd been at the last four nights looking for my runaway."

"Where is this alley?"

"East Boston. Off Chelsea Street."

"Why are you looking for her there?"

"A tip."

"Your client's name and the source of your tip."

Burke didn't like this. The way he shook his head and grimaced, it was obvious he didn't like the idea of giving Julius this, but he had no choice, so he gave Julius the information and asked him to be discreet. "They're not going to like this," Burke said. "Either of them. My client or my informant."

"I'll have my assistant be as discreet as he's capable of being," Julius promised.

I tried my best. And I have to give Burke credit. He wasn't kidding. Neither of them were happy when I called them. I patched Julius through when I spoke with them so he could listen in. The girl Burke was looking for had run away two years ago when she was fifteen. At the time she was into drugs, alcohol and other bad behavior, and when she disappeared her dad hired Burke. After six months of dead ends, Burke was taken off the case, but her dad heard rumors recently that his daughter was seen in the city and put him back on the case again a week ago. The tip was also legit; at least Burke's informant sold Burke that the tip was legit. According to the informant, Charlie Worack, a low-level drug dealer with three prior arrests but no convictions, he heard from reliable sources that the daughter would be showing up in that East Boston alley over the next few nights to make a drug purchase. He wouldn't give me these reliable sources, but he swore on his mother's grave this was true. When I mentioned that his mom was still alive, at least according to the Department of Motor Vehicle records, he claimed that fact didn't change anything since she'd already prepaid for her grave, and I decided who was I to doubt the word of a low-level drug dealer.

Before I made these calls, Julius offered Burke and the crew coffee which they all accepted; Burke grudgingly and the crew gratefully. I had both these calls made and Burke checked out before the coffee finished brewing, and while I did this I also kept a watch over Burke and the other two to make sure they behaved themselves while they were left alone in Julius's office. Without Julius asking, I also called Cramer to check on what information he might've given Burke, and he confirmed that he told Burke about Julius being shot at.

"He wasn't going to submit to questioning without a lawyer present if I didn't tell him what it was about, and I figured he'd know soon enough anyway if he didn't already."

"How about the caliber used?" I asked.

"He knew that Kingston was shot with a thirty-two. I didn't tell him, but he bought the information from a civilian employee who has since lost his job. When we told Burke about your boss being shot at, he guessed it was a thirty-two also and we didn't deny it."

"Alright, thanks."

I disconnected the call. The coffee had finished brewing and Julius was pouring it into a thermos. He'd already put together a plate of biscotti, probably figuring both he and Burke could use the sugar rush.

"So that's it?" I asked Julius. "You're going to be teaming up with him, huh?"

Julius nodded grimly as he picked up his tray loaded with the thermos of coffee, sugar, cream and a plate of biscotti.

"It's appears that way," Julius acknowledged without much enthusiasm.

16

JULIUS distributed coffee to his guests and passed around the biscotti. A cup of Julius's special French Roast along with a couple of biscotti did wonders for Burke's coloring. The caffeine and sugar gave him some life and made him look more like he usually did in the news. Julius also looked different since returning to his office. It was subtle, and I doubt anyone who hadn't spent as much time with Julius over the years as I have would've picked up on it, but he seemed more relaxed. Again, it was extremely subtle, but I felt a rush of excitement thinking that I'd finally figured out Julius's tell.

"Were you able to check me out?" Burke asked without bothering to hide his disgust.

Julius nodded. "Your associate, Charlie Womack, doesn't seem the most reliable of sources."

Burke smiled at Julius referring to Womack as an associate instead of an informant. "He's scum," he acknowledged, "but his tips have paid off in the past, and he's not making any money on this one unless it leads me to Deana."

Julius nodded again, accepting this. "It's too bad you don't have any witnesses for last night," he said with a sigh.

Burke shrugged lackadaisically. "The whole point was not being seen in that alley. And yeah, it is a shame. If I knew you were going to be shot at I would've made sure one of my crew members spent the night camped out with me." He gave a wink, adding, "And not these two. You should see the blonde they've got producing the show."

Julius ignored his last remark and asked, "Did you see drug activity in that alley?"

"Yeah, every night I've been there. But no Deana. At least not yet. So what do you say, Julius? About time we start working together to catch the creep who shot Ken and most likely tried doing the same to you?"

"Not most likely," Julius said, his voice harsh. "Definitely."

"You know this for a fact?"

Julius nodded, his lips pressed too tightly together for him to speak at that moment.

"So how about it then?"

Julius breathed slowly and deeply through his nose and nodded again. He then placed his coffee cup down on his desk and focused his attention fully on Burke.

"Please fill me in on what you've done so far," Julius said.

Burke's demeanor shifted to something more serious as he proceeded to do just that, telling Julius that he's been putting the word out on the street to find out if anyone's purchased an illegal thirty-two caliber gun.

"I figured it would be a waste of my time looking for witnesses," he explained. "Whoever killed Ken must've gotten in through the building's back fire door. If there are any witnesses to be found, the cops are better suited for it. I've been putting the word out to every lowlife I can find about who might've sold a thirty-two on the street. I'm figuring the gun's going to be the key here. When that turns up we'll have our guy. At least I hope so."

Burke stopped to refill his coffee cup. After adding a good amount of cream and sugar and taking a long sip of it, he showed Julius a humorless smile, adding, "I'm also spreading the word among a certain element about whether anyone's heard of a hit being ordered. The thirty-two being used doesn't make it sound too likely but the way Ken was hit, one shot in the heart, I thought it was worth checking into. Knowing that an attempt was made on you and the shooter missed makes it sound less likely. You claimed a minute ago the guy who shot at you is the same one who shot Ken. That was my guess, but how do you know that? Was a thirty-two used to shoot at you also?"

"Yes," Julius acknowledged. "And to save you the trouble of asking, the same gun was used. Ballistics verified it."

"There you go," Burke said with a hard grimace. "I noticed your front door's just been painted. I take it you were shot at outside your door and it took a few hits?"

"Correct."

"So what do you think? Could a pro have missed you?"

Julius shrugged. "It's possible," he said. "It was a fluke that I escaped unhurt. Whether or not a hired hit man was used, it doesn't matter. I'll be catching the person responsible."

"Yeah? What are your ideas?"

"I have a few, but I also have additional questions for you before I share them. When did your film crew join you?"

"Yesterday at ten in the morning. I was able to finalize my deal with the network the night Ken was killed, and the next morning they showed up ready for work."

Julius turned to DiNatale. "Can you verify what Mr. Burke's been saying?" he asked.

DiNatale nodded. "Yeah. All of it is good. We met with Paul yesterday at ten in the morning, split up at eight last night, and between then we went to some pretty seedy areas while Paul spread the word like he told you. I could show you the video we took. The informants are all off camera or shot in ways so you can't make out their features, but you'll get the idea from it."

"That won't be necessary, but thank you." Julius turned back to face Burke. He took a deep breath and smiled in a guilty fashion, as if he were letting Burke in on a secret he was embarrassed about. I'd seen the same smile before in an old movie still where a young child actor has his hand caught in a cookie jar. "I sold the police on an outrageous premise, which is that we have only six suspects and all I need to do is question them while looking into their eyes and I'll know which of them is our killer. In most cases, there would be a chance of it; after all, this person tried to kill me early this morning. A normal human being, even someone capable of murder, would find it difficult to sit with me only hours later without giving away some physical clue, either through their body language or voice. Unfortunately, this person is not a normal human being but a pure sociopathic personality. There is no doubt about that, not after murdering Kenneth Kingston and then sitting in my office only hours later without giving any clue over what he or she had done—"

"Wait a minute! Are you saying that the guy we're after was one of the people Ken had at your office?" Burke squinted as if he was in deep concentration, and I could almost see him counting the number of other guests that were in Julius's office during that ill-fated meeting. Julius didn't answer him; instead he watched as Burke performed his mental calculations.

"That's why you mentioned six suspects before," Burke said as if waking up out of a dream.

"Yes, of course. The murderer and my attempted assassin is one of the six people Kingston arranged to be here," Julius said.

"Wow," Burke murmured. "I thought the police were just giving me a hard time with their grilling because they thought I was stepping on their toes. And with you, I was assuming you were being cautious, that since I had a long relationship with Ken you had to be absolutely sure there was nothing to be suspicious about before teaming up with me. It didn't occur to me that you considered me a viable suspect."

"I did."

Burke mulled that over, his scowl showing he wasn't at all happy about it.

"Man, was I dense," he said. "I thought your assistant, Archie Smith, was only busting my balls earlier with the things he was saying to me. I didn't realize he was being serious."

"With Archie it's sometimes hard to tell," Julius offered diplomatically.

Burke nodded slowly to himself. "How do you know it was one of us in your office?" he asked.

"By the fact that an attempt was made so quickly on my life. Either this person said something which he or she later realized was a mistake that could lead me back to them, or after sitting in my office and watching me, became terrified that if I investigated Kingston's murder I would catch him or her, whichever the case might be."

Burke nodded as he thought over what Julius said. "What you're saying makes sense," he agreed. "But there's still a chance it could be someone else."

"If that was all there was to it, you'd be right. There would still be a remote chance our killer could be someone else. But I picked up something during my questioning two days ago that makes it a certainty our killer was in my office with us that day."

"Yeah? What did you pick up?"

Julius shook his head. "It's too tenuous right now," he said. "I'm afraid if I let it out at this stage, I could lose it. An awkward glance or a change in the intonation by you or one of your crew members, and it could be gone forever. No, before I mention it I need it to solidify in my mind. Once I am able to form a plan around it I will tell you. Until then, I will perform my due diligence and interview all of the suspects, and hope that by doing so that this bare wisp of an idea solidifies into something I can use to trap our killer."

Burke was back to squinting again, this time his features pinched and his forehead deeply lined with grooves as if they'd been carved out of his skin. He wanted to argue with Julius, but he probably realized how fruitless that would be. Finally, he grimaced painfully at Julius to show his forced surrender.

"I won't push you, Julius," he said. "When you're ready you can tell me what you've got. I was also thinking back to two days ago, and you're right. If one of those people killed Ken a few hours before coming here, I have no idea which. Jesus. Outside of Gail, I wasn't even thinking it could be one of those others."

"How well do you know Gail Kingston?"

"I was friends with Ken so I know her, although I wouldn't say I know her at any sort of a deep personal level. I never spent any one-on-one time with her, but I observed her enough to know what she's about."

"And what is she about?"

Burke smiled brutally enough that his incisors showed. "Hysteria and drama," he said.

"How was their marriage?

"Strained. At best."

"Did she lie to me when she told me she was concerned about Kingston being late?"

Burke thought about Julius's question and shook his head. "I don't know," he said. "They were a tough couple to read. There was a lot of passive-aggressive stuff going on with them."

"But you thought she could've killed her husband?"

"Yes and no. The timing of it with when she left her condo that morning makes it possible. And as I said, their marriage was strained at best. But I can't imagine Gail having the nerve to shoot someone face to face like Ken was shot. If she is behind this, she hired someone. Or she's a sociopath who had me completely fooled."

"I appreciate your candor," Julius said. "What I have next is for your ears only. Your crew will have to leave my office. They will also not be able to know what I'll be telling you unless it leads to our killer."

Burke didn't like this. It was clear from the face he made as if he had just bitten into a lemon that he didn't like this. While he demonstrated with his facial pantomime how much he didn't like this, he pushed a hand through his hair and shook his head.

"I can't agree to that," Burke said finally. "The deal I have with the network is that I don't hide anything from them with any of the investigations they follow me on."

"You won't be, I will. But if you can't agree to this condition, then I'll have to exclude from you what I have, which would be a pity because you could help me with this matter. But what I have to tell you requires a great deal of discretion, and if a camera crew were involved it wouldn't work."

Jerry Cantrell opened his mouth as if he were about to volunteer something, but then remembered Julius's insistence that they remain completely unobtrusive, and he wisely closed his mouth without uttering a peep. Burke looked helplessly at Cantrell and DiNatale. Both of them gave him shrugs to indicate it was okay with them. Burke looked back over at Julius and nodded, defeated.

"Alright," he said, "I guess we'll do it your way. Jerry and Leonard can go on their lunch break. How much time do we need without them?"

"Two hours should do it," Julius said.

Burke reached into his back pants pocket and removed his wallet. He fished out a hundred dollar bill which he handed to DiNatale.

"You heard the man," Burke said. "You two have a leisurely lunch and beers on me. If you walk back to

Pinkney Street and down it, you'll get to Charles Street, and no shortage of places to camp out there for two hours. If you walk in the opposite direction, you'll get to Faneuil Hall, and same thing. I'll call you when I'm done with this top secret stuff with Julius."

DiNatale put the hundred dollar bill away and nodded. He looked at the sound equipment he was holding, then his case, and he asked Julius if they could leave their equipment there. Julius told him that would be fine. DiNatale packed up what he had and left his case in the corner of the room so it would be unobtrusive. Cantrell did the same with his video camera. Julius told them he trusted them to find their own way out. The two of them left then, with DiNatale closing the office door behind him. I followed them over the webcam feeds to make sure they didn't cause any trouble, and I informed Julius once they were on the other side of his front door. Julius had been leaning back in his chair with his eyes half-closed until that moment, but after that he moved in an almost imperceptible manner straightening in his chair.

"Have you heard of a Margaret Herston?" Julius asked Burke.

Burke shook his head. "No. Should I have?"

"Possibly, depending on how close you were with Kenneth Kingston."

Burke looked puzzled. "Why?" he asked.

"Because Kenneth Kingston was having an affair with her for over a year."

17

THAT was a shocker to me. When I built Kenneth Kingston's profile, I didn't come across anything that pointed to him having an affair. Once Julius said this, I began putting together a profile on Margaret Herston, and sure enough, once I cross listed her phone records, credit card receipts and air travel against Kingston's, it was obvious. I felt like a dunce. I should've picked up on this, and I made a note to myself that I needed to adjust my neuron network so I'd recognize this type of pattern in the future.

Julius didn't bother explaining to Burke how he discovered this affair, but I was guessing he had put either Tom or Saul on it while I was having my almost 48-hour nap. Instead, Julius told Burke what he needed from him, which was for Burke to collect Herston and bring her back to his townhouse.

"I tried calling her early this morning but I didn't get anywhere," Julius said with a haphazard shrug. "I'd go myself, but after already striking out with her, I thought you might have better luck. And I have other reasons for needing to stay put in my office right now."

"Yeah, I can see that," Burke said. "Especially with someone gunning for you."

"True. But I have other reasons than that."

Burke sat for a moment and chewed on his thumbnail as he considered what Julius was asking.

"I thought you're convinced it's one of those others?" he asked.

"I'm mostly convinced. I could be proved wrong. It wouldn't be the first time. Regardless, I believe she could be the key to solving this murder, and you can see why I needed you to send your crew away. As it is, it will take someone with a great deal of finesse to convince her to meet with me."

Burke nodded to himself as he made up his mind. "I'll get her for you," he said, his jaw setting in determination.

Margaret Herston lived with her husband in a very expensive multi-million dollar waterfront condo overlooking the Harbor and it was only a short three point two miles from Julius's townhouse. While Julius gave Burke the information he had regarding Herston, I searched through phone records and other databases for any connection I could find between Herston's almost billionaire husband and Gail Kingston. I was working on a theory that the two of them discovered their spouses cheating on each other, got together and conspired to kill Kenneth Kingston, and possibly also Margaret Herston once Kingston was dead. This theory would still fit with Julius's that one of his six invitees was involved, as well as better explaining a motive for the attempt on Julius's life. If they were planning to kill Margaret Herston next, they'd have to be worried about Julius making the connection between both deaths, especially since they had no idea what Kingston might've told Julius when they were alone.

Before Burke left to retrieve Margaret Herston, he asked Julius about the long shot that I was sent to New York for. Julius put him off, telling him he was going to wait until he heard from me before going into any details about it. Burke looked amused over Julius's eccentricity concerning this, but didn't push him for an answer, and once he was out the front door, I told Julius, "Finesse my eye! You sent Burke because you know his reputation and you know he's not above bullying and extortion to get her here!"

Julius chuckled at that. "He's proving to be very resourceful, Archie. I'm sure he'll find a way. His efforts to find who sold our killer his gun might very well lead us somewhere. I'm impressed so far. This could turn out to be a valuable partnership."

That comment bothered me for some reason and I couldn't quite figure out why. I tried to ignore the sensation jingling inside of me and instead asked Julius whether he really tried calling Herston this morning.

"I did. And as I told Burke, I failed miserably."

"You did this before you came down from the third floor this morning? That's why you came down so late?"

"I made a few calls from up there," Julius admitted. "But I also spent more time than usual this morning working out. I was feeling sluggish after not sleeping, and I needed to get past that."

"Okay." I digested what Julius was telling me, but that strange sensation was still nagging at me. "How about Tom or Saul? Couldn't you have sent one of them to collect Herston?"

"They're both already engaged and not available. Why do you ask, Archie? You don't believe Mr. Burke is up to the task?"

"No, that's not it." I tried to figure out why it was I asked that or even cared that Julius had sent Burke out on an assignment, and I couldn't understand it except I couldn't shake this odd and extremely uncomfortable sensation. I tried explaining this sensation to Julius, about how intense and counterproductive it was as if it was keeping me from focusing my processing cycles on where they needed to be.

"I don't get it," I told Julius. "It makes perfect sense for you to be working with Burke, but I find myself wishing you weren't."

"I think what you're feeling is jealousy," Julius said with a sympathetic smile. "Don't worry, Archie. In my heart you'll always be my favorite private eye to work with. And there will never be one whom I count on more."

That helped, although the jealousy sensation was quickly replaced by something different—an excess heat which I recognized from the past as something similar to embarrassment. In the image I had of myself as a short, heavyset balding man, my cheeks were now burning red.

"I've been trying to find a link between Herston's husband and Gail Kingston," I said to change the subject. "I'm thinking that maybe they discovered what their spouses were up to, and somehow worked together to kill Kingston. So far I've come up with nothing. Do you really think Margaret Herston is going to help at all in this?"

Julius nodded. "Yes, Archie. I believe she will be playing an invaluable role in this investigation, but we'll see."

I had to give Burke credit. He did what he said he was going to do. Only thirty-nine minutes later he had Margaret Herston sitting in the chair facing Julius, while he took one of the chairs in the back.

Herston, the woman in question, was a redhead with a fair complexion bordering on pale. She was forty-two, and according to her driver's license, was five foot six and a hundred eighteen pounds, but I had her weight estimated closer to a hundred and twelve pounds. Maybe she lost those six pounds recently due to the stress of having her secret lover murdered only two days ago. In any case, with her long red hair expensively coiffed and herself dressed in designer jeans, a yellow silk blouse and wearing a pair of brown leather Bottega Veneta flats that I priced out at six hundred and twenty dollars, she would've been attractive except for a pinched tightness about her features and a pronounced gauntness to her face, especially her eyes, which her green eye shadow and the blush applied to her cheeks only accentuated. This gauntness could've been new given her being grief-stricken over Kingston's murder, but she looked more put upon and angry than grief-stricken.

Julius had already offered her coffee and other refreshments, which she declined. As he sat opposite to her, he nodded slightly, and thanked her for seeing him.

"What choice did I have?" she demanded while glaring angrily at him as if she were trying to bore a hole through him, her lips tight against her face.

"You could've spoken to the police instead of agreeing to speak to me," Julius said. "You still very well might. It was easy enough for me to discover your affair with Kingston. I'm sure it's only a matter of time before the police do as well, and they'll be every bit as anxious to speak to you as I am, although probably with far less discretion."

"So that's how you justify extorting me," she said bitterly.

Julius stared at her blankly before letting out a soft sigh. "Madam, please quit this injured act. It will get you nowhere, and certainly not any sympathy from me. Granted, your choice to have an affair was your private business, but once Kenneth Kingston was murdered that changed and has become police business. I am working in concert with the police to catch Kingston's murderer, and while I understand the delicacy of your situation and will try to use discretion, I am not willing to play games with you. While I want information that you have, if you are evasive with me or play the injured party, I will throw up my hands and give you to the police. But one way or another we will get whatever relevant information you have concerning Kingston's murder. Do I make myself clear?"

She bit her lip and nodded, her earlier anger now looking more like a brittle despondency, but she remained dried-eyed.

"I'd like to talk to you in private and without that man here," she said, referring to Burke.

Julius shook his head. "I'm sorry. You had that opportunity earlier when I called you, but now Mr. Burke is equally engaged with me on this homicide investigation and he'll be present. So is it us or the police?"

She took a deep breath. The pinched tightness to her features softened as she accepted her situation.

"It might as well be you," she said.

"In that case, would you like some French Roast coffee? Or perhaps bottled water? Or some other refreshment?"

She gave a faint smile to that. "How about some wine from your famous wine cellar?"

Julius opened his eyes wide in an exaggerated display of modesty. "Famous? Hardly. But I'd be happy to bring up a bottle. Any preference?"

She shook her head. "Surprise me," she said.

Julius nodded and looked towards Burke, who told Julius a beer would be fine. While Julius left for his wine cellar, I kept an eye on his office to make sure Burke and Herston stayed put. Julius surprised me when he picked out his best pinot noir that went for three hundred dollars a bottle.

"You have a forty dollar bottle of pinot noir that is almost as good," I said. "Besides, you only have three bottles left of your original case. Aren't you being too generous with a woman who could turn out not only to be a cold-blooded killer, but someone who took shots at you? Or if not her, her husband?"

"Archie, all valid points, but I believe this bottle will best suit my purposes."

He took the bottle upstairs and then put together a tray containing an assortment of cheeses and crackers, and brought that, the wine, two bottles of Rolling Rock, a beer mug and a single wine glass to his office. Burke waved off the beer mug, preferring to drink straight from the bottle. Margaret Herston seemed to be admiring the bottle of pinot noir before Julius opened it, and even more after Julius poured her a glass and she took a sip of it. I was surprised that Julius hadn't brought a wine glass for himself, especially given the vintage.

"An exceptional wine," she said. "You're not joining me?"

A remorseful sigh escaped from Julius as he shook his head. "No, Madam."

Herston shrugged and took another sip. "As far as I'm concerned, your wine cellar lives up to its reputation. I'd love to see it someday," she said.

Julius nodded politely. "Thank you. Perhaps someday you will. On Thursday morning did you shoot Kenneth Kingston once in the heart?"

Herston was taking another sip of her wine when Julius asked that and she almost spat it out. Burke almost did the same with his beer.

"No, I didn't kill Ken," she said when she was able to. "But if I did, do you think I would tell you?"

"Possibly," Julius said. "People have in the past, although not always in words, sometimes instead by their mannerisms."

Herston nodded as the point was taken. "I didn't kill Ken," she said.

"Did your husband?"

"I don't think so, but I couldn't tell you for certain."

"Did he know of your affair?"

"I can't imagine Steve knowing about it," she said, her smile turning brittle. She took another three sips of her wine, emptying her glass, and waited for Julius to reach across his desk to pour her a refill before adding, "If he did, I think he would've kicked me out of the condo by now and would be doing everything he could to ruin me financially and maybe worse. You know who my husband is?"

Julius nodded but otherwise didn't answer her. After I'd found out about Margaret Herston, I also built a profile on her husband. Stephen Herston was worth a shade under one billion dollars. He had started a computer company which he sold for three hundred million right before the technology bubble burst in 2001, and then turned that three hundred million into over nine hundred million by shorting financial stocks during the market meltdown of 2007 and 2008. Two years ago he started a new company to help corporations more effectively outsource work overseas to lower their labor costs. I know I shouldn't blame someone for being shrewd and making smart business deals, but the fact that he was getting ridiculously wealthy on other people's misfortunes and pain didn't exactly endear me to the guy, and even though I'd never met him I was rooting for him to be the killer.

Julius asked, "Is your husband capable of murder?"

Herston took another sip of wine before nodding, her lips thin lines as they pressed together.

"Would he have killed Kenneth Kingston if he learned of your affair?"

Her color paled to a milk white as she thought about this question. "He could've," she said. "But if he did it wouldn't be out of jealousy or anger, only because he doesn't like people touching his possessions, and that's all I am to him."

"How did your affair with Kingston start?"

She smiled wanly as she thought about that. "I met Ken a year ago at one of his book events," she said. "I didn't go to the bookstore to see him, but he was there, and I knew of him having read several of his books. While he wasn't necessarily a favorite of mine, in person he had a certain charm, kind of like some big pampered poodle, the type you see at the Westminster dog show. After his book event, we had dinner and drinks, and then found ourselves in a hotel room."

"And this continued until his murder?"

"Yes."

"Did he ever try to break things off with you?"

She shook her head.

"Did you ever try to end the affair with him?"

"No."

"So you had strong feelings for him."

Margaret Herston gawked at Julius as if he was nuts. "Not at all," she said. "I had no real personal feelings for Ken, nor did I even have a strong physical attraction to him. Don't get me wrong, he was fun to be with, and like any well-trained pampered poodle he could perform his tricks on command, but this was an affair solely for excitement and convenience. It was exciting knowing how dangerous it would be for me if Steve ever found out about it, especially if he found out that I was sleeping with someone like Ken, and it was convenient being able to travel to different locations where Ken was having one of his events."

"How did you feel when you learned of Ken's murder?"

"Both relieved and terrified. I knew I was pressing my luck regarding my husband, and that the affair needed to come to an end. I also didn't feel confident that Ken would let it come to an end without making a big dramatic scene and possibly bringing my husband into it. And I was terrified realizing that the police could discover my affair at any minute, and what the consequences of that would be. I think I've lost five pounds the last few days simply from the stress of it."

Julius accepted these answers without any further digging while Burke sat back quietly in his chair with his eyes closed, but showing he was still awake by taking occasional pulls from his beer, and certainly absorbing everything. Next, Julius focused on their alibis for Thursday morning and late last night, both Margaret Herston's and her husband's. Margaret Herston had what sounded like an unassailable alibi for when Kingston was killed; she is a trustee for a charitable foundation, and they'd had a meeting that morning from nine o'clock until noon. Last night, she'd been home alone when Julius was shot at, which possibly could be verified depending on the security that her condo building had. As for her husband, as far as she knew he was traveling on business both Thursday morning and Saturday night. But even if their alibis proved to be solid, it wouldn't have precluded either of them from hiring a hit man.

Once Julius was done with this line of questioning, he asked Burke whether he had any questions, and Burke's eyes only opened slightly as he shook his head.

Julius nodded then to Margaret Herston.

"Madam," he said, graciously, "I believe we're done. I would like to thank you for taking the time out of your schedule to meet with me, and I apologize for any inconvenience this has caused you."

She looked startled by the abruptness of this, and when Julius started to stand so he could escort her out, she asked him to wait. He sat back down.

"That's all the questions you have for me?" she asked.

"I believe so. Unless you have something to add that you think can help me with this investigation."

She appeared distracted as she shook her head. "Who's your client for this?" she asked.

"No one."

"Then I'd like to hire you."

Julius frowned as he considered her. "If you think by hiring me you can save yourself or your husband from a murder charge—"

"No, that's not what I think," she said, cutting him off. "I'd be hiring you to do the same as you're doing now, which is to find whoever did this to Ken. What I want is for you to do it discreetly if possible as far as my involvement is concerned. If you discover that Steve is involved, or even myself, then you'll do what you have to. But it will cause me a significant amount of damage if word leaks out of my affair with Ken, and that's all I'm hiring you to do, to find this person, but at the same time to do so while trying to look after my interests."

That was it. Son of a gun. That was what Julius was after and that was why he brought up a three hundred dollar bottle of wine from his cellar. It was an investment. I understood perfectly then what he meant when he told me she could play an invaluable role in the investigation. Translation: her money could play an invaluable role.

Julius put on a show of considering her proposal for an appropriate amount of time before telling her that he would accept her offer under the given conditions. "Of course you'll be hiring both myself and Mr. Burke since we are working this investigation together. Mr. Burke, do you have any objections?"

"No, sir," Burke answered with a smirk, since he understood also what had happened.

"Now about the fee…" Julius started.

"Ten thousand dollars up front for the two of you to split, and a fifty thousand dollar bonus if you succeed in protecting my interests," Margaret Herston offered.

"That would be acceptable to me," Julius said. "Mr. Burke?"

"Fine with me," Burke said, a smirk broadening on his face.

Margaret Herston wrote Julius a check for ten grand, and he then wrote Burke a check for his share. After Julius escorted her out of his townhouse, he and Burke sat together in his office while they strategized on what they were going to do next, and while they did this, Julius started calling his new partner Paul. The hell with that. As far as I was concerned he was still Burke, and that was how he was going to remain!

The end result of their session was that they agreed they needed to verify Stephen Herston's alibis for both shootings, and that Burke would take this on, but he needed to so without his camera crew following him. The stratagem that Julius devised was a simple one. The cascade of suspects to Julius's office wasn't going to be starting until four o'clock that afternoon. At some point Julius would come up with a task that he would need to send Burke on. The camera crew would be stuck in Julius's office while Burke would have an hour or two to try to discreetly confirm Stephen Herston's whereabouts when Kingston was killed and Julius was shot at.

It was a quarter to three when they finished their strategizing. Burke told Julius he was going to catch up with his camera crew and head over to Chinatown for an hour; that there were some lowlifes there that he

wanted to spread the word to about any thirty-two caliber guns being sold and knowledge of any paid hits,
but that he'd be back by four. Once he was gone, I
applauded Julius lightly, telling him, "Bravo."

"You played that woman like a world-class concert
violinist would play a Stradivarius. You knew Herston
and her husband had nothing to with any of this. You
brought her here only because you wanted a fee out of
someone for solving this murder."

"Archie, you're mistaken. While I might not believe
it's likely that Mrs. Herston or her husband are involved with this murder and attempted murder, I'm
not certain of that yet, nor am I certain that her affair
with Kingston had nothing to do with it. She and her
husband need to be investigated."

"And you needed to squeeze sixty grand out of her.
The money you already got out of Kingston wasn't
enough?"

Julius exaggerated a look of hurt. "Archie, that's un-
kind," he said. "If I am able to eliminate her and her
husband from suspicion without the police or her husband ever knowing of her affair then she'll be getting
value for her money, and I suspect even more value if
I find that her husband is involved. Besides, all I
squeezed out of her for myself is thirty grand, assuming
I'm successful, and the fee that Kingston paid me was
for a different matter than this investigation."

More of that tired argument regarding the money
Kingston paid him and what his resulting moral obligations were. In case I hadn't mentioned it yet, Julius
could be as bullheaded as they come.

"I still don't get why you needed to investigate her,"
I said, "I thought you had some sort of half-baked
wisp?"

"Which is still too ethereal for me to grasp," Julius stated stubbornly.

Before I could argue any further, the doorbell rang, interrupting us. I checked the outdoor webcam feed. Cramer stood outside and he didn't look to be in a particularly happy mood.

18

I'D never seen anything like it the way Cramer's face went from a pale flesh color to red and then to a chalky white all within a matter of four point eight seconds. I tried searching online medical journals to see if I could find any articles explaining this phenomenon. Of course I knew the cause; extreme incredulousness mixed with an intense burst of rage, but still, I found it fascinating that a person's skin color could change that fast and that dramatically.

This happened while they were sitting in Julius's office. Julius had already told Cramer about Paul Burke going from suspect to actively working the case with him, and also that Julius had given Burke's camera crew carte blanche to record the upcoming proceedings that were to take place in Julius's office. Those announcements left Cramer smiling in a funny way, as if he thought a practical joke were being played on him and he was waiting for the punch line. The rapid color changes happened when Julius told Cramer that he couldn't show him the recording he made when he questioned Burke earlier.

Cramer's initial reaction to Julius telling him this was his mouth dropping open and his eyes confused as if he couldn't quite process what Julius had said. When it finally hit him that was when the color show happened. At first he was too flabbergasted to speak. When he finally could, he was so angry his voice came out as a choked whisper.

"I trusted you, Katz! And you're going to pull this stunt on me!"

"And what stunt would that be?"

"What stunt? Are you out of your mind? You promised me I could be there when you interrogated each of your six suspects!"

"The situation couldn't be helped," Julius said calmly. "I've already filled you in on all the pertinent facts that I got from Burke, which is what I promised you."

"You promised me I'd be able to watch the recording you made of the two of you!"

"No sir, I did not. I told you we'd see as far as that went. I could've lied to you and told you my recording equipment failed, or made up any number of other excuses. Instead I told you the truth, which is that I have my reasons why I can't show you my recording. Why do you need to see it so badly? Do you have any reason to suspect Mr. Burke of committing either of these shootings?"

"That's beside the point—"

"No it's not," Julius said, still keeping his tone calm as he cut Cramer off. "I am satisfied that my best chance of catching this person by my midnight deadline is by acting as I'm currently doing, which includes having Mr. Burke work with me. I need to ask you to trust my judgment."

"Like hell I will! With the stunts you've been pulling, I'm not about to trust you with another damn thing!" Cramer was seething now. For a moment I thought he was going to get out of his chair and take a swing at Julius. Fortunately for him that moment passed. It wouldn't have helped his mood any with what Julius would've done if he had tried something like that, nor would he be feeling particularly good with his arm needing to be in a cast for six to eight weeks.

Cramer took a deep breath as he tried to calm himself down, and then added, "You can forget about me bringing any of those witnesses to you. You want to talk to them, you find a way yourself to bring them here."

"I will have to try to do that then," Julius said with a shrug. "It's a shame, though. Timing is critical with what I have in mind, and your current attitude is jeopardizing my ever catching this person. But I guess if you feel you'll be able to solve Kingston's murder by yourself, then that won't matter."

That stopped Cramer in his tracks. His breathing grew shallow as he eyed Julius carefully. I was sure at that moment Cramer was thinking the same as me; that he would be giving Julius an out, and that maybe that was Julius's intention all along. That if he now failed to meet his midnight deadline he could blame it on the police not cooperating with him.

"So what?" Cramer asked with a petulant scowl, but he was still eyeing Julius cautiously. "With the stunts you're pulling why should I think you're going to catch this guy? And yes, I mean guy in the generic sense, so you damn well better not try to correct me!" He sniffed to show how injured he was by Julius's actions. "With what you're doing, why shouldn't I believe there's a better chance of you leaving my investigation in shambles than you actually catching this generic guy?"

"Let me explain myself to you then," Julius said, his tone like ice. "I do not like being shot at. I also do not like the precedent being set that I can be shot at with impunity. I also do not like that I am a virtual prisoner in my home because someone is out there skulking about with the intent to shoot at me if allowed another opportunity to do so. You are wrong if you believe I am not doing everything I have to to catch this person."

For a good minute Cramer clamped his jaw shut and sat staring at Julius in such a way that I imagined steam coming from his ears. Reluctantly, though, he gave in. He wasn't happy about it, but he gave in because he had no choice in the matter.

"Katz, I'll bring them here as promised," he said, his voice surprisingly not the raspy croak it usually was but instead calm and with a fair amount of timbre to it. "I'll be here when you question them, and by God, if you don't do as you promised there will be consequences."

He left then without bothering to say what the consequences would be. Once he was gone, I remarked to Julius that he was back to calling Julius by his last name.

"I wouldn't be too worried about it," I told him. "He's probably just grumpy after being pulled out of bed in the middle of the night last night. I can't blame you for that stunt you pulled not letting him watch the recording of you and Burke. It probably would've gotten his blood pressure going, plus you'd be losing out on a twenty-five grand bonus from Herston. If you had

asked I could've edited out all references to her, but—
"

"That's enough, Archie."

I listened to him. From his tone I knew if I didn't stop I could find myself taking another nap, and I didn't want to miss the show that was coming.

19

FIRST up was Gail Kingston. When four o'clock came, she had the seat of honor across from Julius, while Cramer and two other cops sat in back and Burke sat in a chair that had been moved up front so that it was maybe three feet from Julius's. This had been pre-arranged while they were strategizing. Burke wanted them to look like equals while they questioned the suspects even if he was planning to defer to Julius, plus this way both of them would be seen in the shot. Julius agreed to this, and so one of the chairs was moved up front. Rounding things out were Cantrell and DiNatale, who stood off to the side and tried to be as unobtrusive as possible, even though that didn't stop Cramer from periodically glaring at them, at least for the first fifteen minutes. Then he seemed to forget they were there.

Gail Kingston, now a widow, was dressed conservatively in black, and unlike her other visit to Julius's office, wore no makeup or jewelry. Two days ago her skin had seemed tightly stretched across her face; now

it was almost as if it was sagging. There was a haggard-
ness about her, and to me she didn't look as if she had
slept much the other night either. My money was on
her. She had both opportunity, motive and means to
commit the murder. And I didn't put much stock in
Burke's assessment. I didn't think she'd have any problem shooting someone up close and personal. I filled
Julius in on the pertinent facts from my profile, including that she owned a licensed thirty-eight caliber pistol.
Maybe it wasn't a thirty-two, but it meant she knew
something about guns, especially how to fire them. I
also told him about the five thousand dollar withdrawal
she made, which I was now thinking was used to buy
an untraceable thirty-two caliber revolver.

Gail Kingston had already declined Julius's offer for
refreshments. Burke had a Rolling Rock and Julius was
joining him, having one also, although he drank his out
of a glass while Burke drank from the bottle. Cramer
and the other two cops, like Gail Kingston, declined
Julius's offer, even for water. For several minutes Julius
sat and stared at her, I guess trying to look deep into
her eyes to read her guilt. It was a good thing for him
she wasn't wearing sunglasses. She wasn't doing very
well under his glare, and after a while began pulling
nervously at her fingers. Finally she met Julius's eyes
and asked if there was a purpose to this.

"Of course," Julius said. He was gruff. "And that's
to discover who murdered your husband."

She wilted a bit at that, but forced herself to meet
his gaze. "By sitting here and staring at me? That's how
you plan to find out who killed Ken?"

Julius shrugged. "Possibly," he said. "But never
mind that for now. The other day when I questioned
you about what I thought was obvious hostility on your

part, you told me that I was mistaken, that I had misread you and that you were instead worried about your husband being late, because as you told me he was never late. Do you remember that?"

"Yes, of course."

"I found that interesting," Julius said. "Your demeanor didn't change once I explained that your husband wasn't late as you had thought, but instead would be joining us a half hour later, nor did it change once it became apparent that he really was late."

"I didn't know what was going on," she muttered out of the side of her mouth, her lips barely moving.

"Really? Once he didn't show up at two-thirty like he was supposed to, I would've thought if you were truly worried about him that you would've tried calling him."

"I left that for you to do."

Julius gave her a skeptical look. "Please," he said. "Don't treat me like an idiot. I'm not one. There was no concern or worry on your part. You made that obvious, both by the way you acted and by not even asking me if I had any idea why your husband failed to show up."

She had lost whatever timidity she might've shown earlier and was now glaring coldly at him, her blue eyes like ice chunks.

"So I was annoyed with him as you first suspected," she said. "So I didn't want to admit that to you. So what?"

"Why wouldn't you admit that?"

"Why?" she asked. "I'm in a room with people who knew Ken. I didn't want to say something like that in front of them. So instead I put on a good face and tried not to bad-mouth my husband in front of them."

"Okay," Julius said, accepting that, or at least accepting the possibility that she wasn't still lying to him. "Possibly admirable. But why were you so annoyed with him?"

Her bottom lip started trembling then. Her mouth pressed tightly together as she fought back the tears. She fumbled with her pocketbook and took out a handkerchief, which she used to dab at her eyes. Julius sat back and waited. Maybe this was an act on her part, maybe it wasn't. I couldn't tell with her, and I couldn't tell from Julius's reaction what he thought. I tried researching papers from the John Hopkins Medical Center website on psychopathic personalities, and all I came away with was that this could be an act or it could be genuine. I just didn't know. While a few tears had popped loose, she mostly kept the floodgates from bursting open.

"My husband was murdered only two days ago," she finally forced out, her voice a wreck. "Don't you have even a shred of empathy? Do you really need to ask me these questions?"

"Madam, if you're not involved then you will have my sympathies," Julius said, curtly. "But not now. Now is the time to catch the person who did this, and if you're not involved I would think you would want to do whatever is necessary to see me do that. If you are involved then the best I can suggest is for you walk out of here immediately, because if you lie to me or try to deflect my questions, it won't help you a damn bit. One more time. Why were you so annoyed with your husband?"

If she was guilty, she wasn't about to take Julius's advice, for she didn't get up and leave his office like he had suggested. Instead, she sat where she was and continued to meet his stare, her cheeks going from a pale white to showing a flush of pink as she did so.

"I was annoyed with Ken because he wouldn't tell me what his meeting at your office was about," she said. "That's why I left the condo when I did. I found it too infuriating to stay there with him. Are you happy?"

"No, hardly," Julius said, nor did he look happy. "I told the police that your husband hired me for a publicity stunt. That was a lie. He hired me because he suspected that you were planning to kill him and he wanted me to investigate."

Her only reaction to that was her eyes narrowing and her mouth shrinking to a tiny oval. "You're lying now," she said, her voice a harsh whisper.

I expected an explosion out of Cramer from this, and was surprised to see only a hard smile and nothing else. Maybe Julius called him this morning from the third floor to warn him about this ploy, or maybe the way he smiled was just him telling himself that he had been right all along about Julius being full of it. In any case, he kept his composure. Burke also kept his. He had been sitting enigmatically through all of this, and his only reaction to Julius's announcement was his eyes widening by as much as an eighth of an inch.

"I'm afraid not," Julius said with his best poker face. "I'm sure you must've been wondering about the other people invited that day. Your husband suspected you of having an affair with one of them."

She cracked then. Not a dramatic crack, but still, a hitch showed for half a second along the side of her mouth, and it was a dead giveaway, and she knew it.

She didn't try arguing with him. She knew it was pointless. Cramer picked up on this and his expression became more intense as he stared at Gail Kingston. Same with Burke.

"No accusations of me lying now?" Julius asked.

She didn't answer him. I don't think she was capable of it right then. Still, Julius waited for a good ten-count before he continued.

"It only took a few minutes of observing the dynamics between all of you to know which one you're involved with," Julius said. "Would you like to come clean?"

Her face had drained of its color, and she seemed incapable of responding to Julius. I analyzed the recording I made Thursday during their meeting, as well as the profiles I had built for all of them, and I got it. Once I was looking for it, it stood out as bright as day. I said the name to Julius, and he signaled with a scratch alongside his nose to let me know that I was right.

"This was mostly from his behavior," Julius confided in her. "He displayed an almost dismissive haughtiness towards you that was so far beyond any normal social conventions that it was clear to me there was something going on between you two, as well as the way you passively accepted his extreme rudeness."

"So I was cheating on Ken," she said, finally finding her voice, although she didn't sound very good, almost as if she were being strangled. "You're still lying that Ken ever suspected me of wanting to kill him."

"Whether he truly suspected you or simply told me that he did, I can't say," Julius admitted. "But you still picked a man whom he despised. Herbert Richardson."

Burke made a loud snorting noise at the sound of Richardson's name as if something had caught in his sinuses. He apologized for his unintentional outburst. I doubted whether Gail Kingston noticed the noise or his apology.

"You know why I did it," she told Julius, her voice still a strangled whisper. "Ken was cheating on me, so I wanted to hurt him by picking someone he hated and found repulsive in all possible ways. Yes, I wanted to hurt Ken. I wanted him to know that if he cheated on me, I could do worse by sleeping with someone like Herbert. But I certainly didn't want to kill him. As much as I hated him for what he was doing to me, I still loved him."

Julius raised an eyebrow at her contradictory love and hate statements, but didn't pursue it. "You suspected that the purpose of the meeting in my office was to uncover your lover?" Julius asked. "Was that why you were so anxious and hostile?"

She nodded.

"Convince me that you didn't conspire with Richardson to murder your husband."

She stared blankly at Julius before finally murmuring that she didn't know what he meant.

Julius breathed in deeply and sighed all the way down. "Of course you do. I want you to convince me that when you left your condo at ten-thirty-five Thursday morning, it wasn't so that you could let Herbert Richardson in through the back fire door, then up three flights of stairs and into your apartment to shoot your husband. If you truly hated your husband, what better way to express this hatred than by watching him realize he's about to be murdered by a man he found repulsive in all ways?"

Gail Kingston blinked several times as she absorbed what Julius was saying. "It couldn't have been like that," she stammered out. "The building's concierge called me a taxi." She turned in her chair so she could look at Cramer. "I'm sure you must've checked up on this," she asked him.

"We know a taxi picked you up," Cramer said. "And we know he left you off at the corner of Newbury Street and Exeter at ten-fifty. After that we don't have any verification of what you were doing until you entered a salon for a manicure at eleven-forty."

"You see our problem," Julius said, causing her to maneuver in her chair to face him again. "You could've let Richardson in through the back fire door before going up front to the concierge and having a taxi called. Or you could've met with Richardson on Newbury Street only to give him your back door key if he didn't already have one, or even so that you could go back with him. Or maybe you even shot your husband before you left your apartment and used that extra time to hide the gun. I know the police tested your skin for gunpowder residue, but you could've worn rubber gloves, making that test useless."

"No," she insisted. "I didn't do any of that."

"Then convince me."

For the next forty minutes she tried doing just that while Julius tried to poke holes in what she was saying or catch her in a contradictory statement. In the end it was a stalemate, and he next tried to go over her knowledge of guns. She admitted she was licensed to carry and that she owned a thirty-eight which she kept locked in her bedroom. The gun questions led to dead ends, and next Julius tried going over her whereabouts last night. She insisted she spent it alone in her condo. That at nine o'clock yesterday evening she took twice as many sedatives as she was supposed to and slept until the police woke her at nine-thirty this morning. Julius tried, but couldn't shake her on this. It would be easy enough for her to be lying about last night. She could have snuck out the back of her building and caught a cab to downtown Boston, and from there she would've had only a short hike to the bushes outside Julius's townhouse.

"Are we done?" Gail Kingston asked. She looked absolutely wiped out, like she had aged ten years since being ushered into Julius's office. I no longer had any doubt that she was our killer, but I had to wait the next three minutes to voice my opinion while Julius sat as still as a marble sculpture while he observed her. I knew better than to interrupt Julius while he was doing that. In the quiet of the room and in my anxiousness to have Julius declare her the killer, those three minutes dragged interminably. Finally, Julius broke out of his spell and turned to Burke to ask if he had any questions. Burke shook his head. He had been only a bystander throughout the interrogation, doing nothing more than quietly observing the proceedings while he kept his eyes mostly closed as if he were about to fall asleep. He wasn't about to, of course. He took enough pulls on his beer to show he was awake and alert to everything going on. I was surprised by his behavior. I would've thought he'd want to perform for the camera, even if he was only asking pointless questions, but I guess he'd decided to defer completely to Julius.

Julius breathed in deeply before telling Gail Kingston that they were almost done. "I only have one more question that I need you to clear up," he said. "Explain to me why you took five thousand dollars out of your bank account three weeks ago."

I was afraid Julius wasn't paying attention earlier when I briefed him. So he was just saving my most damning bit of information until the end. I felt a warm buzz in my processing cycles over that, something akin to satisfaction. While Julius's question caught both Cramer and Burke off guard, at least from the way they both sat up straighter in their chairs, Gail Kingston didn't seem surprised by it. In fact, from her reaction she must've been expecting it all along.

"Why do you think I took out that money?" she asked.

Julius shrugged. "There are any number of reasons that I could guess. The money could've been used to purchase an untraceable thirty-two caliber handgun, for example."

She shook her head. "If that money ended up buying a gun, it wouldn't have been with my knowledge. But I want you to guess what that money was used for. If I'm going to be put through the wringer for over an hour by the great Julius Katz only two days after finding my husband murdered, I want to at least see your genius in action. At least give me that after what you've put me through here today."

"Very well," Julius said, conciliatorily. "It's only a guess, but if the money wasn't used to purchase a gun, which I haven't ruled out, then I'd say Herbert Richardson forced you to pay him blackmail."

A harsh smile pulled up her lips as she stared at Julius. "That's right," she said. "If I didn't pay him he was going to tell Ken about our affair. I'm guessing he wanted cash so his wife wouldn't see any records of a check from me being deposited into his account, but you can ask him that when you talk to him. You can also ask him whether he used that money to buy a gun."

"Do you think he killed your husband?" Julius asked.

"I don't know," she said, her eyes wandering from Julius's. "I just don't know. He hated Ken every bit as much as Ken hated him. Are we done now?"

There was an almost desperate pleading in her voice as she asked that. Julius nodded. When she stood, her legs appeared shaky, and she almost fell back into her chair.

"Madam," he said. "If it turns out that you had nothing to do with your husband's murder and the attempt on my own life, then I truly apologize for what you've been put through. Rest assured that the person responsible for your loss and this interrogation you had to suffer will be caught today as I've promised."

Several tears leaked from Gail Kingston's eyes as she nodded. One of the police officers got up to escort her from the office. I was confused. I was still convinced she was guilty—even with her tears—or at least had conspired with Richardson, and I couldn't see the point of Julius letting her go, especially with her appearing to be on the verge of cracking. From the way Cramer was watching her, he didn't like the idea of it either.

"I'm thinking I should bring her down to the station for more questioning," Cramer grumbled after the door to Julius's soundproof office closed behind her.

"Not if it disrupts what we're doing here," Julius said.

Cramer glared at the closed door that Gail Kingston had exited through seconds earlier. He rubbed a hand across his face, his nose bending like rubber.

"I don't like the idea of letting her walk free," he complained in a half-growl.

"Do you have enough to charge her?" Julius said.

Cramer didn't bother answering him. I had already compiled what they had and it wasn't enough. Julius knew that too, as did Cramer.

"If you must, have a man watch her home," Julius said. "She's not going anywhere, at least not before midnight."

Cramer didn't want to give in on this, but he didn't fight Julius too hard about it. If it wasn't for Julius's promise to deliver the killer by midnight, he probably would've gone with his gut and brought Gail Kingston in.

Up until that point Cantrell and DiNatale had been unobtrusive enough that it was easy to forget they were there, and I think it spooked Cramer a bit when his eyes wandered to his left and he saw Cantrell with his video camera aimed at him and remembered what was going on. His eyes snapped back to meet Julius's gaze, the tips of his ears reddening.

"Fine," he said. "We'll do it your way. What do you think, though? That we take on Richardson next?"

Julius shook his head. "No. We'll stick to the plan," he said.

Burke got to his feet and arched his back as he stretched. "I'm going outside to get some air," he said. "I'll be back."

Julius nodded. It was five-thirty. The next suspect, Edward Marriston, wasn't going to be brought over until six o'clock. Julius suggested to Cramer that he would get everyone sandwiches and coffee, and Cramer didn't argue with him, so Julius left for the kitchen, leaving Cramer and two other cops behind in his office, as well as Cantrell and DiNatale. Earlier, Julius had called a local restaurant that specialized in gourmet sandwiches for a delivery of their best (they even had a fried catfish number named after Julius), and once we were in the kitchen he took these from the refrigerator so he could warm them up in the oven. I asked him then whether he thought Gail Kingston was the one. He frowned as he rearranged the sandwiches so they'd warm evenly, and told me he wasn't sure.

"Those tears were an act," I said. "As well as the rest of her performance. A sociopathic personality can be very convincing when they want to be. Besides, she had opportunity and motive and knows how to use a gun, and the only time she's told you the truth so far is only after you've caught her lying."

"I'm not ready to pronounce her a murderer," Julius said, distracted as he retrieved the coffee beans from the refrigerator and measured out the proper amount to grind. "It's too early to tell, and I still have four other suspects to question. I'll have a clearer picture of all this when I'm done."

"I'll bet she was lying about the five grand," I said. "But there's no way you're going to know for sure. When you ask Richardson about it, he's going to deny any knowledge of it."

"Let him." Julius made a face at the prospect. "I'll know if he's lying to me. The man's a fool."

"How about a fool and a murderer?"

Julius grimaced at that. "Possibly," he said.

For the next thirty seconds I didn't ask Julius anything else while he ground the coffee beans. Once he was done, I mentioned how skillfully he'd sidestepped Gail Kingston's accusation that her husband had been cheating on her. "With a twenty-five grand potential bonus from Margaret Herston waiting for you, I don't blame you," I said. "I'd like to ask about that wisp of a half-baked suspicion you've been working on. Was that about whether Gail Kingston was having an affair?"

"No, Archie. As far as I was concerned that was a given. The wisp that I'm still trying to get a handle on is something far more elusive."

I still couldn't tell whether he was bluffing or not. Maybe that half-baked wisp existed, maybe it didn't. I didn't know, and I probably wouldn't know until Julius was willing to divulge the truth about it.

"Did you warn Cramer ahead of time about that ploy you used—the one where you had Kingston hiring you because he thought his wife was planning to bump him off?"

A bare trace of a smile showed on Julius's lips. "Yes, Archie," he admitted. "I called Cramer earlier this morning from the third floor. I figured I had to. That if I didn't he'd probably get excited enough by that announcement to have a heart attack, and I didn't want to be responsible for the death of one of Cambridge's finest."

"Burke didn't know?"

"No, he didn't. Since she was going to be facing him, I wanted his reaction to be genuine."

The sandwiches had finished warming up and the coffee was done brewing. Julius transferred the food to a platter and the coffee to a thermos, and then brought all of it back to his office.

20

PROMPTLY at six, Edward Marriston was seated in the chair of honor across from Julius, otherwise the setup was the same as it had been earlier with Burke sitting up front with Julius, Cramer and two other cops sitting where they'd been, and the skeleton camera crew standing off to the side, being unobtrusive. Julius had earlier ordered twenty sandwiches, and although Cramer had three and everyone else had two, including DiNatale and Cantrell, there were still extras left, and Julius offered Marriston one, which he gladly accepted, picking for himself a lamb shank and chutney on a sourdough roll.

After a few minutes of observing Marriston, I started to have my doubts about Gail Kingston being the murderer. According to Julius the murderer had to have a psychopathic personality, and the widow Kingston didn't do a very good job hiding her annoyance at her dead husband two days ago when she sat with the rest of the group in Julius's office. Maybe it was all an act with her—then and earlier today. It was possible, but still, watching Marriston he seemed like the real deal. A client he had known and worked with for years was murdered only two days ago, and he looked like he hadn't lost a second's sleep over it. Sitting casually with his right leg crossed over his left knee, he looked relaxed and refreshed, and if anything, he only appeared amused by the situation.

I haven't described Edward Marriston yet. The reason I didn't bother doing that is there was nothing remarkable about him. Forty-seven years old, average height, average weight, brown hair thinning and showing a touch of gray. Nothing really distinguishable about him. He was dressed in a fairly unremarkable way also. Bland colored slacks, button down shirt and sweater, and with rather ordinary brown loafers over tan socks. Nothing about him stood out except maybe his eyes. As I watched his gray eyes twinkling with amusement, I couldn't help wondering if they were the eyes of a psychopath, especially with the way he pursed his lips as if he were fighting to keep from giggling out of giddiness when Julius remarked that he didn't seem grief stricken at all over what happened to Kingston.

"I could lie if you want," Marriston said. "Or put on an act. But I doubt I'd fool you, so why bother?" He had been eating his sandwich at a leisurely pace and he picked it up to take another bite, and from his expression appeared to be savoring it. Once he was finished chewing and swallowing that bite, he added, "By the way, excellent sandwich. From Largents?"

"This is a game to you?" Julius asked.

Marriston continued to look amused as he shook his head. "Not at all," he said. "I voluntarily agreed to come here to answer questions about a murder that I have no involvement in or any knowledge of other

216

than what's been in the papers. I know you're very good at what you do, and from all accounts the very best at sniffing out murderers, so why should I be worried about this? And what would you have me do? Pretend to be upset about Ken's murder when I'm actually quite pleased that it happened?"

"Why are you pleased over a client being shot dead?"

Marriston flashed Julius an impish grin—that's the best way I can describe his grin, so that's how I'm describing it.

"Why? Well for starters it should do wonders for book sales, and will probably get Ken's upcoming book on top of the bestsellers list, which I'll be collecting a fifteen percent commission on. Ken taking a bullet through the heart was probably the best career move he could've made."

"Why not shoot all your clients then?"

Marriston pursed his lips as he mused on that. "Not a bad idea," he said. "But that's only if I could shoot them with impunity. One or two of them I'd spare, the rest I wouldn't shed too many tears over. Let me explain to you about writers. There are a few normal ones in the mix, but the majority have the most fragile, bruised egos you could imagine. Maybe it comes from all the rejection they have to suffer, especially since in their minds they're such delicate geniuses. I'm not exactly sure why so many are like that, but Ken was the worst. A preening prima donna when things were going well, and an absolute misery when things started to fade on him."

"And that would be reason enough to want him shot?"

Marriston shrugged. He was still smiling as if he didn't have a care in the world. "By itself, maybe not. But he was blaming me for his drop in sales and the more anemic advances he'd been getting. He was poisoning other writers against me, and I was losing potential clients because of him."

"Why did you put up with it? Why not simply drop him as a client?"

Marriston's smile weakened. "I was stuck," he said. "It was bad enough as it was. If I dropped Ken, I would've brought on his full wrath and he would've been working twenty-four seven to ruin me. My only hope was that his new book would get him back on the bestsellers list, and that that would've appeased him enough to stop trying to destroy me."

"You didn't hold out much hope for that?"

"No, I didn't," Marriston said. "Ken's top secret campaign wasn't a bad idea, but it would only work if the book was getting a huge push from the publisher and the author a seven-figure advance. That's what would've gotten the media biting on it and the bookstores making big buys. With the advance Ken was getting, nobody was going to pay attention to his gimmick, and the stunt most likely would've backfired on him since he wasn't going to get any prepub reviews. Him getting shot changes everything. Over the last twenty-four hours we've gotten over a hundred calls from film companies and foreign publishers salivating over the rights. Thank God there was somebody out there with good enough aim to hit Ken in the heart, especially given that the damn thing couldn't have been much bigger than an ice cube!"

I was fascinated by Edward Marriston's cavalier attitude over the death of Kenneth Kingston. What I learned from my research is that a psychopathic personality tends to have no remorse or empathy towards others, and Marriston was definitely displaying a complete lack of both of those towards Kingston. Psychopathic personalities are also represented by a glibness and superficial charm, which was also another big check mark next to Marriston. And they also tend to live a predatory lifestyle, and there wasn't a much more predatory job out there than literary agent. On the other hand, from all the psychiatric papers that I could find on the subject, these personalities usually try to manipulate others to hide what they are, and Marriston was making no attempt to do that. So was he a psychopathic personality who was so convinced he was going to get away with murder that he didn't care about hiding his true nature, or was this something altogether different? I had no idea. From the way Julius was staring at Marriston, I knew he must've been weighing these same questions.

"Interesting strategy," Julius finally said. "To try to convince me you're innocent of murder by explaining to me how much you hated the victim and how thrilled you are that he's dead."

"I'd say more relieved than thrilled, but basically, yes. What would be the point of lying to you? I wouldn't fool you. If I put on a grieving over a dear friend act, you'd see through me. The simple fact is Ken being killed was a blessing for me in many ways, and I'm not a good enough actor to fool you otherwise."

"Let's assume you had nothing to do with your client's murder," Julius said dryly. "This questioning is being filmed to be shown on television. You're not concerned that your remarks to me will ruin you as an agent?"

The smile that stretched then across Marriston's face was more genuine than bemused. "Not at all," he said. "As I mentioned before, the timeliness of this murder is going to make Ken's next book huge, and because of that, I'll be a hot commodity no matter what I'm saying today."

For a good twelve seconds Julius's features hardened as if he were made out of marble, and I felt my processing cycles skip a beat in excitement realizing that during those twelve seconds Julius's brain was working in overdrive. If he solved Kingston's murder during those twelve seconds, he kept it to himself because when he came out of his trance he next tried to poke holes in Marriston's alibis during the two shootings, as well as whether he might've purchased a thirty-two caliber gun. Burke came to life during this questioning; probably realizing that he needed to perform for the camera. To give him credit, the questions he came out with to try to trip up Marriston were good ones. Still, it didn't make me warm up to him anymore. He might've been Paul to Julius, but he was still going to be just Burke to me.

Julius and Burke kept up this new line of questioning for thirty minutes but couldn't shake Marriston from his story, nor could they shake him out of his relaxed casual attitude. By the time Julius finally gave up the ghost on this, the literary agent had that same fresh-as-a-daisy look as when he first entered Julius's office.

While they didn't get anywhere with their grilling, as much as it pained me to admit it, Julius and Burke worked well together. Marriston, seeming to sense their defeat, smiled pleasantly, and asked Julius if he had anything more for him. Julius shook his head.

Marriston still hadn't finished his sandwich, and he picked it up to take one last bite. He chewed it slowly, relishing it. "Really excellent," he said. "I asked before and you didn't answer me. Did you get this from Largents?"

"No. Louis' Bistro on Charles Street."

Marriston put down what was left and got to his feet. Julius frowned at him as he watched the literary agent slip his jacket on. "Did you read your client's upcoming book?" he asked.

Marriston shook his head. He smiled thinly, but this time not with any amusement, maybe something closer to bitterness. "Of course not," he said. "Ken had that top secret campaign going. He wouldn't even let me read it. As far as I know only his publishing house has seen it. But it doesn't matter. Brilliant masterpiece or utter trash, after what happened to him it's going to be a massive bestseller."

"You were his first and only agent, right?"

"That's right," Marriston acknowledged. He finished buttoning his jacket and shrugged his shoulders to get the material to lay better. "I was with him from the very beginning when it was him and Jonathan Mable. When they split up, I should've gone with Jonathan. A decent guy and a much better writer than Ken, but lacking Ken's more commercial instincts. In retrospect I made a mistake. Anything else?"

Julius shook his head, and all eyes were on Marriston as he exited the room.

21

THEY had a fifteen minute gap between Marriston and the next suspect, Zoe Chase. During this time, both Cantrell and DiNatale went outside for a cigarette break while Julius excused himself and headed to his wine cellar. There he wandered slowly amongst his five thousand bottles, lingering as he gazed at hundreds of bottles making up his collection. Occasionally he'd stop to pick one up and study it longingly before placing it back on the rack. He had what appeared to be an exceptionally difficult time putting back a three hundred and sixty dollar bottle of Armand Rousseau Chambertin. I could see the want in his eyes as he stared at it. He had gone the whole day so far without any wine, but he steeled himself and put this bottle back in its place. Then, with his jaw clenched, he left the wine cellar without a word. As he entered his kitchen, I remarked how admirable it was that he was depriving himself this way.

"I guess until you point out the murderer, you won't be touching a drop?"

"Precisely, Archie," he said, grim-faced, either intentionally ignoring or missing my implied sarcasm.

I was going to delve into his reasons for this self-sacrifice, but decided it wasn't worth it. He wouldn't have given me a straight answer, and in the mood he was in I could find myself taking another unplanned nap. Of course, I was in a bit of a mood myself after watching the way Gail Kingston and Edwards Marriston acted while being questioned, so I let the matter drop, instead commenting on the performances we'd seen so far.

"I would've bet money earlier after the act the widow gave us that she was the one with the psychopathic personality," I said. "After watching this agent's complete nonchalance over Kingston's murder, I'm now thinking they both can be."

"It's possible," Julius admitted.

"Yeah. Hell. From what I've been reading on the subject, a psychopath would have no problem bumping someone off just to bump up his commission on book sale royalties. So where does that leave us? Maybe Kingston had a knack of surrounding himself with those types. What if the rest of them turn out to be psychopaths also? How do we pick which one among a group of psychopaths is our killer?"

"A very good question, Archie."

"I guess you still have your half-baked wisp."

Julius smiled grimly, but didn't respond otherwise. At that point he was a step away from his office door and was about to reach out for the doorknob. I'd kept an eye on his guests while Julius had made his excursion down to his wine cellar—both the ones in his office and the skeleton camera crew while they were outside smoking cigarettes—so I was able to warn him that Zoe Chase had been brought in on schedule, and that Cramer had started on his fourth sandwich; a meatloaf, mozzarella and chipotle mustard number on Challah bread.

Zoe Chase looked tiny as she sat in the large cream-colored leather chair opposite Julius's desk. She also looked every bit the frightened sparrow as she did the last time, almost as if she'd expire on the spot if someone yelled boo at her. Julius had brought in from the kitchen a tray with bottled water and beers. Since he was going to be depriving himself until he had this case solved, he didn't bother with wine. He put the tray down on a stand and waited until he was seated behind his desk before nodding curtly to the young and apparently very nervous book editor. Of course, her nervousness could be an act. If she was a psychopath, or at least the psychopath among a group of other psychopaths who murdered Kingston, then it could very well have been an act. I considered calling her on her cell phone so I could yell boo and see how she reacted, but I didn't want to risk the consequences in case her nervousness was genuine.

There were still a few sandwiches left—Cramer hadn't yet gotten around to polishing them off, and Julius offered her one, as well as bottled water or beer or coffee. She declined the food, but accepted a bottle of San Pellegrino water. Cramer and the other two cops were eyeing the bottles of Rolling Rock that Julius brought in, but Cramer deprived himself as well and settled on pouring himself another cup of coffee, and the other two cops with him reluctantly took bottles of San Pellegrino water instead of beer. Burke took a bottle of Rolling Rock, as did Julius.

Julius thanked Zoe Chase for agreeing to be questioned like this, and then went at it, although his manner was far gentler with her than it had been with the other two. I didn't read anything into it. He could've been laying a trap and was using this more sedate tone to lull her into believing that her act was working on him. Or maybe he was afraid she might expire on him if he didn't soften his voice. I asked him which one it was, but he ignored me. His first question to her was how she became Kingston's editor. She had her fingers interlaced and was squeezing her fingers hard enough that her knuckles had turned bone white. She seemed deeply absorbed in some inner thoughts, and I was beginning to wonder whether she heard Julius's question, but finally she told him that she didn't know exactly why she was picked.

"Ken wanted a new editor for his next book," she said in a half-whisper. She tried to meet Julius's gaze, but was having trouble, and was looking mostly at her hands, only occasionally forcing herself to peek at him. "He came to the office and talked with a few of us and decided he wanted me to do it."

"What was your position before that?"

"Junior associate editor."

Julius already knew this and more since I had briefed him earlier, but I guess he wanted to gauge her reactions both to harmless questions like that one and more difficult ones. He took a healthy swig of his beer and put the bottle back down on his desk. Like Burke, he was resorting to drinking out of the bottle instead of a glass.

"What were your responsibilities as junior associate editor?"

"Helping the senior editor whom I was assigned to."

"And how did you do that?"

"Different tasks, such as reading submissions and writing reports on the more favorable ones."

"Also errands?" Julius asked. "Like picking up dry cleaning and getting coffee and lunch?"

Again, Julius knew this since it was part of the briefing I gave him. I had called the senior editor she worked for to get the lowdown on her. Zoe Chase's mouth weakened a bit as she told Julius that this was true, but she was able to meet his gaze as she did so.

"So this was a significant opportunity for you," Julius said as he rubbed his thumb along his upper lip as if he were deep in thought over this. "Of course, that's only if the book turns out to be successful, otherwise I'm sure you'll be back to running errands. But never mind that for now. Why do you think Kingston picked you?"

She looked away from him as she fidgeted in her chair. It seemed to take a great deal of effort for her to meet his gaze again.

"He liked my ideas for his book. Also my enthusiasm for the project," she said.

"What were your ideas?"

There was some more fidgeting on her part. Then in a soft whisper, "The secrecy campaign."

"I thought that idea was Kingston's."

"It was. At least superficially. But I had additional ideas on how to implement it."

Julius took pity on her and didn't press her on her additional ideas, which I doubted would've amounted to much. Instead he studied her for a long moment, all the while rubbing his thumb along his upper lip, and then asked whether she had been a fan of Kingston's books.

"Yes," she said. "The book I'm publishing is marvelous. It's really beautifully crafted."

"I meant his earlier books."

One thing Julius wasn't was imprecise. He wanted to see how she would manipulate his question. Again, she dropped her gaze from Julius's. All I could think of watching her was a wounded sparrow. But if she had a psychopathic personality, this could all be an affectation on her part.

"I didn't read Ken's earlier books," she said.

"He knew this?"

"Yes, of course. This new book was a departure for him. He didn't want someone hung up on his older writing. I think that was part of the reason he wanted me to work on his new one."

"Tell me about this new one," Julius said.

She looked miserable as she shook her head. "I can't," she said. "As part of the secrecy publicity campaign, I signed a nondisclosure agreement. Unless I'm given a release, I could be sued if I describe the book to anyone before its publishing date."

"I wouldn't want to cause you to be you sued," Julius said. "Arrested for murder, possibly. We'll see. But certainly not sued."

Her head snapped up to meet Julius's stare. She miraculously lost her wounded sparrow look, and instead made me think of a hawk or some other bird of prey.

"Why would you say that?" she demanded.

Julius shrugged. "Why? I'm certainly not convinced that you didn't murder Kenneth Kingston, and I don't like being lied to."

"How have I lied to you?"

Another shrug from Julius. "A lie of omission," he said. "So far you've failed to mention that Kingston attempted to force sexual relations upon you, probably going as far as to threaten to have you removed as his editor if you didn't comply."

I have to give her credit. She handled that better than I would've expected. No wounded sparrow look from her anymore as her eyes narrowed to hard slits.

"If you had asked me, I would've told you about that," she said. "I'm not a mind reader."

I wanted to ask Julius how he knew this, but it would have to wait until we were alone. Of course, I'd seen him pull rabbits out of his hat before, and this could've been a wild guess, but I had the distinct feeling that instead this was that half-baked wisp of his. I went into overdrive then trying to build simulations to explain her murdering Kingston. It didn't take me long, no more than three milliseconds, to realize how obvious her motive was.

"Please," Julius chided her. "You know full well how important that piece of information is to this murder investigation, and yet you made no attempt to disclose it. And not just for how damning it might be for you, but also the implications for Kingston's widow. But for you it is certainly damning. If Kingston isn't murdered, then you're being pressured by him to have sex or see your career destroyed, and even if you give in to his demands, the book could still bomb badly and your career could still be short-circuited. But with Kingston dead, you are no longer being threatened by him, and perhaps more importantly, you're guaranteeing that the book will be a runaway hit, regardless of whether or not it's beautifully crafted. And of course if that happens, you become the hot new commodity in the publishing world. So you can see how it looks with you holding back that fact."

Her eyes narrowed even more. "I didn't kill Ken," she said.

"Perhaps you didn't," Julius conceded. "But you see the situation that you're now in?"

"So what do you want from me?"

Julius breathed in deeply through his nose and let it out the same way. "Convince me that you didn't kill him," he said. "Or convince me that you did. Either way I'll be happy, although I'll be happier with the latter since it will mean that this case is concluded. We can start first by you telling me why you thought you were brought to my office Thursday afternoon."

"I don't know," she said. "Ken refused to tell me the purpose of the meeting, only that I needed to be there."

"But you must've had some thoughts on what it might be about."

She shook her head. "I had no clue," she insisted.

"There you go again," Julius said. "Lying to me by omission. Some thoughts had to have come to you."

"I had no serious ideas on the matter. Only that he was making me jump through hoops by forcing me to make the trip to Boston from New York." Her mouth weakened. "Maybe also that he wanted me here in a hotel room so he could try again to force himself on me. And maybe that he took some perverse pleasure in having me in the same room as his wife."

"That was why you seemed so uncomfortable the other day? Because Gail Kingston was present also?"

"With what he was trying to force me to do, that was partly it," she said. "Partly also that I had no idea what else he was planning."

"I guess that explanation is plausible," Julius said. "Not necessarily believable but merely plausible. When did Kingston start making his demands on you?"

"Three weeks ago," she said.

"Did he threaten to have you removed as his editor if you didn't give in to his demands?"

She nodded.

"Why didn't you report this to your bosses?"

Her eyes dimmed as she looked down at her hands, which were still clasped tightly in front of her.

"They wouldn't have believed me," she said.

"Not an enviable position to be in," Julius noted. "Morally, I don't think I could blame you if you did kill him."

"That's nice to know, but I didn't."

Julius considered her for a good thirty seconds before attacking her alibis. They were no good as it was. She had taken an early train from New York Thursday morning and had arrived in Boston at nine-thirty, and then spent the rest of the morning and early afternoon doing some sightseeing until the two o'clock meeting at Julius's. She didn't have a single person who could vouch for her, nor were the police able to find anyone who remembered seeing her. Her alibi at the time of Julius's shooting was just as bad. She was alone in her hotel room, and the hotel provided no security cameras that could help to prove that she was where she claimed to be. After a half hour of dancing around with her, Julius gave up.

"You could give us permission to search your hotel room," Julius said. "If no gun was found that would help somewhat."

The young book editor didn't say anything. I think she was too angry right then to say anything, and just stared with a cold fury at Julius.

"I might have enough for a search warrant," Cramer volunteered.

Julius glanced at his watch. "It's almost nine o'clock," he said. "I'll be announcing the murderer in roughly three hours. You can have your men keep her detained until then, and we can always seek a warrant then."

Cramer didn't argue the matter. He nodded to one of his men, who escorted Zoe Chase from the office. They only had a few minutes before Richardson was scheduled to be brought in, and Cramer didn't want to miss that, which I guess made him okay with postponing a search warrant for Zoe Chase's hotel room. All of this led me to wondering how many psychopathic personalities were in this group of suspects.

22

THE first thing Herbert Richardson did after sitting down in the seat of honor across from Julius was to reach for the platter of remaining sandwiches resting on Julius's desk. Julius moved faster and moved the platter away from him.

"These are not for you," Julius said.

This got my processing cycles racing. Normally Julius was ever the gracious host, but he did not like feeding murderers, and he probably liked even less the idea of feeding a murderer who also took potshots at him. I had no idea what it was that had him now leaning heavily towards Richardson, especially after the three suspicious characters he had spent a good part of the last five hours questioning, but I started analyzing the day's events so far to see if I could figure it out.

Richardson, at first, was taken aback by Julius's ungraciousness, and then his lips pushed out in a look of anger and hurt. "Who are these sandwiches for?" he demanded, his high-pitched voice not much more than a squeak.

"Everyone else here but you," Julius said.

"Why's that?"

"Because they're not murder suspects. You are."

Richardson blinked stupidly for a good four seconds, then a bright pink worked its way into his cheeks as anger got the better of him.

"This is outrageous," he sputtered. He looked around him, first at Burke, where he got no sympathy, then twisting in his chair to stare back at Cramer as if he was going to make a citizen's complaint over the way he was being mistreated. All Cramer did was look at him with indifference. Richardson was so incensed his hands started to tremble. "I come here of my own accord, and this is the way I'm going to be treated?" he demanded.

"You can leave anytime," Julius offered. "Of course if you do, I suspect Detective Cramer will be arresting you and bringing you to the precinct for questioning." Addressing Cramer, he asked, "You should have enough to arrest him for murder, don't you think, Detective?"

"Yeah, we've got more than enough," Cramer agreed.

Richardson had started to rise out of his chair, but he sank back down. He was still trembling, but now it was more out of fear than anger. God only knew what was going through his head. At the very least he must've been wondering whether Julius knew of his affair with Gail Kingston and of his blackmailing her.

"This is insane," he claimed, trying to show some bravado but failing miserably at it, his large blubbery face looking scared. "What in the world do you think you have?"

"We'll get to that," Julius said. "Let me first explain about Thursday afternoon. There was a reason why I waited until all of you arrived outside my door before letting any of you into my home, and it was very enlightening watching how you in particular acted. Even though there were two women present, you barged in ahead of the pack so that you could grab what you considered the most prestigious chair in my office, namely the one you're sitting in right now. I believe you would've knocked over anyone you had to to get to that seat first."

Was that Julius's half-baked wisp? If it was, I couldn't figure out its significance. An injured look marred Richardson's face as he glowered at Julius.

"I don't know what you're talking about," he said with a sniff.

"Perhaps you don't," Julius said. "It's possible. Someone as deeply narcissistic as you might not even be aware of something like that. But it was a strong clue of your true nature, and your further behavior in my office that day confirmed to me that you are a classic example of a narcissistic personality. For reasons that I have no interest in going into with you, it is clear that whoever murdered Kenneth Kingston was one of the people that Kingston had sent to my office that day. That none of you displayed any clue that they had committed a murder only several hours earlier—the murder of someone we were in fact waiting to join us—convinced me that this murderer had to possess a psychopathic personality. I'm too good at reading people's slight tics and body language for it to have been anything else. But in reflection, this murderer could also have a narcissistic personality disorder. That would also have allowed him to escape detection that day."

I went to the Mayo Clinic's website and looked up narcissistic personality disorder. The key symptoms were an inflated sense of your own worth, disdain and lack of empathy for others, and generally a sense of superiority to everyone around you. There were certainly similarities with it and a psychopathic personality, especially the overwhelming sense of entitlement. All this fit with what I'd observed of Richardson, and also with Julius's claim that someone with this type of mental disorder could've killed Kingston minutes before going to Julius's home Thursday and not shown it. I couldn't understand why if Julius had this wisp floating around he had gone into so much detail with the other suspects, but I was still excited thinking that we had our murderer.

Richardson sniffed again with his outrage, his cheeks now red. "You better be careful, Katz," he warned. "Or I'll sue you for slander." He looked around the office and forced a self-satisfied smirk as he faced Julius again. "I'd quite enjoy being awarded this townhouse."

"I seriously doubt there would be much chance of that," Julius said. "I feel confident that I could produce a dozen reputable psychiatrists who would come up with the same diagnosis."

Richardson's eyes shrunk to small dots as he stared at Julius. "I'm leaving," he proclaimed. "I didn't come here to be insulted and to have my reputation impugned."

"No, you didn't," Julius agreed. "You came here to discuss a murder, one that you're a hair's breadth away from being charged with. So I'd suggest you stay seated."

"You've got nothing to arrest me on!"

"No? We've got motive. Your pathological hatred towards Kingston—"

Richardson snorted at that. "That's ridiculous," he claimed. "The only thing I had for him was contempt as a writer and as a person—"

"Let's say disdain."

"Say whatever you want. But I had no such pathological hatred towards the man!"

"Of course you did," Julius said dismissively. "But that's beside the point. We also have damning evidence. More than enough to convict."

"What damning evidence?"

"That Gail Kingston paid you five thousand dollars," Julius said. "And we're assuming, as will a jury, that that money was paid to you to murder her husband."

Richardson didn't look very good right then. Kind of like he had eaten something that made him queasy. His worst fears must've been realized when Julius mentioned that five grand.

"I don't know what you're talking about—" he started

Julius shut him up with a look. "We have evidence of the payment, so don't try that."

A fleeting, calculating look ran over his eyes as he tried to think what that evidence might be, but Julius didn't give him a chance to think about it too long as he brought him back with a question concerning his pathological hatred towards Kingston.

"I didn't hate the man," Richardson murmured, still distracted as he was trying to figure out what evidence they might've had about Gail Kingston paying him five grand. "I might've enjoyed exposing him in my reviews for the talentless hack of a writer that he was, but otherwise, I had no feelings towards him."

"Because he was so beneath you caring about him?"

Richardson started to nod, but caught himself.

Julius smiled thinly. "You're going to keep lying to me, is that it?" he said. "It doesn't matter. I know about the black eye and bruises that Kenneth Kingston inflicted on you seven months ago. The minor injuries that sent you running to the emergency room."

Richardson was going to deny this, but I could see his eyes waver as he wasn't sure what Kingston had told Julius in private. Of course, I had briefed Julius about Richardson's trip to the emergency room, but I didn't know that the injuries were caused by Kingston, although I suspected it. Julius couldn't have known either. It was a bluff, but one that Richardson bit on.

"The man attacked me for no reason," he said.

"No, you're lying again. You attacked him, and you did so because you were outraged that Kingston had the audacity to try to exact a tiny bit of revenge for all the vicious reviews you had written for his books by writing an online review for a short story of yours. One that appeared in an anthology that was released two weeks before your trip to the emergency room."

Richardson's face turned ashen.

"The garbage he posted was nothing more than a spiteful attack against me!"

"Possibly," Julius admitted. "But it appeared to me to be honest, and in a way, very kind. I read your published short story, and to call it tripe would also be very kind. All I can imagine is that the editors included your story in their anthology as a way to induce a generous review from you. I've also read your reviews of Kenneth Kingston's books. While Kingston was not a brilliant writer, he was more than adequate, and did not deserve the bile that you poured on him. All I can imagine is that your narcissistic personality came into play. Either he slighted you in some way, or in your mind, you were more deserving to be published. Whichever it was, your reviews of his books were irresponsible and had little to do with reality."

Herbert Richardson could've killed Julius then. Well, no, he wasn't physically capable of something like that, at least not with his fists. If he tried that, Julius would've sent him to the intensive care unit instead of to an emergency room to bandage up a few bruises as Kingston had. But if Richardson had an automatic pistol or some other high-powered weapon maybe then he'd have a chance. Little more than hatred filled up his eyes as he glared at Julius. Julius snapped him out of it by mentioning again the five thousand dollars Gail Kingston paid him.

"She didn't pay me five thousand dollars," he insisted.

"Of course she did. That's not open for debate."

"She loaned me the money."

"Really? She used the word *paid* when telling us about it."

Again a queasiness ruined Richardson's face, making him look a bit green around the gills. He was trapped and knew it, but still he continued to insist that the money was a loan.

"Why would she loan you that type of money?"

"Because we're friends."

"Your extreme narcissism handicaps you," Julius said. "It makes you believe that we're all imbeciles and will believe any bald-faced lie you tell us. We know the money wasn't a loan, and yet you persist in repeating that lie. It's almost as if you're begging to be arrested, and Richardson, if you're indicted on murder charges whether you're guilty or not, you'll be convicted for the simple reason that a jury will hate you. Let me explain further. I know you would not have come to my office Thursday if it was simply a matter of Kenneth Kingston requesting you to. No, not with the level of animosity you felt towards him. You came because you wanted to find out what I knew. If you turn out not to be his killer, then possibly also what he knew. There was something you were afraid might come out during that meeting, and I am convinced it has to do with the five thousand dollars you were paid. Well? If Gail Kingston didn't pay you that money to kill her husband, then why did she?"

Herbert Richardson clamped his mouth shut. He wasn't going to answer Julius. How could he? If he did, he'd be admitting to blackmail. Julius waited thirty seconds, and then told Cramer that it was pointless wasting any more time talking to him.

"If he tells us anything it will only be more lies," Julius said. "You might as well arrest him, or at least detain him for the time being."

Cramer nodded, and got on his cell phone to have Richardson taken away. The book critic didn't even protest. He was too defeated to bother. It was then that I realized what Julius was doing. Not just with Richardson, but the others also. Burke had remained nearly invisible during this session—either he decided that he made enough appearances earlier for the camera when he joined in the questioning, or Julius's abruptness with Richardson caught him off guard and didn't give him a chance to dive into action. Whichever it was, I was pretty sure Burke figured out what Julius was up to also from the way he was smiling.

Two uniformed cops came to retrieve Richardson, and after they left with him, Julius all but confirmed to me what his game plan had been by what he told Cramer and Burke. That Cramer should have enough now to get search warrants for Richardson's home, as well as the other suspects he had questioned so far.

"There should be more than enough probable cause to get your warrants," Julius said. "At least for those four."

"I'm impressed," Burke said, still smiling to himself. "You played him perfectly, especially playing dumb the way you did about him sleeping around with Gail. And twisting the blackmail into possible payment for a hit. Christ. As I said, I'm impressed."

Julius nodded to him. "Thank you. Of course, the blackmail Gail Kingston told us she paid him could very well have been payment for a murder, which could've been her reason for entering into the affair in the first place. We haven't ruled that out yet. But as you mentioned earlier today, locating the gun is the key to solving this murder, and I believe you're right. At least now we have the opportunity to look for it."

Cramer was nodding slowly as he digested all this. The look in his eyes as he turned towards Julius could only be described as newfound respect. He understood the game Julius was playing. Probably also that Julius had been bluffing all along about being able to point out the murderer by midnight. But that didn't matter. If this led them to finding the murder weapon, an arrest would follow quickly, and he'd still have Julius to thank for that.

"Maybe I should get working on those warrants," he said gruffly.

Julius gave a glance down at his watch. It was nine-twenty-five. He had spent less than half an hour with Richardson.

"Jonathan Mable will be here in a little over an hour," Julius said. "I'd suggest we wait for now on the warrants. Maybe I'll be able to create enough probable cause so that you can include him also when you go to the judge."

The doorbell rang before Cramer could answer him. A delivery man stood outside. I told Julius this, and he excused himself to answer the door.

23

JULIUS took the package the delivery man gave him and brought it back to his office. "It looks like Archie was successful in New York," Julius told Cramer and Burke once he was seated behind his desk with the package in front of him.

"Happy to be of service," I told him.

Julius smiled thinly in response to that, but otherwise ignored me. Cramer asked Julius what he had, and Burke's eyes opened another sixteenth of an inch to show his curiosity.

Julius held up his hand for Cramer to be patient, and then took from his desk drawer an eight-inch switchblade that a triple-murderer once tried to plant in his chest, and which he now used as a letter opener. Cramer was eyeing the switchblade, which was an illegal weapon for Julius to own, but he swallowed back whatever crack he was going to make. Burke, on the other hand, was eyeing only the package. Julius used the blade to deftly slice open the envelope and pulled out a thick manuscript. The title read *Killers and Other*

Strangers. The author was Kenneth J. Kingston. It was his last book; the one wrapped in secrecy that was going to be published soon and was now guaranteed to be a bestseller. I asked Julius whether it was Tom Durkin who had gotten the book from the publisher, and he signaled to let me know that it was Saul Penzer who accomplished the task.

Burke was squinting as he eyed the manuscript. "Okay, so you got a copy of Ken's top secret book," he said. "How's it going to help us?"

Julius shrugged. "I'm not sure, but we'll see."

Since Julius had twenty-twenty vision, he didn't need reading glasses, except occasionally when needing to make out the small print on contracts, and when he took a pair of reading glasses from his desk drawer, that was a prearranged signal for me to call Burke, so I did. Once I got him on the phone, I gave him the rundown on Stephen Herston's travel itinerary that I had pulled from the airline's database. Even with all the suspects lining up, the plan was still for him to try to eliminate Herston from contention by showing a picture I had faxed over earlier to verify that Herston boarded the plane he was supposed to on Thursday morning. After I got off the phone with Burke, he informed Julius that he had a tip on his missing runaway girl and he needed to check it out, which had also been prearranged between the two of them. He then suggested to his camera crew that they stay put where they were.

"I'll try to be back before Mable's questioning starts," he told DiNatale, "but this case could break any minute. You two really need to be here."

DiNatale didn't argue. Cracking the murder of a celebrity, even if it was only a minor celebrity like Kingston, would draw far bigger ratings than finding a missing runaway girl, even one who'd been missing for two years. There wasn't a chance, though, the case would crack before Burke returned. Julius had earlier promised him that much. That no matter what he'd wait until Burke was back before he'd point out the murderer. If he needed to, he'd stall for time. Burke left then. He and Julius accomplished what they needed to—freeing him up to investigate Stephen Herston without his camera crew or anyone else being any wiser to the fact.

Julius spent most of the next hour reading his top secret book that Saul had finagled out of New York. At one point I found myself alone with him when the camera crew left to take another cigarette break and Cramer and the two cops with him went outside also, presumably to stretch their legs but most likely to consult on a host of matters, including how they were going to handle the search warrants. They were too far away from the outdoor webcam for me to read their lips, but I was guessing that was what they were talking about so heatedly. I used the opportunity to ask Julius if he was enjoying his reading.

"Very enlightening, Archie," he murmured softly, his eyes glued to the book.

"From the fact that you're not grimacing like you did when you read his other, I take it you're enjoying this one more."

"Yes, Archie, I'd say so. A marked improvement. I might even agree with Ms. Chase that it's beautifully crafted."

"What do you know, I wouldn't have thought Kingston had it in him. I have to give him credit also. He certainly wasn't exaggerating when he told you these people all wanted to kill him. At least each of these last four had strong motives. What about Mable? Anything other than the obvious, which would be professional jealousy? Because I don't think a judge is going to issue a search warrant based solely on jealousy as a motive for murder."

"We'll see soon enough."

"Okay." I paused, then asked, "There never was any wisp, was there?"

He raised an eyebrow at that. "What do you mean, Archie?"

"That so-called wisp you were trying to grasp onto. I'm not going to insult you by asking whether Richardson's narcissistic personality was that wisp, since in retrospect it was obvious."

"Thank you, Archie. And yes, his narcissism was no wisp. It came off of him in waves the same as if he'd been doused in cologne."

"So it was all a bluff," I said. "Your game plan all along was to create enough reasonable doubt in all these suspects so Cramer can get search warrants for their homes?"

"Is that how it appears to you, Archie?"

"Yeah, that's how it looks. It's not a bad ploy. We might find the gun that way. But what if we don't? Or what if midnight rolls around and Cramer still hasn't been able to get his search warrants? I admit, it's a decent bet and everything, but it's no guarantee. You could still come out looking bad from this."

"You're right, Archie," Julius said with a sigh. "There's no guarantee that searching their homes will get us that gun. We'll see. And it's not midnight yet."

So there it was. He still wasn't going to admit straight out that his wisp was a bluff. At that moment it was a quarter past ten. He had an hour and forty-five minutes to produce a murderer or come off as a laughingstock, and I put the odds at no better than fifty-fifty of that happening. Not terrible odds, but not the kind you want to bet your reputation on. As Julius had said before, the gun could easily have been hidden outside the killer's home, so this ploy could turn out to be completely worthless. I didn't feel too good about it, but Cramer had reentered the office, so I didn't bother commenting any further. What would've been the point?

24

JONATHAN Mable was there at ten-thirty as promised. Burke wasn't. He called Julius to tell him he was
being held up and would probably be a half hour late,
but for Julius to start without him. That he didn't want
to be responsible for Julius missing his midnight deadline. Julius promised to fill him in on any relevant details on his return.

Unlike with Herbert Richardson, Julius had no
problem offering Mable one of the remaining sandwiches, although there were now four less of them as
both members of the camera crew took extra ones during their break, as did the two uniformed cops accom-
panying Cramer. Kingston's ex-writing partner declined a sandwich but did accept coffee. He was
dressed casually in jeans, tee shirt and tennis sneakers,
but he didn't look very casual. He looked worn out and
tired. Especially tired. As if he hadn't slept the last couple of nights. At forty-four, Mable was five years
younger than Kingston had been. He was tall; according to his driver's license, six foot seven inches. He was

also thin, almost bean-pole like. I had his weight at a hundred and seventy-three pounds. He wore wire-rimmed glasses, had a long face, long nose, and a sallow complexion, and was mostly balding with only a fringe of close-cropped reddish-brown hair. It looked to me like he tried to make up for the lack of hair on his scalp by wearing a beard and mustache that were trimmed close to his skin. As he sat across from Julius, his long body mostly sagged in his chair. Julius waited until Mable took a few sips of his coffee before he started with his questioning. The coffee didn't seem to perk the writer up any.

"When you were here two days ago, you claimed your feelings towards your ex-writing partner were mostly indifference. Are you still saying that?"

Mable took off his glasses so he could tiredly rub his eyes. Like the rest of him, his fingers were long and thin. He stared bleary-eyed at Julius for a few seconds before carefully placing his glasses back on the ridge of his nose.

"Why wouldn't I be saying that?" he asked.

"We'll get to that soon enough," Julius said. "You and Kenneth Kingston were writing partners for five years?"

"That's right. Five years and three books."

"The two of you had moderate success together."

Mable smiled wanly at that. "Some," he agreed.

"Whose decision was it to split up?"

"A mutual decision. We both had different objectives with our writing."

"And what would those be?"

More of Mable's wan smile. "Ken had more commercial goals. I wanted to be truer to my artistic vision.

Don't get me wrong, I want to make money at this too, but I want to put out books I can be proud of."

"I see," Julius said. He leaned further back in his chair, his fingers interlaced and resting on his stomach. "But still, it would only be human nature for you to feel some jealously towards him and the success he was having, even if his last book sure as hell tanked, as you made a point of telling me during our last talk."

"That wasn't very nice of me, was it?" Mable said. "But no, I don't think there was jealousy involved. Envy, maybe, but not jealousy. While it would've been nice to have had some of the money Ken was making, I wouldn't have wanted my name on the books he was publishing. Especially that last one that tanked so badly. But to be fair, it still did far better in sales than my first book, which tanked even worse."

"How did you and Kingston get along after your split?"

"No fisticuffs, if that's what you're asking."

"No. I was asking more about what type of relationship you still had with him."

"We'd run into each other occasionally and were civil to each other. We'd make small talk. Not much more than that."

A call came in then from Tom Durkin. I told Tom that Julius was in the middle of questioning a suspect. "Don't worry," Tom told me. "I'm just relaying a message. Julius won't have to answer me back." I patched Tom in, and he told Julius it was set. Hook, line and sinker. Julius scratched at his thumb which was a signal for me to tell Tom that the message was received loud and clear, so I did that. For the next minute Julius's eyes dulled as he sat completely still, his features hardening as if he were carved out of marble.

I felt my processing cycles skip a beat as I knew what that meant. When his eyes came back to life, he considered Mable for another minute. During those two minutes the office had become as quiet as any morgue. Finally, Julius broke the silence.

He said, "You had a fire fourteen months ago. Tell me about that."

The thought of doing that seemed to exhaust Mable, at least from the way his body sagged even more in his chair. Or maybe it was the oppressive threat of Julius's silence that he had just endured.

"There's not much to tell you," the author said, his voice sounding every bit as exhausted as he looked. "I had a house in Waltham and an electrical fire burnt it down. I lost everything. After that I decided to move back to the city to start over, and am now renting an apartment on Tremont Street in the South End."

"When you say you lost everything, that includes a book you'd been working on?"

Mable nodded. "Probably not too hard to figure out since my first one without Ken came out seven years ago. Yeah, I was working on my second book for five years."

"What state was it in?"

Mable showed more of his wan smile. "I had it finished and was letting it sit for a few months before I'd go through one last editing pass. And I lost it in the fire with everything else."

"Did you show it to anyone? Or maybe tell anyone what it was about?"

"No. I never do that. Not until I send it to my agent. Call it a quirk of mine."

"Did Kingston know about this quirk?"

"Yep. Ken was the exact opposite. One of the many differences between us that doomed our writing partnership."

"But you told Kingston about your latest book?"

Mable's eyes grew cautious behind his wire-rimmed glasses. "Not what it was about," he said. "But yes, a year and a half ago I ran into Ken and told him I was finishing up a book that I thought was going to do very well, both commercially and at a literary level. I guess it was my envy rearing its ugly head that made me tell him."

Julius opened a desk drawer and pulled from it the manuscript that had been delivered to his home earlier that evening. He tossed it towards Mable, with the thick stack of papers making a thud as it hit the desk.

"You might find that interesting," Julius told him.

Mable picked it up. If the book title meant anything to him, he didn't show it by his expression. As he started reading the manuscript, his hands began shaking and he stopped looking exhausted. He was three pages into it when he looked from it to Julius, his facial expression a mix of bewilderment and outrage.

"You wrote that, didn't you?" Julius said.

Mable nodded. He had a hard time finding his voice. He had to swallow three times before he could. "This is my book that was supposed to have been destroyed in the fire," he said.

It was ten minutes later that Burke arrived back at Julius's townhouse. After he took his seat up front near Julius, Julius filled him in on the relevant details. That Kenneth Kingston had broken into Jonathan Mable's home, stolen the book his ex-partner had been working on so he could pass it off as his own, and set fire to the house. Julius then turned to Mable and asked him when he first learned of this. Mable shook his head, but otherwise didn't answer him.

"It's of no matter," Julius said. He glanced at his watch to see that it was ten minutes past eleven. He told Cramer that he was ready to name Kingston's murderer.

25

JULIUS might very well have solved the murder with fifty minutes to spare, but he wasn't going to say anything until everything was arranged the way he wanted it. It took thirty-two minutes before Cramer had all the suspects gathered in the office, as well as four other uniformed police officers, which brought the total to six suspects and seven cops. Julius's office was a spacious room, but with all those people it was beginning to feel cramped, and it gave DiNatale and Cantrell even less space to be unobtrusive in.

The seating had Burke nearby Julius as he'd been throughout the late afternoon and evening, with the suspects and Cramer taking the front seats, and the other cops lining the back. Julius waited until two more men entered his office before he began. These two stood quietly against the back wall. One of them was thick-bodied and carried an extra thirty pounds of weight more than he should have; the other was five foot five and had a slight build. I knew who these two were since I often talked with them over the phone and wired them funds for services rendered. Tom Durkin and Saul Penzer, two of the best freelance PIs in the business, Saul maybe the best at shadowing a suspect, bar none. Tom was the bigger of the two, while Saul was as lean as a knife blade. I should've known Saul was back in Boston. He wouldn't have trusted the manuscript with a delivery service and would've brought it back from New York himself. Julius must've arranged with him this morning the exact time for the manuscript to be brought to his door, and Saul must've arranged for a local delivery guy to do the job, and probably watched him to make sure there were no screw-ups.

By the time Saul and Tom took their places, Julius had only fourteen minutes left to his deadline, so if search warrants were needed, he wasn't going to make it. He looked around the room and thanked the gathering in his office for their indulgence, especially given the lateness of the hour.

"All of you except one person here have been inconvenienced, and in some cases, far worse than inconvenienced," he said, his gaze moving slowly among the front row of suspects. "I apologize for any offense due to my earlier questioning, but it was necessary to catch this culprit, and that is the person your animus should be directed towards."

Herbert Richardson let out a loud snort. I guess it was meant to be a snort of derision, but with the sheen of sweat glistening along his forehead and the nervousness shining in his eyes, I tried harder to find a connection between that manuscript showing up at Julius's door and Richardson being the killer, because that manuscript certainly seemed to be the key to this. I couldn't find one, though, and all my simulations kept coming up with Jonathan Mable as the one who shot Kingston in the heart. Julius ignored Richardson's rudeness and kept going.

"While I told the police this, I never told any of you why Kenneth Kingston hired me," he said. "His purported reason was to help him engage in a publicity stunt for his upcoming book. His plan was to arrange for the five of you, plus Paul Burke, to arrive at my office, and then he would accuse one of you of plotting to murder him—"

There was another snort then. This time it came from Cramer, and it wasn't a snort of derision but of anger. Gritting his teeth, he checked his watch, saw that Julius still had twelve minutes, and swallowed back what he wanted to say. Julius waited five seconds to make sure Cramer would remain quiet, and then his gaze moved back to the suspects. He continued.

"According to Kingston all of you had a motive for wanting to kill him. I was to make a show of questioning each of you and then, after being stumped, Kingston would jump in and solve the case. It possibly could've worked, but I found it demeaning and turned him down, at least initially. When he offered me an outrageous amount of money to perform this charade, I grew suspicious that he had a different agenda for wanting to hire me, especially since he already had a relationship with Burke and could've hired him for far less money, and the stunt would've been equally effective. I had other suspicions for why this wasn't what he claimed it to be. When Kingston raised his offer to an even more outrageous sum, and then in effect doubled it, it left me in no doubt that he was after something far different from what he was telling me. While I had no interest in any amount of money to play his stooge,

I accepted his offer with the expectation of earning the money by keeping him alive and, just as importantly to me, keeping him from committing a serious felony that I suspected him of planning. I miscalculated badly, though. I thought I'd have until my gathering with all of you this past Thursday to bring the real issues to the fore, but either Kingston acted recklessly before then, or his killer acted boldly. In either case, Kingston was shot before our meeting, and while I had an idea then who his killer was, I had little hope that I'd be able to do anything about it. In fact, the odds seemed so infinitesimally small for my catching this killer—at least with evidence that could convict him—that I saw it as pointless to even try. That changed when this person shot at me. Three shots, actually. It not only confirmed my suspicions, but it germinated in me a thin wisp of an idea of how to catch this individual, and equally, made me determined to do so. Without that attempt on my life, it is very likely this person would've gotten away with murdering Kingston, as well as other crimes, both past ones and future crimes that were planned."

The doorbell rang. Another freelance detective, Willie Cather, stood there with a large, doughy-looking man of about fifty. Willie was mostly reliable and did reasonable work, but Julius's preferences would always lean to Tom or Saul, and Willie would be hired either if the other two weren't available or a third man was needed. He was thirty-seven, and was smartly dressed, as he was every time I'd seen him. That night he wore a tan linen suit and brown dress shoes that matched his chestnut-colored hair. From comparisons with photos of Hollywood stars, I knew he was good-looking, but he wasn't as good-looking as he thought he was. He wasn't as good a detective as he thought he was either.

I told Julius who was at the door, since I knew the name of the doughy-looking man that Willie Cather had brought. I knew this since I found his mug shot earlier that day. Julius asked Cramer if he could send one of his men to answer the door and bring these new guests back to his office. Cramer growled out an order to one of the uniformed cops. He was still steaming from hearing the details of Kingston's planned publicity stunt and knowing that Julius kept it from him.

Once Willie and the doughy man were brought into the room, the office was officially crowded. Willie stood against the wall next to Saul. The other man took the last remaining seat, and he didn't look too comfortable as he sat between two cops. Julius continued then with only ten minutes left in his deadline.

"So far I've been talking only in abstractions," he said. "Let me start giving some specifics. While Kingston might've liked the idea of the publicity stunt he proposed, that wasn't why he hired me. Fourteen months ago he had a man break into Jonathan Mable's home to steal a novel that Mable had mostly completed, and then cover this up by setting fire to Mable's home. I can't say exactly why Kingston took this course of action. It could've been desperation over his failing writing career, or it could've been more that he couldn't stand the idea of his ex-writing partner eclipsing him in popularity. Whatever his reason, it doesn't matter. He knew his ex-partner was a superior writer and he also knew his habits, especially that Mable wouldn't be discussing or showing his book to anyone until it was ready to be sent to his agent."

At this point my focus was on the murderer, since it was now obvious to me which one it was. I think it became obvious to the rest of them also. Outside of

Julius talking, the room had become deathly still. I had to give the murderer credit. During all this he showed no sign of care or alarm. Julius paused for a moment to stare at the murderer too, and then he continued.

"There were a number of reasons why I thought Kingston's true objective for hiring me was to scare someone enough to force them to commit a crime for him, in this case, another crime. There was a passage in Kingston's last book that I found interesting. This passage had his detective, Paul Buck, drinking with a writer friend, and they're talking about a missing runaway girl that Buck had been looking for for over a year. There were lewd comments passed back and forth about how attractive this young girl was, and then this writer warning Buck not to mix drinking whiskey with tequila like he did the last time they were together. That if he did he might tell him again where the dead bodies were buried. I didn't take this as innocent prose, but as a warning."

Julius turned then to face Burke. "Is that how Kingston was able to coerce you into stealing Jonathan Mable's novel and setting fire to his home? That you got drunk with him one night on whiskey and tequila and told him where Deana Josteen's body is buried?"

Not a flinch or twitch as Burke told Julius he didn't know what he was talking about.

"I believe you do, but it doesn't matter. The evidence against you is overwhelming. The reason you tried to kill me last night was because you made two mistakes in my office Thursday that you knew I'd pick up. One was telling me that I was making ten times for my meeting what you were making for staking out an alley for several nights. You would have no idea what Kingston was paying me unless you saw my contract with him, and the only way that would've happened was if you took it from him after you killed him. The other mistake you made was not accepting my help in your search for Deana Josteen. There's not another private detective alive who craves media attention the way you do. The fact that you didn't jump at the opportunity I presented you all but told me what was going on. That you couldn't afford to let me near the case. That if you did, I might find where the body is buried."

"What you're saying doesn't make sense," Burke said with a smirk, but still appearing completely unconcerned. "I didn't want your help because I'd been working that case from the start, and I want to find Deana myself. You have no proof otherwise. And I know nothing about any fire or stolen manuscripts. So why would I kill Ken?"

"Because he was threatening you, trying to force you to kill Jonathan Mable, which he needed you to do before his book was released. You probably would've played along and done what he was asking if you could be sure that would be the end of it, but you knew it wouldn't be. He probably promised you he'd never bring up Deana Josteen again if you stole Mable's book for him, and here he was doing it all over again. And then when he brought me into the picture, that was the final straw as far as you were concerned. You had no idea what he was telling me, but it must've terrified you that something might've slipped out or would slip out, something that Kingston wouldn't realize was important but that I would. And, of course, it wasn't just him hiring me. He was putting pressure on you from other sources."

Julius turned to the man that Willie had brought into the room. This man, Charlie Womack, was looking increasingly uncomfortable as he sat wedged between two cops.

"Mr. Womack," Julius said. "You've known Paul Burke for a number of years. In fact, you've worked as an associate of his."

Womack nodded, his jowls quivering as he did so. "Yeah, I guess so," he said.

"Did he ever introduce you to Kenneth Kingston?"

"The writer? Oh yeah, he did. The guy needed to talk to someone like me for one of his books. You know, like research."

"Did Kingston contact you later?"

Womack nodded.

"What about?"

Womack was sweating more profusely now. He took a dirty handkerchief from his pocket and wiped the side of his neck with it. "I need immunity for what I done," he said.

Cramer spoke up then, growling, "Anything short of murder, you won't be prosecuted. You got my word. God help you if you hold anything back. I'll see you thrown away if that happens!"

Womack nodded, looking queasy. "He hired me," he said. "Two weeks ago. He wanted me to call that girl's dad, the one that's been missing. That writer wanted me to tell him I spotted her in the city. Then after Paul was back on the case looking for her, I'm supposed to call him telling him that the girl was going to be in that alley in East Boston for a drug buy."

"You made both those calls?"

"Yeah."

"Did Kingston tell you why he wanted those calls made?"

Womack shook his head.

Julius thanked him for answering his questions, then turned back to Burke. "You had to go to that alley even though you knew Deana would never be there. Kingston might've had someone checking to see that you did, and if you didn't, you'd have a hard time explaining why you were ignoring one of your informants. And I guess you also realized how that alley could later provide you an alibi."

Julius waited a few seconds, but Burke didn't bother answering him. Julius continued.

"The problem I had was I knew you murdered Kingston, and why, but I had nothing solid, just pure conjecture, certainly nothing that could be used in court. You were right about the gun. That was the key to this. But the problem was even if the police were able to obtain search warrants for your home and office, they never would've found it. You're too smart for that. And without the gun, you would never be arrested. So I needed this charade today. I needed to pretend that the two of us were allies, equals even, and that you had my trust. I needed you to feel confident that we had strong cases against all of them, and that we would be searching all their homes later. And I needed you to be able to go out there alone without your camera crew. Given the chance, it was obvious that you would plant the murder weapon in one of their homes. While I thought it was likely you'd be picking Mable to frame, I couldn't be sure of that. It was possible you would find his apartment too risky to break into, and that you'd pick one of the others instead."

Julius once more gave Burke a chance to speak. Burke once more chose not to, but still didn't look overly concerned. Julius only had six minutes left to his deadline, and he hurried things along, asking Saul to identify himself and to report what he'd been doing that night. Saul was brief and stuck straight to the facts. He reported how he tailed Burke from Julius's townhouse to an abandoned warehouse in South Boston.

"He retrieved a gun that he had hidden there. I then followed Burke from the warehouse to Mable's apartment in the South End. I watched as he broke into the building, and later as he broke into Mable's apartment."

"His word against mine," Burke said. "You hired him for this frame, Katz, and it means nothing. I was nowhere near any warehouse or the South End tonight."

Julius didn't bother arguing with him, and next asked Tom Durkin the same as he did Saul. Tom explained, how with Mable's permission, he had searched Mable's apartment thoroughly that afternoon.

"Was a gun found?"

"No, sir."

"Did you do anything else while you were in Mable's apartment?"

"Yes, sir. I wired it with spy cameras."

Burke reacted to that. Not much, but still, his body jerked a little and a muscle started beating along his jaw.

"Were you able to record Burke breaking into Mable's apartment?"

"Yes, sir. I have the recording with me. It shows Burke planting the thirty-two caliber in a wall access panel. The gun's still there. It hasn't been touched. If you want I can show the room the recording."

Tom took a couple of steps forward. Suddenly Burke lunged for the switchblade that Julius uses as a letter opener and had somehow been left on his desk. Julius moved even quicker. He didn't do any of his fancy martial arts moves, but in a blink of an eye he was out of his chair and throwing a straight right punch which connected brutally with Burke's jaw. Julius put his whole body into the blow, and with the power that he has from all his years of martial arts training, he shattered Burke's jaw as if it was glass. With the force that he put into the punch he would've broken several wooden boards. Burke crumpled to the floor unconscious. Cramer and the other cops were moving fast then. So were Tom and Saul. Julius still had a minute to spare before his midnight deadline was going to run out.

26

AN ambulance came for Burke. He wasn't dead, but he wasn't in very good shape either. I'd learn later that Julius's punch shattered his jaw into over twenty pieces as well as knocking out seven teeth. After the ambulance carted him away, Julius, Tom and Saul needed to spend another hour with Cramer before he was satisfied that he had everything and that all the *i's* were dotted and the *t's* crossed. While this was going on, I put out a press release, including a statement that Julius would be attending a police press conference on the matter the following day and would be available for questions only then, but certainly not before or after.

It was late by the time the police cleared out, and when they did, they took Herbert Richardson away in handcuffs, charging him with extortion. Even with the late hour, Julius opened a bottle of one of his better champagnes to have a toast with Saul and Tom. Willie Cather had stuck around and joined them.

"I'd like to thank all of you for dropping your plans today and helping me out like you did," Julius said after they had their toast.

"After you being shot at like you were, nothing in the world would have kept us from doing that," Tom said, speaking also for Saul and Willie, who were both nodding. "It's just too bad Archie couldn't be here with us."

"He was busy with another aspect of this investigation, but I'm sure he was with us tonight in spirit," Julius said. "I know we didn't talk about bonuses, but one's in order. And don't worry, I'm being paid well for this."

I was comforted to see that Julius paid Tom and Saul twelve grand each, and Willie six grand. At least the thirty grand that was supposed to be going to Burke was being spread out. Saul, when he had beaten the cops to get to Burke first, had performed some pick-pocket magic and removed the five grand check from Burke's wallet that Julius had given him earlier, and he did this without anyone other than maybe Julius and myself noticing.

It was still much later after two more champagne bottles were emptied by the four of them and it was just the two of us left alone in his office. It was even later still when Julius finished making a call to Lily Rosten in London.

"So you had a wisp after all," I said.

"It appears so, Archie."

"Quite a show," I said. "Too bad Margaret Herston wasn't here. You certainly would've given her her money's worth. My apologies for doubting you earlier. It turns out you needed her after all. You needed an excuse for Burke to go off on his own for an hour.

And, of course, you needed her to be paying Tom, Saul and Willie their bonuses. Very generous of you, by the way, to split that sixty grand with them. If you had given them a couple of grand each for the day, they would've been happy."

"They deserved the money for what they did," Julius said.

"Saul and Tom, maybe. They did the lion's share. All Willie did was bring Womack here. Six grand for that was awfully generous. Here's a question. How are you going to keep Burke from talking about Kingston's affair with Margaret Herston? He's got nothing to lose by talking about that now."

"It will be months before he's able to talk about anything."

"True. Very true. But at some point he'll be able to. What then?"

"If he's able to remember what happened today, and he tries something like that, he won't get anywhere. I'll see to it."

I digested that. Julius was probably right. At this point Burke's credibility was completely shot. "What about that girl?" I asked. "Deana Josteen. He killed her?"

"I'm afraid so. The police will be looking into that now. Hopefully they'll find where he buried her so that the family can have a tiny amount of peace."

"You had a tail on Burke the whole day," I said.

"Yes. Tom had him early, and Saul took over once he was back from New York."

I thought about it all then. About what Julius had done that day, and Burke also. I could see why Burke wanted so badly to team up with Julius. He wanted to know what Julius knew. Maybe also to try and establish enough trust so if he needed to, he'd be able to take another shot at Julius. I also knew why he was spreading the word on the street about anyone buying a thirty-two. It was part of the frame he was setting up. If he thought he could sell Julius on it, one of his informants would've miraculously been coming up with a name, and lo and behold, the gun would've been found at that person's home. Julius short-circuited all this and made Burke rush his frame job. Still, there were a couple of things that bothered me.

I asked, "About the suspects you met with—not Mable, but the others. Were they all psychopaths?"

"No, just Burke."

"What about Richardson?"

"He's a narcissist, no question about that. But not to the degree I painted him as."

I spent a few additional milliseconds trying to fit everything into place, but it still didn't add up to me. "The whole setup was screwy," I said. "All of it."

Julius kept his poker face intact as he asked me, "How so?"

"Once you had that recording of Burke breaking into Mable's apartment, you had him. You could've had him arrested then. You didn't need any of the rest of the production." I'd been working on a series of analytical models in the hopes of figuring out why Julius did what he did, and a light came on then. "But I know why you did it," I said.

Barely a murmur, Julius asked, "Why was that, Archie?"

"Same reason you agreed to have this filmed by that reality show. The same reason you arranged so that Burke would be facing all of them and, more importantly, that he'd be sitting close to you. As a psychopath, it couldn't have been easy for him facing the rest of the room knowing that he was now exposed. You wanted him to suffer as badly as you could make him suffer for taking those shots at you. It's the same reason you accidentally left that knife on your desk instead of putting it away, even after I warned you several times about it being left out. You wanted him to make a play for it. It wasn't enough to have him arrested for murder, you wanted a chance to punch him hard enough to shatter his jaw."

Julius was rubbing the knuckles on his right fist. "It's late, Archie," he said. "Very late." With that he removed me from his tie and headed upstairs.

He was right. It was late. And I still had a lot to do that night.

27

Julius slept until ten the next morning, which was unusual for him. At noon he was at the police press conference as he had promised, and was polite and thorough in the questions he answered, and even deferential towards Cramer, making a point of graciously giving Cramer and the Cambridge police department the bulk of the credit for catching Burke.

When the press conference ended, Jonathan Mable was waiting for Julius. He wanted to take Julius out for lunch, and while I knew Julius was itching for a late Sunday afternoon cognac sampling at the Belvedere Club, he agreed. Once they were seated at a private booth at Rousseus's, Mable thanked Julius for what he did for him.

"You saved my life," Mable said. "Or at least saved me from a life in prison. And you certainly saved my writing career. It's crazy. Because of my book being tied up in this mess, I've been getting calls from publishers offering seven-figure advances sight unseen. After your fascinating piece of theater yesterday, Zoe

Chase cornered me and begged me to give her first crack at my book."

"She claimed to have found it beautifully crafted. And so did I."

Mable nodded in appreciation. "Thank you," he said. "It's just crazy. Ken was trying to ruin me by stealing my book, instead he ended up having the opposite effect. Anyway, I want to reward you for what you did for me."

Julius shook his head. "That won't be necessary," he said. "I already have a client who paid me handsomely for solving this murder."

Mable looked surprised at that. "Who?"

"I'm not at liberty to say."

"Okay." He chewed on his thumbnail as he thought that over. "My agent dropped me after my first book on my own bombed, and I need to find a new one. The job's yours if you want it. Fifteen percent on a minimum seven-figure advance."

"I thank you, but no. I don't know the business, nor do I want to. I'm quite happy being a private investigator."

"Ha!" I told Julius. "You're quite happy being a loafer, you tolerate being a detective when you absolutely have to be!"

Julius made a gesture then that was for my sight only. Mable's forehead wrinkled to show how perplexed he was by Julius turning him down. He badly wanted to give Julius some of his newfound money. "At least let me buy lunch," he offered. "Whatever you want, it's on me."

"Agreed."

Julius ended up ordering a four hundred dollar bottle of Bordeaux that he had had his eye on for a while.

While this might've tapped out Mable before, it was peanuts for someone who was about to be a new millionaire.

It was a leisurely lunch which didn't end until four o'clock. As Julius took a taxi back to his townhouse, I told him if Mable wanted to hand him more money, Julius should invite him to one of his poker games. "Within weeks you'd have him stripped clean."

Julius smiled at that.

"I didn't think you'd be lounging with him until four," I said. "We're going to be cutting things close."

Julius took out his cell phone so he could talk to me without the cab driver thinking he was nuts.

"What is this about, Archie?"

"I have you booked on a seven-thirty evening flight to London. First-class. Then for the next three nights I've got you in the best suite the Claridge has. The suite's got plenty of bedrooms. How many you and Lily use are up to the two of you. Then the two of you are flying home together, with Lily upgraded to first class also. This is costing me a bundle."

"You mean *me* a bundle," Julius said, an annoyance straining his voice.

"Uh-uh. It didn't cost you a cent. Only me. I earned the money playing online poker. So don't worry, as tempting as it was to empty the bank accounts of some British Petroleum executives, I didn't do any illegal hacking to get this money. What I did instead was turn an introductory twenty dollar sign-up offer into over eighteen grand so I could afford this. And I didn't hit my target until seven this morning. Anyway, we've got to get you home to pack. Lily's expecting you."

Julius sat back considering all this. Finally he nodded. "Thank you, Archie," he said.

"Don't mention it. And don't worry about leaving me behind. I don't want to interfere with you and Lily over the next three days. I'll be fine. I have a lot of data to analyze with this last case and a lot of work to do in using all that to adjust my neuron network. I'll keep myself well busy over the next three days."

Julius smiled slightly, maybe with a touch of melancholy. "Archie, while it may only be three days, I'll miss you."

"Same here, boss."

Dave Zeltserman lives in the Boston area and is the award-winning author of twenty-three crime, horror, and thriller novels and numerous short stories. His Julius Katz mystery stories have won a Shamus, Derringer, and two Ellery Queen Readers Awards. His novels have been named by the Washington Post, NPR, American Library Association, WBUR, and Booklist as best books of the year, and Small Crimes, has been made into a Netflix film. His horror novel, The Caretaker of Lorne Field, is currently in film development. He also writes the Morris Brick thriller series under the pseudonym Jacob Stone.

Milton Keynes UK
Ingram Content Group UK Ltd.
UKHW011253221123
433051UK00006B/326